TRIS
SELLERS

Copyright © 2019 Tristan Sellers

All rights reserved.
No part of this publication may be reproduced, stored in or introduced into a retrieval system or transmitted, in any form or by any means—electronic, mechanical, printing, recording, or otherwise—without prior permission of the author, except for use of brief quotations in a book review.

This book is a work of fiction. Names, characters, organizations, places, incidents, or events are either products of the author's imagination or are used fictitiously. Any resemblance to actual events, locales or persons, living or dead, is entirely coincidental.
Edited by Jordan Rosenfeld

Cover Design and Interior Formatting by Qamber Designs and Media

ISBN: 978-1-7333478-1-5

To my family: without your unwavering support,
I would never have completed this work.

To my editor, Jordan Rosenfeld; You transformed my maddened
scribbles into a maddened cohesive narrative.

To Jacqueline: You are my hero.

SHE'D CHOSEN THE NAME Yakuza because it was violent. And she loved violence.

She straddled him now, and wasn't even leaning on his neck that hard. Even so, he couldn't get her fingers away from his windpipe. He struggled ineffectually at the straps of the top she hadn't wanted to take off because she didn't feel like it. She didn't know his name, and was now in the process of making sure she'd never need to. There was some totally garbage pop playing on his little phone speaker by the bed that he must have thought would enhance the mood between them. She didn't agree. She knew she had looked so perfect standing there. If only he'd known to look a little bit closer. He was trying to reach for the phone now. Good, turn that shit off.

Too late for forgiveness though. Totally garbage taste equaled a totally garbage life culminating in a neat little death.

Or maybe he wanted the phone for another reason. It occurred to her that he was trying to call for help. Funny. Not like he could talk. Or breathe. Not long now. His red face was blue shifting. He'd be very dead soon.

She gazed around the apartment as his struggles grew more feeble. He had a nice place. She'd agreed to come back here because his shirt had buttons on it and didn't have any wrinkles. It was a nice dark color. That meant he took care of himself. That meant he *could* take care of himself. That meant he had nice things, and the money to buy more.

And this apartment. She briefly considered redecorating as he left scratch marks on her forearms and chest. She twisted her head so he couldn't reach her face. She caught her own reflection in the large window by the bed.

Occluded hazel eyes on an angular face framed by black hair just long enough to be styled up into a coif when it wasn't askew from the act of strangling. She had strong features, she would say striking. Eyebrows a little thick, a sharp upturned nose. Her lips were still a little dry from all the drinks she'd put away. She wasn't vain, or at least she didn't consider herself vain. It was just that everyone else in the world was ugly.

He finally got a hand on the phone and slammed it into the side of her face. A tiny new crescent scar blossomed red in the glass before her. She paused for the barest second, eyes wide in the mirror. She shook her head. Disdain and mock disappointment in her laugh as she leaned more heavily into him. Bracing her knees against his shoulders, she pulled very, very hard on his neck. He didn't manage to make a sound as the arm he was preparing to swing again spasmed and his head came off. She held it in both hands like a potted plant. She'd definitely need to redecorate.

Jacqueline awoke, not quite screaming. The details of her reality came back into focus as all the lights she'd left on while sleeping erased any doubts that lingered there.

Her apartment was small, and not very nice. She'd moved three times this year. This one had bare walls with no furnishings and even fewer shadows. Nothing to inspire the imagination. No windows. It did have a very large metal door with a chair wedged under the handle.

She boarded in the sub basement of her building, next door to the super and the boiler room he tended. The boiler room didn't have a proper boiler anymore, just a squat grey cylinder that didn't make too much noise and took up half the space the old boiler had. A minor historical society had made a fuss when the old machine was dismantled. Nobody else much cared. Hot dry air blew through the vent in her ceiling. She never needed more than a sheet for a blanket.

She began her breathing exercises as she sat there, tangled in the sheet. In through the nose, out through the mouth. Inhale for five seconds. Hold it for five seconds. Exhale for five seconds. She'd quit drinking a week ago, but still felt hungover. She rattled her hand across the detritus on her bedstand—pills, pills, badge, gun—until she gripped the last one tight, finger on the safety, the tension of it pushing back. She held her breath as long as she dared. Her life wasn't ruined yet.

"At least until you tell someone," she said out loud, letting out her breath all at once. She put the gun back down and began to relax. What had the killer called herself this time? Yakuza. Another name change. Every three encounters, like clockwork. Right on time. She reminded herself to make a note of it later.

At the very least, lurid as they were, her dreams of Yakuza were easy to depart. Dreams about the other one, Yaqui, were much harder to wake up from.

She stuck both feet out of bed at once and landed some feet away. The space directly in front of and beneath her crummy futon was reserved for the little faces staring back up at her through char-grey eyes with expressionless lips. She picked up the pencil by the sketches and put it back under her pillow. She needed to separate them at some point. There'd been no common link in the faces she'd seen in either of the dream scenarios. Other than the ironclad sensation that what she was seeing was real. But she'd never admit that, least of all out loud. Even less so to herself. She blinked, and returned to the comfort of routine. She didn't have a kitchen, but the water in her bathroom faucet had no safety settings. This close to the boiler room, it would scald if left on long enough. She left it running, overflowing a chipped mug. After about a minute, a teabag transformed the boiling mug into breakfast.

She'd organized her apartment recently. Instead of one large pile, there were now three: clean clothes, dirty clothes, and several black garbage bags filled with takeout trash. Her "Police" windbreaker looked lonely hanging in her closet next to her dress blues, vacuum sealed.

She rifled through the first pile. She didn't want to let herself be introspective. *Think too much about your situation and you might realize just how crazy it sounds. Might want to turn yourself in. Then you'll never have to think too much. The pills will take care of that for you.*

Jacqueline had given boilerplate reasons for her sick days, things that could be easily explained away. She'd never mentioned visions. You could be depressed or anxious all you wanted and nobody would care. These things happened to many people. With this in mind, she prepared for work.

Jeans, old boots, a tank top. Black turtleneck and then her police jacket. She wiped her hair out of her face and tucked the rest behind her ears. There were no mirrors in her place—another reason she liked it so much. She glanced back at the sketches. Her face was the only one she couldn't see. She never needed to. She'd know her suspect on sight. She winced and brought a hand to her face. It came away red-tipped from her cheek. Dripped.

"Motherfucker," she said.

She looked around the tiny room. Nobody here but her. She put up her collar. Avoided the dozens of eyes on the floor.

She slammed the door behind her.

The rain fell horizontally. Jacqueline had no defense against it, but it made her feel alive. The dreams were always warm, bringing with them a sense of artificial comfort that lingered into her waking moments. This disturbed her more than anything. A dream that felt more real than her, more enticing than food in her stomach or air in her lungs was the most dangerous thing she could think of. Warmth was not to be trusted. Comfort was not to be trusted. The rain was cold and unforgiving, her head pounding, her breathing ragged and red-tinged. The taste of copper as sharp as if this was her first mile. She wouldn't have it any other way.

Her gut rumbled as she passed by the street vendors. The one she liked most had just opened for the day. Vegetarian pho. Rico knew her well. There was already a sealed plastic bowl waiting on the counter for her. She replaced it with some cash and continued down the road. The soup warmed her hands as it sloshed gently against the sides of the disposable Tupperware.

Jacqueline had a strong memory that flared crimson every time she smelled meat. At one point or another, everyone got an idea of where their food came from. You might visit a farm, or a butcher's, and maybe you'd see red. So much abhorrent death going into your food would surely leave a bad taste in your mouth. Sometimes, it felt like only she was able to hold on to that idea. There again, she didn't really like to talk to other people. Maybe if she did so more often, she'd have a better idea of where to look for leads on the unfortunates Yakuza left in her wake.

She scowled. It had been too dark to see the victim's face clearly. Part of her really would have liked a better look. The rest of her was glad she hadn't gotten one.

Her routine drew her onward. She turned the corner off Amigara street and the rain began to abate, but the cold remained. She felt freeze-dried in the wind-chill. She hadn't hunched over for the rain and she wouldn't for the wind. The precinct loomed before her. She gripped the massive wrought iron handle with a numb hand.

Jacqueline tried not to focus on any details as she made her entrance into the station. The weather attacking the windows made the busy office feel like a snow globe—all the colors too bright and surreal. It was also unseasonably warm, perhaps because of the bodies crowded together.

Another plus, she thought bitterly as she shouldered

past a street preacher on overtime. He was ministering to a woman wearing too little for the weather who just looked grateful to be inside. Whether she'd actually been working or just walking home, it hadn't mattered when VICE had picked her up. She and the preacher were cuffed to the same bench. They both smelled terrible, like days of neglect occasionally sterilized with alcohol. Everything smelled terrible, even the smells she recognized as ordinary, public. Jacqueline was offended by all this humanity. It wasn't usually this bad for her, but in close proximity and in great enough numbers the feeling was overwhelming. The more something reached out to her sense of compassion, dug at her personal judgment, took advantage of what should have been an automatic reaction of goodwill, the more she pulled away. The gravest offender of this crime came into view as she approached her work area.

"GOD FIRST, AND EVERYTHING ELSE WILL FALL INTO PLACE," proclaimed the plaque as Jacqueline set her soup down on her own desk right next to it. The sign rested by a heavy peacoat, hand muff and pink pillbox hat on the desk of Desk Sergeant Pinkerton. Although, she preferred "Mrs." if you had to be formal. Mrs. Pinkerton had recently been promoted and her husband was now retired from the force. She was in her mid-forties, plump, and pleasant. Shrewd attention to detail and a gift for visualizing faces had drawn Jacqueline to the force. For Mrs. Pinkerton, it had been a handiness with background checks and after-action reports, and her husband. He'd been a detective—how good a detective Jacqueline had never had the chance to discover.

The Mrs. had signed on not long before Jacqueline enlisted. Jacqueline had also attended Mr. Pinkerton's retirement party. Half of it, anyway. She'd felt out of place and disappeared before the gold watch made an appearance.

Surprisingly, Jacqueline didn't feel out of place often. She felt in place when she was working. She was perfectly capable of talking to people in a professional capacity.

She was exceedingly confident in her ability to deduce and reason effectively. Less so in her ability to handle the complexities of happy hour with the other detectives. She didn't feel comfortable drinking, at least socially. Drinking alone had been easy, but difficult to stop. Talking about things other than work or 'getting to know' other people was likewise perilous. Near the beginning of her career, she'd tried to use what she knew of logic and applied-psychology to 'problem-solve' potential friendships. After multiple nights without calls, three outings that only seemed to exist in other people's photos, and dozens of awkward silences, Jacqueline had written the set of attempts off as disastrous. She'd been too embarrassed to re-examine what had led to her perceived failure. Perhaps it was because outside of work she had trouble focusing on the present.

"Good morning, Jackie!" said a matronly voice that wafted across the desk like fresh baked fudge. Mrs. Pinkerton's face was still perfectly smooth after fifty years, living proof that you were only as young as you felt. Mrs. Pinkerton always seemed to feel good. She shared that feeling with others often, whether it was new recipes or hair care secrets. Her long mahogany tresses framed her sparkling eyes like a dryad parting the reeds. Jacqueline opened her mouth but with no intent to say anything.

"Woah. Jackie, you look terrible! Did you get any sleep last night?" Mrs. Pinkerton demanded.

Thoroughly disinterested in prolonging the conversation, Jacqueline tried to play off Mrs. Pinkerton's concerns by smiling. Her deskmate's eyes widened. Jacqueline's ears, still feeling sensitive, heard a creak as the little wound on her cheek came open. Three little red confetti crystals of dried blood floated down past her field of view.

Idiot, she thought as the unnatural smile sat on her face, unsure of what to do with itself. *Idiot, you never smile.*

Jacqueline and Mrs. Pinkerton had worked together before, and like their desks, their investigative instincts fit together perfectly. It had always been obvious to Jacqueline that Mrs. Pinkerton belonged here. She'd stayed on the force after her husband departed not just out of duty, desire for more pay, or even the simple fact that she had decades left to offer the workforce. She had stayed, clearly, because she was good at her job. She'd taken on a lot more responsibility since her husband's departure, and "good at her job" now encompassed rather a lot of different aspects of information gathering and personnel handling.

Fortunately (perhaps) for Jacqueline, this keen-eyed work ethic did not seem to extend to personal relationships. For Jacqueline it felt naive to see the good in everyone, but today it stopped Mrs. Pinkerton from looking too close at "Jackie's" affairs. Like watching a wave crash against a cliff face, Jacqueline could see concern for her wellbeing erode any sense of suspicion as Mrs. Pinkerton approached at speed with a miniature first aid kit. She'd procured it from the multi-drawer war chest of a desk that housed everything from her chocolates to last year's blotter. Jacqueline braced herself. Not for pain, but for physical contact.

The sting of alcohol on a fresh wound was actually one of the few sensations Jacqueline cherished. It was a cleansing feeling. Jacqueline liked feeling clean. She did not, however, like being tended to like a child with a scraped knee. More than anything, she did not like being touched. She recognized this for what it was, though, even if Mrs. Pinkerton didn't; this was the price she was paying to avoid talking about her night. She sat dutifully, as if waiting for her portrait. After about a minute, Mrs. Pinkerton stepped away from her work with an empty bandage wrapper and a smile.

"You don't have to say anything," she said in what she probably thought was a comforting tone of voice.

"No shit," Jacqueline accidentally said out loud. Even the staunchly polite Mrs. Pinkerton looked startled. It was her turn to be speechless and Jackie's to say far too much.

"I'm sorry. I...have to go. To the restroom. To clean up."

"Jackie..." Said Mrs. Pinkerton, uncertainty creeping into her sympathetic tone.

"I HAVE TO GO."

She left the dumbfounded Samaritan in the dust of her wake and made a beeline for the restrooms.

Jacqueline stood over the sink, breathing heavily. Where had that outburst come from? She looked up at the mirror. The cold water dripping off her face stung her wound.

"You know where it came from, don't you?" she asked her scowling reflection. It wasn't like her to speak out of turn, or so spitefully. She wouldn't ordinarily have liked to waste the energy. But there was someone else she knew who'd go to great lengths for spite. It was her favorite thing to do.

Her wound throbbed. The bandage was too hot. Everything was too hot. She winced, twitching her cheek. She spotted something peeking out from underneath the gauze. A little dark web of veins, almost black. A bruise? No, she didn't just see it move. Surely it wasn't spreading. Slowly, she brought her hand to the dressing.

She began to pull at it. The lights overhead flickered. Lights could flicker for no reason, she reassured herself, everything was fine. Just as the bandage came away, she doubled over in pain. Her skin was on fire. Her eyes shut reflexively against hot tears and a sharp lump in her throat. *No. No no no.* She put a numb hand to her face. Felt something there, tearing through the skin. Metal. Cold as ice from the night wind. *No, that wasn't right. Stop. Stop it.* She tried to pull at the thing. It itched.

"Is that new?" said a voice from behind her. A man's voice, one that Jacqueline didn't know.

"The chain is," she heard herself say. Herself, but not herself. The words came out of her mouth but not in her voice.

"No, the stud," Jimmy replied.

Yaqui looked down at her hand. Something was on it. Something she couldn't see, but had to get rid of. She chuckled as she tugged it off. Felt right, liking popping bubble wrap or scratching an itch.

Jacqueline screamed silently as she watched her hands tear at her flesh like wrapping paper. More flesh underneath. Almost identical, but not hers. Her face cracked like an egg in the mirror. Underneath, the same face, but not her face. Her mouth screamed in the sink, broken. The one on her face smiled and spoke unbidden.

"The chain is brand new. The Panama Canal of my face, from nose to ear, and you're like, let's stop at this basic-ass archipelago."

Yaqui turned around. Jimmy had some decorum, at least, lace-curtain mama's boy that he was. He was waiting at the door of the restroom, out of the night wind but inside the limits of Yaqui's privacy. He shrugged his big shoulders.

"Some people are cool just going to Hawaii for summer vacation," he said, smiling with his big stupid face.

She mock shrugged back. The shoulders on her studded leather jacket were very expressive.

"Some people are cool drinking eight dollar coffee and wearing shirts with TV show quotes on them. Also those people aren't cool."

He laughed, but then his eyes narrowed a little.

"You ok? Been in here a while..."

Yaqui licked her mouth a bit. Dry.

"Yeah. I think it's worn off. Saw some weird shit. Transcendental. A real trip."

She laughed it off.

"Now tell me what you think of my chain. It means a lot to me."

"What does: my opinion? Or the headgear itself?" He grinned as he sidled his leather clad linebacker bulk closer.

"To reiterate, what do YOU think?" she answered.

"Hmmm..." He rested his arms on her shoulders.

"Get the fuck away from me," Jacqueline breathed sweetly.

"What?" he said, eyes wide in clear bewilderment.

He pulled away. Yaqui shook her head.

"Sorry. Dunno why I said that...ummm...let's go meet up with the others. I'm sure they're eager for a good time. Heaven forbid they have one without me."

The concerned look didn't leave Jimmy's face. He tried to paper a playful tone over the cracks of disquiet in his voice.

"Agreed. I'm starving, and the night is young, but I can't have a good time unless I know you're okay." She blinked and vented a frustrated sigh, blowing her hair out of her face. "And I *don't* know that," he added, gently stepping on her protest.

"We had it all to ourselves. / It was only me and you. When we were livin' on the moon / every day was something new," she recited in a singsong voice.

"Aaaaagh," Jimmy said without any real anguish.

"You're always playing that song." He laughed.

"I know. So that's how you know I'm okay, okay?"

He crossed his arms, and she shoved him in the shoulder.

"Come on! Do I have to walk a straight line too? Because it'll keep right on going out that door without you, you fucking twonk," she said with an air of finality.

"Fuck, I don't know. Maybe."

Her stomach dropped three inches, and her heart climbed toward her throat. She was genuinely taken aback at his response. He knew it too--he'd always had big eyes, like mirrors. She could see her own hurt look in them. He rubbed his lantern jaw, trying to summon the words he needed.

"Look, I know it's clichéd to say but, I'm worried about you. Not just cuz I don't like seeing you strung out; but when you are, I've gotta wonder where it's coming from. Is it me?"

She pursed her lips at him. He pursed his back. They

were actually a little fuller than hers. She'd always been jealous, but he loved to share them. His red hair, which he kept longer than hers, fell down over one of his eyes.

"I know that's a selfish thought, but you've never given me any bullshit, so it's only fair that I'm straight with you. That's just where I'm at."

He towered a full foot over her. Hanging his head like this, he looked like a willow.

"...S-sorry," he said.

She squared her jaw. Put her hand on his cheek.

"I'm fine. And I'll prove it to you."

She tugged at his sleeve.

"Let's go. Everyone's waiting for us."

She started walking forward and tripped. Before she'd even finished falling, the first words out of her mouth were a flustered, "Don't say anything!"

Her legs suitably tangled, she finished falling on her ass and whipped a glare in Jimmy's direction, daring him to speak. His lips were pressed thin as he knelt and put a hand out. And then, something very curious happened. Her leg, not done acting out, spasmed forward and kicked Jimmy in the face.

"Jimmy!" she said, horrified.

"Oh my god! Oh my god oh my god, I'm so sorry."

Her guts squirmed in embarrassment. He was sitting on his ass now too, holding his nose.

"I didn't mean to—"

She stopped when she heard him laughing. He put up his hands in fake surrender.

"Fuck it, right?" he said.

"Night can't get any worse."

She chuckled along with him, but her guts were still squirming. Like something was trying to get out.

He helped her up and she didn't let go. They held hands out the door and down the street. Up ahead, their mutual cohorts awaited them, eyes full of hope for the festivities the night would bring. Lights twinkled around them, out of focus like Christmas eve in the rain. She swayed a little as a head rush washed over her. She found herself fascinated by their faces. Little details stuck out like pearls in the seafoam of the evening.

"Let's get something to eat," said Jimmy as the crowd settled.

Her mouth opened to say yes, but the myth of Orpheus and Persephone clamored and clawed for attention at the back of her mind. She was hungry. Yet part of her really did not want to swallow what was coming next.

"Who's Persephone?" she mumbled angrily, her eyebrows knitting. *Someone from one of those dreams?*

"Hmm?" said Jimmy.

He gave her a quizzical look and then shared it with several of his friends. Her friends. Why couldn't she remember their names?

"Nothing, um, yeah!" she said, her voice cracking.

Was this uncertainty just anxiety? The subtle wrongness hiding behind everything, was she making it worse by overthinking it?

"Where should we go?" said *Nat*. The younger woman's nickname jumped to the forefront of Yaqui's mind like a tripwire had set it off. An artist. She worked her ass off for her name, for recognition. Impossible to forget. Remembering was a balm for the angry red haze of unknowing that Yaqui was dealing with.

"Let's try the pretzel place on Temple Street," said a face which she matched to a name with some momentary difficulty. *Tommy*. Easy enough when it was sitting on a nametag most of the time. He'd pulled so many waiter shifts at so many different restaurants that he always knew where and when to get the best bite in the city. Not that he wouldn't trade that for a better way to make ends meet.

"The guy next door, with the hot dogs? He started selling pretzels to steal business. So of course pretzel guy starts selling hot dogs, and they're WAAYYY better!" Tommy enthused.

"What a cruel twist," said Jimmy.

"Where'd you say this place was, Tom?" said Nat.

Tommy blushed and deflated a little bit.

"Oh, ah, I only ever heard about it. I just love a good story."

Nat shoved him grumpily. The group groaned in mock anger, but Yaqui raised a hand demurely for silence.

"On Temple Street? I know the place. They just cleaned their grill. That's why their stuff's so tasty."

Another cheer went up, and Yaqui led the procession down familiar streets. The pavement was wet, but the rain had let up for the night. The unseasonable warmth hinted that it might return before sunrise, though. The bubble of heat felt ready to burst into more humid downpour.

Temple Street was as busy as ever. Most of the tourists had gone back to their hotel rooms to nurse their jet lag, but business was still bustling. The goods on display were hand crafted and cooked, with pride as the special ingredient.

They arrived at the tiny restaurant without incident. Jimmy's muscles were deterrent enough for any night-time weirdos even without Nat's reputation for a mean punch. Nobody but Yaqui noticed the group of young men give them a wide berth in passing. One group entering, one leaving. Without thinking, she locked eyes with the tallest one. Tanned. Shaved bald. Mean blue eyes with dark circles of no-sleep. Alarm bells went off in her head, and she had no idea why. She glanced at a movement from his hands. He zipped up his jacket, the outline of a shape that might have been a holster briefly visible before it vanished. His face remained cold and impassive as he turned away. Something was not right. The door's bell jingled, and he was gone.

"I think...I knew that guy," she said with some difficulty.

As the rest of them sidled up to the counter, Jimmy shot a glance over his shoulder at the retreating ruffians and then donned a concerned frown.

"From where? He doesn't look like his own mother knows him."

"Think I came across it in a report," Jacqueline said.

The confusion did not leave his gaze.

Yaqui panicked. Where were these thoughts coming from? She'd come out tonight to spend time outside her own head, but her problems had given chase. The acid probably hadn't helped, but that was hours ago. And she'd never gotten anything like this before. Flashes of memory from somebody else who felt REAL. *I'm Yaqui*, she told herself. *I'm Yaqui and I need to finish this conversation with my boyfriend so he doesn't think I'm crazy.*

"A, a news report," she threw in hurriedly to cover herself.

Jimmy chuckled in agreement.

"He looks the type. Glad he didn't have anything to say, then. C'mon. Let's go eat."

Jimmy joined the others. She stalled for a moment, wrestling with thoughts on what to do about the bald-headed man with the gun. Should she turn him in?

...Wait, turn him in? Like, to the cops? Like, *talk* to the cops? In person? Holy shit, fuck that. She shook her head and laughed under her breath. Acid made things feel unreal, but as long as she could remember what was real for *her,* she'd be fine. Yaqui brushed away the cobwebs of unfamiliar thoughts as she joined her friends. She stared at the menu in bright primary colors. Her nose wrinkled at the smell of grease. She heard her mouth say,

"Is there anything without meat in it?"

Her eyes widened a little and she tried to bite back her question. But it was too late. The unfamiliar thought had become unfamiliar words.

"Yes!" said Nat, clapping her hands excitedly.

"I knew you'd come around. Ooh! We can do a cranberry cleanse tomorrow. And I think I've still got some kale from the farmer's market. Do you wanna come to my yoga class too? I'll drive you."

"Ok, that just sounds sarcastic now," said Tommy.

"I'll get the coffee!" Nat added, the note of desperation in her voice taking on a minor key.

"*I'll* get the coffee. Right now," Yaqui replied.

Time to sober up. She unfolded a wad of bills and waved away all the words around her as she paid for everyone. She rubbed the tiny ridges on the money, felt them scratch back like invisible fingerprints. Touch made Yaqui feel more real, less like she was in a dream. She didn't want to think about dreams, given the kind of stuff she'd seen in them the past few weeks. She also definitely didn't want to have a freakout here. A little food would ground her.

"And a classic cheese pretzel, please, Raymond," added Yaqui.

"Easy done," said Raymond from behind the counter.

She tapped her feet idly as the hum of conversation blended with the hum of the fluorescent lights and the hum of the refrigerators and the hum of the air conditioner. Outside, the rain returned. A squall she hoped would burn itself out as quickly as it had arrived. Yaqui had always hated the rain. She slipped deeper into the groove left by the hypnotic rhythm all around her.

Yaqui snapped out of it as she was gently jostled by her friends grabbing their orders. Someone pressed a warm cheese pretzel, still moist through the butcher paper, into her hand. She took a paper cup of coffee in the other as she and the rest exited AMERICAN PRETZELS. The hot food and drink felt really good in her hands as the cool night air returned.

Her friends clustered around her as they all took shelter under the storefront's cloth overhang. As the rain began to give way to fog, her anxiety fled and scattered to the wind. What had she even been worried about? She took a drink of coffee and nearly choked on it.

"Who ordered plain black coffee?" she coughed.

Nobody answered at first. Nat shot a quizzical look her way and Tommy deliberately avoided her gaze. Jimmy's voice came from behind her.

"You did," he said.

The wave crested, the tide of anxiety rolled back in.

"No," she heard herself say.

Jimmy leaned in.

"Listen, if you wanna call it a night..."

"That's not what's happening," she replied angrily. Not at him. Not sure who she was angry at. Yaqui definitely didn't want to call it a night and return home. She didn't sleep much these days, and when she did, she didn't like what she saw. She'd always liked horror movies, but the gore was incessant and always in first-person. She'd stuck to comedies for a while but it hadn't helped. She took a bite of her pretzel to calm her nerves. The effect was immediate, electric, and the exact opposite of what she'd been expecting. Her mouth revolted at the salt and grease and cheese in the pretzel. Images assaulted her mind of factory farms, flies and feces. Bile burned the back of her throat as she forced it down. She swayed as it settled in her stomach. She looked up, anger at the visions directing itself like lightning, at random.

The hairs on the back of her neck prickled. She felt sick and kept glancing at her fingernails to check her blood oxygen level. They remained pink and her pulse remained steady but her body kept telling her something was deeply, deeply wrong. Behind her, there was the unmistakable click, flash, hum and echo of an industrial fluorescent light turning on in the basement of a hospital that wouldn't show up on any map. The kind of place you didn't get to leave without a sized-to-fit black bag. Leather straps tightened and a child whimpered. She screwed her eyes shut. *This isn't really happening. I'm with my friends. I'm safe. I'm*

I'm

A metal helmet came down on her head and clamped into place. Built-in screws bored through her skull and crackled with electricity.

She half-screamed and opened her eyes, batting away the vision of the past like so many cobwebs.

A stranger stood across from them, in the middle of the street, in the middle of the rain. She looked like someone's school teacher. All soft curves and softer pastels. Long chocolate hair. No raincoat, but totally dry.

"Who is that?" Yaqui said distantly, still reeling.

"Who?" said Nat, in between bites.

"Sweetie, you know who I am," said the stranger with a worried tone in her voice.

"What the fuck?" Yaqui said.

"What? Hmm?" said Tommy, looking around.

"She looks kinda like one of my high school teachers... Ms. Perkins?" Yaqui said, shouting the last part.

"It's...Pinkerton. Mrs. Pinkerton? You remember, right, Jackie?" said the stranger in the street.

"Who the fuck? What do you want? What are you standing in the rain for?" Yaqui yelled.

The stranger didn't answer, just wrung her hands and looked back at her with a mixture of pity and confusion.

"There's no one there," said Jimmy quietly. Yaqui's eyes widened. She shook her head.

"No," she gulped. Time was trying to stop. She could feel the particles in the air scratching her insides. The light was turning bitter and blue, disappearing. The stars blurred into each other and winked out until there were only two of them. That same toxic unnatural blue.

"Stop," she gasped. The world felt claustrophobic. These people were crushing her, hemming her in. A maze of bodies becoming a vise. She shoved past the group, into the street.

An oncoming car honked and skidded to a halt a few yards away. The driver, an old man, got out with deep valleys of concern wrinkling his face. She knew him about as well as the stranger in the street, but for some reason wanted his help even less.

Sound was disappearing from the outside world. The only noise that wasn't muted was her heartbeat. It sounded like a party from downstairs that would keep her awake forever.

Her friends were closing in around her. Her anxiety had reached its peak. Her pulse was screaming, a flat whine. Her friends moved into position like a pack of wolves. This was their fault. They were in on it. They'd conspired to bring this moment to her. She tried to shout 'Get away from me,' but all that came out was vomit.

She felt like the sky was trying to pull her into it as she threw up her soul. Technicolor static and unhappy noise streamed out of her mouth. Super massive weight pulled at her from every angle, but she was hollow and there was nothing left inside of her. All she'd ever been now lay pooling at her feet. She looked up at her own face, and she wasn't there.

Jacqueline blinked. She was clean, if not dry. Alive. Whole. Lying in the linoleum hallway leading out of the bathroom. And there, blocking her escape was Mrs. Pinkerton. Jacqueline felt as if she'd just washed up on shore, and the woman opposite was the rock that shipwrecked her. Mortified did not even begin to come close to describing Jacqueline's feelings. Mrs. Pinkerton had doubtless seen everything, and who knew what she'd heard. Retreat was not an option. She'd already been in the restroom for god knew how long, and Mrs. Pinkerton was blocking her only other escape route. Jacqueline's eyes gravitated towards the window. It was so invitingly free of well-meaning interference.

"Jackie?"

Her eyes snapped back. She couldn't believe she'd just considered the window. She was really losing it. Needed to talk her way out of this, which was not her strong suit.

"Listen, Elaine," she began.

"It's Clara," said Mrs. Pinkerton.

Jacqueline's resolve vanished. She climbed to her feet. The fact that even her precision memory had betrayed her was the whipped cream, cherry and syrup on top. Hell, it deserved its own dish. Her stomach twanged. She was seriously regretting skipping breakfast now. At least she still had her bowl of soup waiting back at her desk. She smiled as she began to feel more herself. The smile became a grimace when she saw Mrs. Pinkerton's reaction to her unpracticed use of the expression. It was the kind of smile that brought on a wince for the onlooker. Like the site of a car crash.

She had to collect her thoughts. She tried again.

"Mrs. Pinkerton, Clara, please. I don't know what you think you saw—"

"Jackie. You don't have to worry. Your secret's safe with me. But...you need help."

Jacqueline's spirits sank even further.

"I can't in good conscience ignore this."

The walls were closing in around her.

"I know things have been rough for you. I'm not blind. But this can't happen again."

Jacqueline wanted to shout at her. Tell her this was different. This was *real*. All she could think about was getting to her notes. Taking down the new details that she'd learned about Yaqui. A pearl of resolve formed in the filth of her dilemma. She had to figure out the truth, whatever that was.

Say something.

"I promise. I'll get help. I'll go see a doctor."

"Today," said Mrs. Pinkerton.

"Yes. Today," Jacqueline lied.

"I'll drive you," said Mrs. Pinkerton.

Fuck, she didn't say.

"Okay," she said.

"Just let me head back to my desk real quick. I'd like to at least pretend to get some work done today."

Her laugh was even worse than her smile.

Mrs. Pinkerton winced, but nodded.

"Take all the time you need. Nobody is forcing you to do anything. I just want to make sure you're safe," Mrs. Pinkerton said.

"Thank you, Clara,"

Fuck you, fuck you, fuck you.

Jacqueline made to move past her, and Clara reached out for her arm. A harmless gesture, Jacqueline thought too late. She flinched away with a jerk and a sharp intake of breath.

"Sorry," she said as Mrs. Pinkerton pulled back.

"No I'm sorry. This must be very hard for you. I'll do better to remember to respect your personal space issues," said Mrs. Pinkerton.

Out of one side of your mouth, thought Jacqueline. *Meanwhile, I'm your prisoner. One word and I disappear. Section eight. Disgrace. Padded room,* she thought. *Worst of all, I'll never prove any of those people are real. Never catch...her,* she didn't think. Didn't dare think. She wasn't doing the same thing as admitting what she'd been seeing was real, she told herself. Now all she had to do was not admit it to her doctor, again. If she were lucky she wouldn't end up in a straitjacket anyway.

"Thank you," she tossed over her shoulder.

Jacqueline thumped back into her seat at her desk. Her soup was cold. She glared at it hatefully. She could reheat it, but then it would smell like all the other food that had been cooked in the microwave. All the meat. The inadequacy and the razor thin missed opportunity grated painfully. Not just because she'd missed it hot, but fresh. Unmarred by negative experience. Reheated food *tasted* reheated. It tasted like failure. This wouldn't even be the first time *this week* she'd worked without eating. Work was more important. She could make it. *Third time's the charm.* She tried to focus on something else.

Jacqueline pursed her lips and stared at nothing as the office bustled around her. She'd had a waking dream. That had never happened before. She could write off regular dreams; they only happened at night and only while she was sleeping. This was a new and malignant breed of

Not Okay. If these...visions. No, these *episodes*—Fuck! No. Fuck no. She wasn't going to keep *that* word in her head long enough for whatever coroner performed her x-ray to give those little dark spots nice accurate names.

...*Situations.* If these situations could come at any time, without any discernible trigger, she was truly fucked if she couldn't uncover their source in time. Best get to work, then.

She removed a file from the bottom drawer with a small key she'd taped to the back of a picture frame on her desk. Analog. Away from prying code. You couldn't be too careful these days. She hadn't looked at this folder for a while. She'd been subjected to a primetime horror show of Yakuza's greatest hits for several weeks now. She was ashamed to admit she now preferred that bloody litany to Yaqui's idyllic adventures. At least there wasn't any danger of not wanting to wake up from a nightmare. Of her self disappearing. Jacqueline was a passive observer in Yakuza's nightmares. In the dreams of Yaqui, it felt like she was sinking in quicksand. Warm, familiar quicksand.

Jacqueline focused back in on the present. "Quicksand isn't real," she said to herself.

She flipped to the back and paused over the sparsest dossier in the file she'd built. She grimaced and added "Latest alias: Yakuza. Scar; right cheek."

Yakuza was elusive. An extremely adept predator— no, a parasite. Deadly. Her nature always hidden until it was too late. Jacqueline never saw anything she could use. An endless string of nightclubs and bars that were either poorly lit or in danger of giving her sensory overload, with their blinding strobes and deafening music. Yakuza didn't seem to like looking at faces either, or at least making eye contact. Jacqueline shuddered when she remembered the other woman literally clawing a suitor's face off. These bodies weren't discovered. With or without heads. What was she doing with them? And what was the connection between them and her? To Yaqui? Was there any? And what was her real damn name? This file was nothing but questions.

Yaqui's file was much thicker. She updated the larger sheaf with her new jewelry and the assumed aliases of her group of friends. She reexamined a sketch of a young ginger-haired man with a strong jaw. She added a few freckles she'd missed before. Underneath, she wrote: "Jimmy." She looked up from one face to find another staring at her. How long had Mrs. Pinkerton been sitting there? She stashed the file.

"So," she stuttered.

"How...much did you hear?"

"I don't know what you're talking about, dear," said Mrs. Pinkerton too quickly. Jacqueline squared her jaw and swallowed the silence between them.

"With respect. I know exactly what *I'm* talking about. Please refrain from acting like you do not."

She felt a little light headed from her retort. Mrs. Pinkerton didn't look up.

"It's because I respect you, Jackie, as a friend and fellow officer, that I can't do that," Clara said quietly. A beat cop walked by, headed for the restrooms.

"I don't know what to say to that," said Jacqueline, who legitimately didn't. Lack of conversation in daily life was something of a limiting factor there. Mrs. Pinkerton, who'd followed the bathroom-bound officer with her gaze, snapped it back around to Jacqueline.

"You should make that appointment as soon as you can," she said. There was an urgency in Mrs. Pinkerton's voice she'd never heard before. Jacqueline didn't trust the idea that she was being "helped" purely out of good-natured altruism. There was something like real fear in Clara's eyes though. *Maybe bad-natured altruism.* Anything to get Mrs. Pinkerton off her back.

Jacqueline logged into her desk terminal and pulled up the contact page for her psychiatrist. She hadn't returned for a re-up in some time. The pills didn't stop the dreams.

"Then give me something to stop sleeping altogether," she'd yelled in frustration.

"You are exceedingly lucky that my regard for doctor-

patient confidentiality exceeds your obsession with red flags, Ms. Ueda," he'd retorted evenly.

That had been weeks ago. The thought of trying to face the doctor again after she'd shouted and stormed out made her heart hurt and her head dizzy.

"Jackie, I'm sorry. Really, really sorry. But however you want to do it, we have to leave the office right now. Otherwise you might get in trouble and I won't be able to help you," said Clara.

Oh fuck, what did I do, thought Jacqueline. *I must have done something while I was under. Something crazy.* She punched keys as fast as she was able while Mrs. Pinkerton skewered her with those eyes full of concern. *Something noticeably crazy. Visibly crazy.* She looked down at her hands. Shaking. Visibly shaking. Noticeably shaking. Blood all over them.

No.

A head clasped between them.

No.

She screwed her eyes shut. Hit the enter key. Sent her notice of appointment availability. Nice. Normal. Boring. She opened her eyes.

Clean. No skin caught under her fingernails. Nothing there. Never anything there. *I didn't do anything.* Get a grip. *What did I do?*

Mrs. Pinkerton had grabbed both of their coats. She offered a hand, just outside Jacqueline's personal space.

"Thanks," she said, and breezed past her, almost but not quite putting a grateful hand on the other woman's shoulder.

"Let's go get some breakfast," said Mrs. Pinkerton at earshot decibel.

Jacqueline nodded. As they stepped into the lift, her phone emitted a ding. The doors were closing as she glanced at the screen. An email notification. The captain would like to see her at her earliest convenience in his office. The doors closed just as she heard a frustrated voice say, "Someone get—"

Jacqueline didn't drive very often, if she could help it. Too many variables to contend with on the open road. She was thinking of selling her car. It had been some time since she used it. The city had a robust public transport system, and it wasn't like she was a beat cop. On the job, she mainly dealt with after-action and follow-up investigations. Even with this in mind, she was able to keep her wits about her. Memorizing turns, street names, exits, correlating them with the fastest route in her mind. She had an extremely minor panic attack therefore when Clara took a suboptimal turn.

This is it, said a little voice in her head she only half-hoped was hers. *She lied to you about everything. She's not taking you anywhere except for your last stop ever. You're dead. You're fucking dead. Do something.*

"Ummm...my phone has a map app. If that helps," Jacqueline finally managed.

"Oh, thank you! But that's fine. I know where we're going."

This did not inspire confidence. *Why did you even get in her car?* said the inner monologue. *Perhaps you knew what you'd have to do once she found you out.*

She glanced over at Clara, eyes fixed on the road ahead. *Now's your chance. Three Thursdays ago a prowler tried to rob her as she was getting out of her car. She said she drove him off with the gun she keeps in the glove box. Don't go for yours. She'll expect that. Would take too long. Hers is a .38 special. No safety.*

Time actually seemed to crawl as she reached, with glacial slowness, for the compartment button. Out of the corner of her eye, Clara frowned and began to look her way. *Think fast, kid. Don't let me get in your way.* No, this was insane. *Relax. You don't have to pull the trigger. Just point it at her empty fucking head and tell her where to go.*

She could see Clara's mouth begin to form the word "hey."

"I need a tissue," she heard herself say.

"Oh," said Clara at normal speed, shattering the petrified moment.

"Here you go," she added, deftly reaching into the purse by her feet.

"Elaine had a pretty bad pollen allergy so I'd always keep these handy."

A flashbulb went off inside Jacqueline's head.

"Elaine was your daughter," she said.

Clara smiled warmly.

"Yes, that's right. She'd be glad you remembered."

Jacqueline took the tissue. She dabbed at the sweat on her brow as mundane details left no room for paranoia in her mind. Clara's daughter was real, so much more real than thoughts that came from nothing and could only feed on each other.

"She came to the office one day," she said.

Clara nodded, "She liked you. Thought your jacket looked cool. You were very busy that day, but I think the two of you would have gotten along swimmingly."

Something clicked. It was the way Clara used the word "would." Jacqueline cast her eyes downward. Of course. That's why she'd remembered that name for her. It had been the one name Clara had spoken into Jacqueline's hazy periphery the most. Even towards the end. Perhaps especially.

"She had a coloring book. One of those really complicated ones. For adults," said Jacqueline.

Clara chuckled. "Oh yes! She was always so bright."

She laughed again.

"I don't know if you saw, but she was watching you at work in your sketchbook. And, you have this, I dunno, *way* about you when you get really into your work. Where you cross your legs and stick your tongue out a bit. Just a bit, and—" She laughed again.

"She sits herself down right next to you and just has you down to a T."

Her eyes crinkled with the light of mirth. She cocked

her head to the side and stuck out her tongue a bit. Just a bit. More pleasant laughter. Jacqueline smiled with her eyes. A good memory.

"That was a good day. I did actually notice her there, but if she was anything like me...I know I hate being interrupted at work."

"Yeah. That might have been the best day she had in a...while," Clara replied.

"...Thank you," she added.

Jacqueline looked down at the glove compartment. She scowled. She couldn't believe what she'd been considering. Perhaps the situations she'd been having were just leaving more of a mark than she'd realized. She felt dirty. She looked up and was greeted with the sight of a large neon-lit sign fizzling a little bit in the mid-morning rain and fog. It had incorporated images of food into some of its lettering. A fried egg for the "O," for example. This was no doubt humorous to someone.

"Oh," said Jacqueline as they pulled into the parking lot.

"You uh, weren't kidding about breakfast," she said.

"Well, you almost certainly skipped eating again this morning," Clara said.

Jacqueline swallowed. She really had to be more aware of when she was being watched.

"That, and breakfast is the one thing I never kid about," joked Clara.

Jacqueline decided to try and lighten the mood as well.

"Do you, um, wanna use the handicap spot? I think I qualify."

She knocked on the side of her head for effect.

Clara tsked.

"Oh, Jackie. That's not funny. Come on now."

Jacqueline tried to take her foot out of her mouth.

"Fuck. You're right. I'm sorry."

She paused.

"Shit. I mean, shoot. Sorry again. For cursing. So much."

"Hey," said Clara, parking the car.

"It's ok. Take it easy."

She put out a hand that was clearly used to resting comfortingly on shoulders, but stopped just in time. She hesitated, and then pulled it back into a fist hanging ambivalently in the air between them. Jacqueline looked at it. The rain drummed lightly on the roof of the car. She gave it a bump.

Pools of quiet yellow phosphor interrupted the busy grey light from the rain outside. Jacqueline knew the diner pretty well, in the sense that she knew all diners like it. It had an atmosphere of emptiness she enjoyed. As if she'd just missed a party—another thing she enjoyed doing. This one in particular, she had not set foot in. Name brand in everything but name. People were always talking about eating there, but she was pretty sure it wasn't a chain... yet. She'd have to look hard for something on the menu that wasn't processed.

They took a booth in the corner of the restaurant facing the door. Rather, Jacqueline took it and Clara followed. She sat opposite Jacqueline with her back to the entrance. *I'll just have to watch our backs for the both of us.* She decided not to mention to Mrs. Pinkerton why she'd chosen to sit at this vantage point. It would not help her case. *Not to mention she saw me doing...god knows what I was doing. I have to find out. Play along with teatime for now. What is she hiding? What won't she tell me?*

"So doc," she tried,

"Give it to me cold. How much of a headcase am I?"

Clara scoffed, but not unkindly.

"Really Jackie, you've got to stop talking like that about yourself. Besides, I'm not sure this is the best place to be discussing that," she said just above a whisper. *Strike one. Damn. No way around it.*

The curtain of pretense dropped. Jacqueline took a deep breath.

"I'm going to need you to start being straight with me immediately. You had no right to drag me along on this adventure. I was perfectly capable of taking care of this problem myself and further, I did not want to go but I was made to feel like I didn't have a choice and what's worse is I feel like you knew that and used it against me."

Her sotto voce outburst had rendered her light-headed again. Her throat was hot and dry. Her eyes were salty. Clara leaned back, eyes wide like Jacqueline was about to hit her. Despite Jacqueline's reservations the words kept coming. She'd spent so long behind a dam of silence, and now she was drowning because she'd never tried to swim.

"But more than anything, I need to know what happened because *I have no idea*. I am Fucking terrified that I'm losing my mind and that I might have—"

She swallowed the word *killed*—

"Hurt someone without realizing it."

They stared at each other as the waiter approached. Heavily tanned. Slick black hair.

"Hey there, guys! My name is Tommy. I'll be your waiter this morning. Can I start you off with anything?"

Clara blinked and tried to compose herself.

"Yes. Um—"

Jacqueline piped in without thinking. "Two coffees. One black, no sugar. One with vanilla half & half, one sugar, one stevia. Two eggs sunny side up, runny yolk. One side of wheat toast, one side of bacon, extra crispy and two sausage links. I'll have a vegetarian breakfast burrito."

Tommy was commendably fast on the uptake, jotting down notes. Clara a little less so, dumbstruck apparently, as Jacqueline recited her order for her, and so perfectly. She looked down at her phone, trying to think of a response she could use to delay her "urgent meeting" with the chief. She looked back up to find Clara staring at her, goggle-eyed. *Fuck. Shouldn't have snapped at her like that.* She hoped Clara wasn't too upset.

"How did you...?" said Clara, waving a hand in the

direction of the retreating Tommy.

Jacqueline blanched. *The order.* She shouldn't have known it so well. Or at all. Regular people didn't pick up that much through casual observation, much less retain it perfectly for an indefinite length of time. An eidetic memory made her weird, brought more attention her way. *Shouldn't have said anything.* Why couldn't she have just waited? Now she had to explain. Or try to, anyway.

"Umm, you've brought take-out from this place to work before. You always got the same thing," she attempted softly.

Clara shook her head a little.

"I've been here maybe three times. And it's not like I was putting my order on the bulletin board."

"Four times," said Jacqueline before she could stop herself. Clara sat back, mouth agape.

Jacqueline shrugged, resigned. "I can remember... everything. Perfectly. It gets...heavy sometimes. The weight of every memory piling on, like...snowflakes. But it's the one thing that's never failed me. Now you know why remembering stuff correctly is so important to me, I guess," she added lamely.

"I suppose I do," replied Clara.

"Alright then. When I found you in the restroom you'd uh, made a mess."

Jacqueline stared at her blankly.

"What does that mean? Did I shit myself? You need to give me specific details," Jacqueline said.

Clara frowned and pursed her lips.

"Please," said Jacqueline.

"You kicked a pipe. Out of the wall, from under the sink. You were talking to someone who wasn't there, and then you fell over...and then I think you started seizing because your foot shot out while you were sitting there. One kick was all it took. You've gotta show me your leg workout." She laughed weakly.

"God," Jacqueline said, bringing her hand to her temple. She hung her head, staring into the middle distance.

"It's, it's not that bad," Clara soothed. "Those pipes were ancient. Coming apart anyway. And a little water never hurt anybody."

Jacqueline looked up.

"But you see the problem, right? I couldn't account for my own actions. What happens next time? When does it happen again? These are questions I don't have answers to. Living like this is completely unacceptable," she said.

"What are you saying, Jackie?" said Clara in an extremely worried tone.

"It means I'm basically a fucking werewolf, Clara. And given the choice between a straitjacket or being loose on the streets, I'd take a bullet."

That was easier to say than she'd thought it would be.

Clara's figure quivered like a mountain about to become a volcano. Her face, ordinarily the picture of serenity, was now closer to wide-eyed demon than grinning cat.

"Jackie!" said Clara angrily, doffing her inside voice.

"Hey, keep it down," said Jacqueline, looking around the empty restaurant.

"YOU keep it down! You—*you* can shut *up!*" she said matter-of-factly.

"Oh?" said Jacqueline bemusedly, savaged by the proverbial puppy.

"That's right. You know what, I'm glad I decided to 'drag you along' today. It's a good thing I *did*, because shame on you, Jacqueline Ueda! Don't ever say anything like that again. Why, we're going to—and just what is so funny?"

Jacqueline couldn't keep the laughter in.

"You finally used my name. My real one. I—"

She didn't finish the sentence— *hate being called Jackie.*

"...Really prefer being called by my full name."

"Oh," replied Clara, the fever of her ire broken. "I didn't know that."

Tommy returned arm in arm with their food. He was rather good at balancing. Silence prevailed as the dishes came down for a landing, one by one. Jacqueline looked down at her plate as Clara set a napkin in her own lap. She looked up from the French fries she hadn't ordered.

"Do you want my fries?" she asked.

"Sure," answered Clara.

"You forgot the hash browns in my order," she smiled.

"The—" Jacqueline plumbed the depths of her memory.

Clara laughed pleasantly.

"I can never help myself. I always eat them first, before I get back to the office or the house."

"Thank you," said Jacqueline, pushing the little plate over to Clara.

"You're welcome, Jacqueline," said Clara. Jacqueline smiled just a little bit and took a bite of her burrito.

ANTIHISTAMINE. DISINFECTANT. MAGAZINES, MOSTLY about experimental alternative treatments. Much the same as the last time Jacqueline been there. And the time before that, and so on. *A lot of children here today.* Thinking back on it, there had always been at least one when she'd visited. Her psychiatrist shared the building with a neurology clinic. She shouldn't have been surprised Clara knew the way to the place so well. Thank god she hadn't wanted to stay. Well, that wasn't true. She'd had to be convinced that she didn't want to stay. There had nearly been a hug.

Jacqueline watched a doting mother dab drool away from the mouth of her chair bound child. One of the child's eyes met her own. She looked away. Stared at the wall. Ugly sea green. Mottling in the stucco like little continents. Swamp planet with tiny ocean. Uneasy peace.

"Dr. Folsom will see you now," said a voice to her left.

Finally. She hadn't expected to be seen, really. She'd just hoped for proof that she'd been, to get Clara off her back. But here she was. On such short notice, too. She followed the nurse past the sign-in desk and down a very clean, well-lit hallway. Hospitals had always made Jacqueline feel at ease. They were places of singular purpose ironing out the messy details of the world into clean linen, neat stitches and crisp documentation. She swallowed as she passed an orderly pushing a cart of medicine bottles. A foul, dry taste assaulted her sense memory.

And pills, of course. One could not forget the trail of scrips she'd left in her wake. And here was the source. Dr. Folsom had a large and imposing oak door with his surname and title on a bronze plaque. Art deco font. Real engraving, not screen printed at a copy store. The picture of ostentatiousness befitting a pusher of his position. She raised a hand to knock, but before she could make a sound she was interrupted.

"Come in!" said a jovial transatlantic accent with a dash of honey and about a pound of gravel. She'd made no noise, hadn't even knocked. Yet he somehow knew she was there. Jacqueline shrugged, and sighed. Typical of him to start the mind games ahead of time. She'd played them before though, and always won. In she went.

Into almost complete blackness. Nothing so dramatic as the door slamming shut behind her on its own happened, but her every instinct screamed at her to run. She tried to take in her dim surroundings. The windows had been nearly wallpapered over with pages of notes. Stuck together. Illegible.

A new shape in the corner drew her attention. Far more frightening than any boogie man she could come up with was something so out of place it might as well have been a hallucination.

A blanket fort. Constructed out of torn-off curtains and rearranged furniture. She took a step forward and her ankle caught on something. String. Tripwire. Moment of vertigo in darkness. Reflexes kicking in. Floor. Roll. Hand on gun. Wind overhead. Loud noise. Wood against wood. Door slamming. More darkness. Eyes adjusting. Rope creaking. Chair hanging from ceiling. Draw the gun. Aim it at that stupid fort. Safety off.

Sharp pain in her right hand. Not enough time to process noise before a-

blow to the side of her head. Falling over. Consciousness fading in and out. Stay awake. Something touching her face. Cold. Metal. Wet. Her own blood. Coppery scent of it.

"I didn't think I'd see you again," said Dr. Folsom's voice from above her. His golf club rested against her forehead. Her pulse was going wild. Loudest thing in her ears.

"After what you did to me, I expected you to be in the wind. A psychotic break of that magnitude typically precipitates a complete departure from the previous self. Wanderlust. Vagrancy. A paranoid desire to remain 'on the run,' as it were."

His face was starting to come into focus. She really wished it hadn't. It was off kilter. It floated above his dress shirt with the rolled-up sleeves and the tacky tie like a Picasso painting in the dark. She had to be dazed. One of his eyes was higher than other. Both looked so shiny in shadow. Moons. Coins. Those deep sea fish with the lures. Something fell into place in her head. Maybe jostled loose from the blow. Funny.

"This isn't really happening," she said out loud.

"Now I'm really hurt," growled Folsom. He leaned forward. She could see a jagged line of stitches bisecting his face now. Right between his eyes, almost diagonal.

"Look at what you did *to my face.*"

"I am looking," she said serenely. "And the more I look, the less trouble I'm having believing this is just some fucked up fever dream. I probably fell asleep in your waiting room. I mean, look at you. You're a monster."

He gritted his teeth.

"I would choose my next words very carefully, were I you," he said.

"Okay," she said, annoyed. "You aren't real. You're a metaphor for the consequences of my unfulfilled responsibilities or something. This whole room, this whole situation is a farce."

"I could not agree more," said Folsom, and pressed the putter into the flesh of her damaged wrist. White hot pain. Stars behind her eyes. Gasping for breath. Not crying out. Clenched teeth.

"Better now?" he said. He straightened up, leaning back on his club.

"You really don't remember, do you? You walked *right* through that door, without an appointment, mind you. Walked *right* up to my desk," he said, his voice crumbling,

"Tossed it aside like a toy, and *took* my face in your hands like you were peeling an orange and just *pulled* and *pulled* and *pulled* and *pulled*," he nearly shrieked. He looked right at her, as fear returned with the pain.

"I nearly died. Should be dead, really. But you didn't finish the job. Shouldn't be surprised, given your issues with commitment."

He leaned close. Jacqueline tried to look away, but he forced her chin back and up.

"Days of unconsciousness. Weeks of recovery. Nearly a month of silence. Haven't taken on any clients since I got back. Couldn't afford the distraction. I needed to plan, figure out how to get you back here. I've paid for it. Literally, mind you. This office was almost due for repo when you called on me. I couldn't believe my luck. I hadn't outed you yet. Hoped that would lull you into a false sense of security. And here you are. Fully armed, no less."

He picked up her gun, not taking his horrible eyes off her.

"Your paranoia has gotten worse, it seems. Looks like I made the right call."

He wagged the weapon at her condescendingly. He had no trigger discipline. Jacqueline was beginning to hyperventilate.The air scratched at her lungs like sandpaper.

"You're well overdue for a refill," he said. He stuffed a hand into a pocket in shadow, dropping the club as he rooted around. Desperately, she tried to piece at least two thoughts together beyond *let this not be real* and *I don't want to be here*, respectively.

"Here we go," he burbled, rattling a pill bottle free.

He thought *she'd* done this to him.

"It's your favorite. I got your favorite."

It had to be Yakuza. She'd graduated from murder to torture. From live shows to audience participation. She knew Jacqueline's doctor. Maybe knew where she worked, lived. Maybe knew everything. The abyss looking back.

"A nice little cocktail of amphetamines and this

year's most fashionable chemical runoff. Forty capsules of oblivion." He dropped the bottle onto her stomach.

No.

It was time to stop. There was time she couldn't account for. Vivid dreams that felt like memories. Evidence of violence staring her right in the face. For the first time in his career, her doctor was right about her. Perhaps he'd been right all along. It was time to stop running.

"Now," he said with an air of anticipation. "You're going to take all of those. The lot. If they don't kill you, you'll have a nice little episode, and we can have you committed without all of that trial and accusation business."

He cocked her gun inexpertly.

"Or, if you'd prefer a more direct approach, we can say there was a struggle, I managed to wrestle your gun away from you, et cetera, et cetera."

He pointed the gun right between her eyes. There it was. The bullet and the padded room. She held up the pills, pills that represented a trip to the padded room. They always had. In any context, taking pills was like admitting defeat, admitting she was crazy. She couldn't see the padded room, but knew it was hiding inside the bottle. Regular fear lingered from dealing with a mad doctor, but now there was something deeper. Existential, in her bones, the fear that he might be right. The fear that this is where her story was meant to end. Worse still, she'd be responsible for how it ended. Here was the choice. Far too early. *No.* Just in time to stop her before she hurt anyone else. *Reach for the club. He'll see it coming. Shoot you in self-defense. Neat. Like a puzzle. Quick. Painless.* She inched her fingers along.

"I've just decided," he added thoughtfully, "That I'd prefer for you to take your medication after all. It's important to the process of closure that you suffer just as much as I did, please."

That settled it. She continued to move her hand. The sprain started to itch, down to the bone, where she couldn't scratch it.

"Otherwise!" he intoned, "I'll have to shoot you in the stomach, legs, that sort of thing. You understand."

She froze. Her skin felt too tight.

"That's it. Off you pop," he said as she began to fiddle with the lid. Her insides were clenched so tight she felt as if she might snap her own spine. She tried to focus on opening the childproof lock while ignoring the sensation of her bones grinding against each other. His hand holding her gun started to shake.

"Can't. Can't get. It off," she forced out. His breathing, so loud.

All sound cut off. His face contorted into shouts, features distorting like he was in a high wind. Everything muffled, cold. She felt an arm stretch. Inside of her. Up her throat. Rising like bile. A fist curled involuntarily in the throes of a yawn. Coming to rest just beneath her larynx. She was already dead. Had to be dead. Wished she was. Her skeleton pitched itself forward. The rest of her body went with it. Collided with the other body. She was a silent movie starring a series of confused images. Impacts fell upon her, along her arms. Inside her fists. Again and again. Dimly felt something in her hands. Rigor mortis grip closed on the objects. Intimately familiar. A gun and a bottle of pills. Instinctive. Swing the gun toward the light. Arms framed against it like a trebuchet. Pull the trigger. Let fly. Black on gold. War at dawn. Moving toward the horizon at light speed. Fire. Fire. Fire.

She was on fire. Bursting through the bullet holes into a blank sprint. Blank thoughts. Legs propelling her forward into the blinding white. Hair gone. Clothes gone. Skin and flesh burning away behind her. Leaving behind nothing but muscular action and

And

And

And it wasn't like she went looking for trouble. Yaqui stumbled at a wicked head rush. Worst fucking time to smoke, shit. Her lungs were burning as she ran.

Not like she'd known. If Yaqui'd known some psycho asshole was going to give her shit for no reason, then yeah of course she'd'd've waited.

"Get the FUCK back here! HEY," screamed the guy chasing her. She got one good look at him over her shoulder before she turned a corner out of Dead Cat Alley onto Glacier Street. Jesus fuck. It was that fucking skinhead from the pretzel shop. One look at him and now he was after her like a fucking horror movie.

"Help! Fucking HELP. Somebody help me!" she screamed, out of breath. No doors opened.

"Fuck this I am NOT getting murdered," she said to herself. She ran up to one of the little suburban doors. Letting her momentum carry her, she aimed her boot right by the door knob.

The top hinge nearly came off as she fell over herself into the threshold of the little home. Nice living room. A scream rose from the kitchen nook. The grandma there looked almost as mean as Yaqui's prospective killer. The old woman's outfit was all hard angles. Shoulder pads, horn rim glasses, a beehive that was more of a hornet's nest. Yaqui saw the psycho running up the drive. Same bald head. Same denim jacket. Same sour scowl on his light brown features. Same gun. She slammed the door and pushed the grandma-looking couch in front of it. She grunted, suppressing a small scream of her own as she held the couch in place against the thug's collision. A side table carrying a copy of *Little House On The Prairie* fell over.

"Let me in You NARC PIECE OF SHIT," he shouted.

"Fuck you," she cried back, "You're fucking crazy!"

"I am calling the police!" said the old woman whose house she'd invaded.

"The police are being called," she relayed, hoping to drive him away.

"You would, *Jacqueline*. That's right. I found you out. You're fucking dead. Dead."

"My name is Yaqui, asshole. Fuck off. You've got the wrong person."

He slammed against the door again, but the couch held fast.

"I SAW you kill three of my guys," he said after he caught his breath,

"Did a little digging. Wasn't cheap. But you're good for it, right? I heard the cops got a lot of money this year."

"I am calling the Poliiice!" the woman in the kitchen cried again.

"THEN CALL THE FUCKING POLICE," snapped Yaqui.

"Hello?" said the homeowner frantically. She was already on the phone. The thug kicked at the door again before speaking,

"I don't know if VICE actually got clearance to kill people or if you're dirty or what, *but I don't fucking care.* We are *paid up* with you fucking pigs. I know your goddamn face now. You're ffffucked, hear me?"

Sirens blared down the street.

"Fuck-!" said the voice of the thug as it disappeared into the distance.

Thank god. She guessed somebody had been listening to her after all. Beaten Ms. Manners here to the punch. Speaking of which...

"You can relax now. He's gone," said Yaqui, catching her breath.

"Yes but You're NOT," the woman said unkindly. She looked like she did everything unkindly. She'd hung up when she heard sirens but was now redialing, having realized her mistake.

"Hey, come on, look I'm sorry about your door—"

"You scraped up my floor with the couch," she hissed, covering the receiver, "Hello? Yes I know this number just called. No, I can hear them outside. I'm not deaf. No, you're not listening—"

"Why don't you have scuff-pads? Fuck it— I'll pay for it! I'll pay for everything, just *hang up the phone,*" Yaqui shouted, at the corner of frustrated and frantic.

The old woman pursed her lips and narrowed an appraising glance at her before hanging up.

"Alright," she said finally,

"Say I believe you...cash," she enunciated with an air of finality.

"Okay. Can you drive me to the bank?" Yaqui enunciated back.

"I heard some of what your boyfriend was yelling out there. Junkies like you always carry cash, right?" She said this as if she were very clever to have figured this out.

Yaqui wouldn't say she was speechless. There was a lot she would say.

"I have a fucking name. If you want to see dime one from me, you will use it. I know you heard it because you heard enough to talk shit."

"You brought a dangerous criminal to My Neighborhood, came into My Home, scratched up My Floor—you don't *get* to make demands," the woman fired back.

"Some psycho was trying to kill me. I just didn't want to *die*. What the fuck is your problem with that?" said Yaqui incredulously.

The old woman shook her head and grimaced like she was correcting a wrong answer on a test. "You're trash. You've got nobody to blame but yourself for the situation you're in," she said with relish.

"Don't act like you know me," said Yaqui as her fists clenched.

The old woman leaned over the kitchen counter.

"You *reek* of weed," she nodded, eyes wide. Yaqui's cheeks grew hot.

"I don't have to take this," she muttered.

"Hey!" the woman shouted as Yaqui scraped the couch some more moving it away from the door. She clack-clacked towards Yaqui in her thick plastic heels. Yaqui shoved the couch into the woman's ankles with a mighty scrape. She went over like a tree, bouncing her face off the couch and landing flat on her back.

"You'll pay for this!" she said from the floor in agony.

"Sure, if the bank's still open," said Yaqui with a cold

smile, and ducked outside into the bright sunlight.

Jacqueline blinked against the glare. She looked around the downtown intersection. Five or six people weren't too busy to stare at her. She took in the glass storefront of the coffee shop she was standing in front of and the wreckage of tables and chairs within. She snapped her head around at movement in her vicinity.

"You ok, lady?"

He looked like he worked construction. Old. Fat. Balding. Big beard, graying. Thin little mustache. Calluses on his hands. Also, he was too fucking close.

"Back. Up," Jacqueline said curtly, raising the gun she hadn't let go of. The old man cried out and nearly fell over himself backwards. He put out a hand to cover his face.

"Please," he sputtered.

Jacqueline recoiled as what she'd just done hit her. She spun around. More movement. More people backing away. More people beginning to notice. She swallowed the words: "Don't Move." Forced the gun back down to her side. She shunted all her fight-or-flight instincts into a single outlet and bolted. The sun was setting. She stuffed the gun back in her jacket. Her hand hurt. Fingers red and white from gripping the gun too long. Nobody followed. She took as many alleyways as she could, heading for the railway. Down the steps, too many people on their phones. Too many people looking her way as she passed.

Jacqueline bought her ticket without incident. Got on the muni railcar without incident. Sat down without incident. She sat very still as the railcar rattled along the tracks and tried not to have an incident. Another incident. She looked down at her feet and imagined no floor there. She wished it were true. Wished she could just fall forward and be dashed into six billion pieces. Disappear.

A single, dry, half-hearted sob escaped her.

Jacqueline wanted to vanish. She knew Yaqui was fake. Knew it like bad news at sunrise. Yet she wanted nothing more right now than to cease to exist and become a part of this other self and her life. Turbulent as it was, at least it wasn't hers.

She looked up at the lights overhead. They were louder than they were bright. Buzzed like bug zappers. She realized she was falling for another kind of trap. Even the strife present in these waking dreams was meant to draw her in, make her care about this fiction more than the real world. This time had been even worse. She'd slipped right into this other world. Her thoughts and wants perfectly in sync with the narrative she was feeding herself. It wasn't even that she'd been worn like a glove; she'd *been* a glove in the pocket of a coat in the closet. Barely even a witness. At least an observer would have the agency to be able to stop watching.

This was the kind of discussion she'd like to conduct from a red couch. Not that she'd ever come close to admitting this level of dysfunction in her brain, but she would have liked the option. As it was, her therapist was insane and wanted to kill her. She could only hope he wouldn't come after her again. She looked straight ahead at her reflection in the window.

"I'm crazy," Jacqueline said out loud. Her reflection stared blankly back at her. It did not answer. Neither did the three or four other people in the muni railcar. They were likely used to people talking to themselves. She felt the inside of her jacket pockets. She was still carrying the choice around with her, in there. The pill and the bullet. She looked back up at her reflection.

"...That's what you want, isn't it?" she said slowly. No reply. But she knew she was right. Even if the things she'd seen weren't real,

"They aren't," she said.

Even if they aren't. These impulses and...situations are coming from somewhere. This other self. Whatever wedge of her brain was doing this to her knew how she'd react, what she'd do next. She took out the pill bottle. *Suicidal ideation.* If she "cured" herself, the other side would essentially die. She put the pills away. Brushed against the gun, hesitated, hurriedly pulled her hand out. Folded them both in her lap. Her wrist still hurt. That and the pills at least confirmed where she'd been, if not what she'd done.

She sighed. She admitted she hadn't felt truly happy in quite some time, but...was this her subconscious going to work on putting her out of her misery? She looked down at the holster in the crook of her armpit. Should she even have this? She stood up.

"I'm still a detective."

This got the attention of a few people, though they had sense and self-preservation enough to turn away almost immediately. She had been manipulated up to this point. This otherness wanted her mad, gone from the face of civilized society. Well, if she was going to be mad, she might as well retain the ability to end it all on her own terms.

She walked to the door. Looked out the little window but avoided her reflection's gaze. Waited for the muni railcar to slow down. Spotted the sign showing the stop she was at. Same as it ever was. She shook her head.

No. No, this wasn't her stop. Wasn't anywhere near her home. Why did it feel so familiar? Whose stop was this? She looked again at the sign.

Glacier Street. She licked her lips. Dry. So dry. She could see it clearly in her head. The path that would take her home. Up and out of the station. Down a few streets she knew like the back of her hand, and into a warm, well lit—

The doors clanked open loudly, and she hurriedly stepped back.

Up, out and into a stranger's home. A place she had absolutely no reason to be. That'd be it. She'd be done, if she wasn't already. The doors closed. She watched the stop speed away. Hers was still a while out.

There might have been answers up there, she thought.

"No. Just strangers. Can't risk it," she said. One of the other patrons coughed.

When Jacqueline finally got off, night had fallen. It was that special kind of bitter, freezing cold right after it rains. She followed the mist of her breath home.

"Jackie? Oops, I mean, Jacqueline?"

Jacqueline squared her shoulders and took a deep breath before turning around. Cold air burned her lungs and nose.

"Heeyyy," she tried to say with some enthusiasm.

Clara waved hello and walked closer. She had a muff around her hands to keep the cold off her fingers.

"Hey you," she said warmly,

"How are you feeling? Any better?"

Jacqueline wasn't sure how to respond to this. Rather, she was quite capable of responding, but not in any way that would make her sound sane. She'd have to stall. She raised her eyebrows in surprise.

"What are...you doing here?" she attempted lamely.

"I just got off," Clara replied, indicating the precinct station up the street with a shrug.

Right. That hadn't worked. Of course it hadn't worked. What were you thinking? Now you have to tell her everything. Only you don't have anything to tell her. *Push her down the stairs.* There's not that many people around. *Push her down the railway steps. Shoot the witnesses.* It's dark. Not too many will have seen you. *Shoot anybody who saw you. One bullet left. They'll never catch you. Never let them catch you. Put the gun in your mouth. Put the fucking gun—*

"Jacqueline?"

She blinked. Stared at Clara, staring at her.

"Oh, uh," she rummaged around in her coat. Brushed against the gun.

"Yeah, um, shi-shoot," she mumbled, checking her pockets.

"Did your doctor's visit go well?" Prompted Clara helpfully.

Jacqueline really wanted to say no. Thankfully, she produced the pills first. Her wrist twinged again as she pulled them free.

"Ta-daa," she winced, rattling them around.

"Oh, good," said Clara. And that seemed to be the end of it.

Wait, really? She was almost a little insulted. Hatred bubbled up inside her. All that talk about being her friend. All that bluster about respect and wanting her to be safe, and this is what it all amounted to? She wanted Clara to ask more questions, to probe deeper. If this is what being her friend meant, she didn't want Clara to respect her boundaries. She wanted to be found out. She wanted to be helped. *Please help me.*

"Well," said Clara only a little uncomfortably after Jacqueline had stared at her without saying anything for one minute,

"I'd better be getting home."

Jacqueline shook herself.

"Oh yeah, of course. Sorry. Haha. It's these... little guys." She shook the pill bottle again. "They make me a little spacey. Hahaha." *Lame excuse. Meds for seizures or psychosis take weeks to kick in. She'd know that. Would she know that? Maybe she'll realize I'm lying. Maybe she'll want to actually help me.*

"Hahaha," said Clara. "...Well. Good night," she added. *God damn it.*

"Good night," said Jacqueline. *Fuck you.*

Clara walked down the steps to her own waiting muni car. Alone again, Jacqueline walked toward home. Amigara Street.

She stopped at the AllNiteDrug on the way there for a flimsy knockoff arm brace and the strongest painkiller she could get over the counter. A power bar made her stomach feel a little better. The power bar had a paper wrapper: *Locally sourced protein!* The young man behind the counter had a big mustache.

Outside now, away from the headache-inducing fluorescent glare. A movement caught her eye as she was putting away her wallet. She looked up. It was her reflection. Her colors stood out boldly in the black window. The space was for lease. Empty. She looked into her eyes.

Empty.

"Fuck you," she said.

"You're garbage," she said.

"You made yourself Clara's problem. She's not your mother," she said.

Who is your mother?

She threw the bottle of pharmacy painkillers at the window. They bounced off and rolled into a storm drain. She looked at it for a second. She went back inside and bought some ointment instead. And another power bar. She was hungry.

Jacqueline lay on her bed and stared at the ceiling. She ate the last bite of her power bar and crumpled up the wrapper. She threw it on the garbage pile. She thought about what she'd seen today. About what it meant.

If she assumed at least 70% of the things she saw weren't real, she was left to wonder why her brain was showing them to her. What did they mean? Where did they come from?

Some things were easy to place. The thug who'd been chasing Yaqui was obviously a manifestation of her fear of being caught. Triggered, likely, by confronting Doctor Folsom.

Reliant on the notion that what you saw in his office actually took place.

She massaged her wrist through lightly gritted teeth. She reached over and rubbed a little more ointment on it.

"If it wasn't real, my course of action is the same.

Nothing."

Say the nightmare in the office wasn't real. Being chased through the streets was?

"One does not presuppose the other. It's more likely that neither took place."

And it's most likely of all that it is still happening. You can't trust what you see anymore. You're crazy.

She pinched the nerve between her ulna and radius. The pain took her breath away and left spots dancing in her eyes.

Synesthesia.

"That's the wrong word. But I already thought about that. I know what blunt force trauma looks like. This wound isn't self-inflicted," she choked out.

No response.

"The cut on my face might be, though. If we start putting stock in things like limbic resonance, we've already lost."

Her internal dialogue was silent.

"The rest is cut and dry. My waking dreams featuring the thug came from my memories of him in a lineup. Just another face to regurgitate."

He said she killed his men.

"No, 'he' didn't 'say' anything." The allusions to Yakuza were too obvious to miss. Another manufactured connection.

We established Yakuza is you.

"We didn't est… There is no WE. Nothing is established. My mind is making connections where none exist. Looking for meaning where there isn't any. There's no mystery to solve here. I am alone in my head."

I am alone.

"I am alone."

She began her breathing exercises.

"I am alone."

Jacqueline fell asleep.

She was home. Well, in a home. She felt a little funny here. Getting all sorts of impressions. A lot of mesoamerican stuff. Imported. A lot of jade, though that was hidden away where people couldn't see. Even the black hardwood walls had been felled near the Amazon, varnished with a mixture of their mother sap and a touch of formaldehyde. Homesick or just ostentatious? Ceilings were pointlessly tall. Nothing up there but view.

Nice place, definitely. Too bad she couldn't stay long. It was big. Really big. Parts of it were underground. Garage might be useful later. She'd need to hotwire whatever she took. Not wasting any time looking for keys. Something old. She'd always wanted to drive one of those really fancy old cars. Now did she want red...or yellow? She wasn't sure she wanted to be noticed on the way out. She hoped just being here would be enough. Maybe she'd take a black one. Black was cool, too.

"Batman," she said out loud.

Someone said something off to her left. She looked around. A blonde woman with a pinched face looked at her.

The woman said something again. It didn't seem important so she ignored it. She looked around the foyer some more. There was a really big staircase. More dark wood. It divided the house in two, kinda. On the right, she could see a fountain set right into the ground. Inside. Bet that was tough to clean. Big skylight. Dark wood doors leading to all sorts of places. Lots of dark wood all over the place, really. Left half of the house had a big glass double door leading out to a walled-in garden. Another slice of a different country. None of the plants were native. There was a particularly strong impression around the doorframe. She caressed it, and memories came off it like dust. The dust formed into images. The child entered through it, years ago. Eyes big and full of cautious optimism with a patina of fear. She'd been given a stuffed bear that still smelled of plastic. The owner followed behind her. He was young in this vision, but the way he thought about things made him seem old. Silver on his mind, always, soon it would show in his hair. He was talking into a phone and saying words that were only occasionally important to her. He said "appearances" a lot. Names, as well. The name of the child in particular. It was new to the child, but she'd get used to it. Soon the child would barely remember that it wasn't her first one.

She moved so she could see out the door beyond the visions. Beyond, the garden had disappeared and all that was left was a murky look into the child's past. She frowned. She didn't like the way the place she was seeing made her feel. She could see a starkly lit laboratory, almost like a theater cast in chrome and green tile and fluorescence. The child was also here, strapped to a chair. She was wearing a silvery helmet that covered her eyes. She was panting and crying, trying to concentrate. Two other children who looked a lot like her, but translucent, tried to arrange some blocks on a table across the room. But they were half formed, and couldn't manipulate the blocks properly. As the little ghosts vanished, the child's head slumped forward and she fainted. She heard a voice say it was no use and this was the last time. Utterly useless, he said. A man walked into view and *She*, the only *She* that mattered, the audience here, tried to get a look at *oh, hello...*

The blonde woman with the pinched face had walked over to her and now stood in her way. The vision of the past vanished. That wouldn't do. She tried paying attention to the woman. It was really difficult. People were so boring when they weren't talking about her.

The woman asked where she'd been.

"Out," she replied.

The woman asked if she was high again. Could she even remember her name, the woman asked.

She looked around the room for inspiration and saw a painting at the top of the stairs. Three people posed in it like prize dogs, staring like deer. The blonde woman was in it. An old man with brown skin and silver hair and a silver mustache was in it, the owner. Oh! And the child was in it. She looked great. She wondered if the dress she was wearing in the painting was around the house somewhere. It was so pretty and white. She had to have it. White dress, black car.

The woman asked if she was even listening. Ah yes, still there. Annoying. She looked at the painting again. Her eyes, which were perfect (like the rest of her), picked out the little gold plaque under the painting. She read one of the words printed on it.

"Meredith," she said.

The woman said no, that was *her* name but that it was good she could remember any name at all. Meredith looked at her a little longer after she was done talking. Meredith's pinched face was framed by straight platinum bangs, sharp like the rest of her. She looked at Meredith and saw how her hair used to be black and curly and she saw how much Meredith hated herself and cut at herself to hollow herself out and make herself beautiful. Not important, but interesting. She looked back.

Meredith sneered and said it was nice to see she'd stopped wearing all that ugly jewelry. Meredith said she was lucky it had only left one scar, scars were so ugly. Meredith looked down at the yellow silk top and black bike shorts she was wearing.

Meredith asked why she was dressed like that. She perked up and pointed at the painting.

"Where's that dress?" she asked.

Meredith scoffed and said that if she thought Meredith would be seen in public with her, with her face like that then she could think again. Meredith told her to at least put some makeup on over the scar if she was serious about going out with them. Meredith added she could do it after she was done whoring around with her little friend upstairs. He'd been let in through the servant entrance and was waiting for her in her room.

She smiled. Perfect. She walked away and headed up the stairs. Meredith made a disgusted noise. She paused halfway up, seriously considering doing something about that noise. She didn't want to hear it ever again. The ambient bass around her began to hum in earnest. Her fury thickening the air.

No. She had one thing she'd come here to do. She couldn't let herself be distracted. She'd timed it all so well. She didn't want to do it the other way. Not yet. Not if she didn't have to. Besides, she'd need a witness for this next bit.

She finished walking up the stairs. Green carpet up here. Really thick. She took off her shoes. It felt really nice. Such a shame she couldn't stay here. Lots of nice things. She looked at the paintings and clay figurines everywhere. She wondered how much she'd be able to fit in her new car and then winced.

There was that annoying scratchy feeling again. An impulse cut off by logic. She shouldn't waste any time here afterwards. She needed to be gone, and quick. She couldn't *wait* for all of this to be over. She didn't want to wait to have anything ever again.

Music emanated from the door at the end of the hallway. Big oak door. Lighter stain than all the rest. Still very pretty, though. She didn't know the song, but wouldn't mind getting to know it.

"When we were livin' on the moon..."

It was catchy. She pushed the door open. Hmmm.

Less nice things here. More little girl things. A laptop was playing that nice little song from the floor in a corner. It was the newest thing in here.

The strong-looking man with the red hair who sat on the bed said he'd picked her favorite song for her.

The child used to spend a lot of time here, she bet. But not anymore. A collage of magazine cutouts on the wall by the door. In just the right spot for a beam of sunshine from the big window opposite. The cutouts were all of female faces. The biggest one in the middle only had one eyebrow. She walked past the red-headed man sitting on the bed. There was a little white desk with ornate fretwork around the edges and on its two drawers.

She pulled one of them open by its gold ring. Old drawings that read like voodoo dolls. Poorly drawn people with their faces scratched out and their names struck through. There was also a handwritten essay:

"Where do I see myself in five years?"

The essay had been folded and unfolded over and over. It was accompanied by a surprisingly detailed drawing of a flooded field at sunset. Ochre and crimson, pomegranate. The man on the bed said something. She realized he'd been talking since she walked in.

He asked a question. She could tell by the way his voice went up at the end. She turned to face him. My, but he was big. Not a problem for her. It meant he'd be less likely to run at first, which would save time. She dropped the papers on the rich green carpet and padded closer. Her attention was totally on him now. What an honor for him.

He said he was happy she'd messaged him. He hadn't recognized the number at first. Did she get a new phone?

"Yes," she said, which wasn't a lie. The phone wasn't hers originally.

He hummed absentmindedly. He remarked that it had been awhile since he'd been here. He thought she hated this place?

She shrugged.

He said it was nice to see her again, at least. He was sad she'd missed Nat's gallery exhibition. It had been totally Mucha (some nouveau artist). He got it, though. She needed time to get better. He looked away. She didn't like that. She grabbed him by the chin and pulled his gaze back. Not too hard. Not yet.

There were those words again. 'Not yet.' Ugh.

He looked up at her and said he was sorry. He was so sorry. He was sorry for not seeing anything wrong sooner and not doing everything he could to help. For not doing anything, actually.

"I'm sorry too," she said. That seemed to work. He hugged her about the middle. Wrapped his big arms around her legs. Laid his head on her stomach.

"There, there," she said. She patted the back of his head.

He said ow, and laughed a little. She drew her hand away. He looked up at her and smiled. She smiled back. She was really good at smiling. She shifted, and sat in his lap. Rested her arms around his neck. He really liked that. Brightened up.

He'd talked to Tommy recently. Apparently, Tommy had seen her with her mom at the diner the other day. He thought she and her mom hated each other.

She raised an eyebrow.

"Wasn't me," she said.

He'd thought that seemed weird. He said that it must've been some other old woman and another stunningly beautiful little lady, then.

"Must," she said. My, but she was feeling chatty today. The impressions were strong here. She could actually see ghosts of the child dancing around the room. Mostly sitting on the bed. That and near him. Had to be the connection. He wouldn't have lasted nearly this long otherwise. Anyone else less interesting to her would be dead, dead, dead.

He said it was probably kind of funny to get an order made special by Tommy, when you were some rando who didn't even know him. She nodded.

He asked if her hand was better, since he didn't see a bandage, but she was already losing interest. Maybe she'd timed it wrong. She looked around a little more while he droned on. Timing was the tricky part. The Other One didn't always get to see what she was doing in sequence. Her eyes fell on a dresser opposite her desk with a mirror above it. Her face lit up. She leapt off his lap and pranced over to it. She looked into her eyes. Looked for that telltale spark. She smiled. Almost naturally.

"Hello," she said.

From behind her, he asked what uh, what were they doing now?

She gripped the dark wood around the silver. Pushed

back. The wood creaked and resisted, but not for very long. Old nails bent as splinters and petrified puffs of sappy air touched the outside world again.

Whoa there, he said.

She'd angled the mirror so the Other One could see everything. See her face. See her smile. She'd been practicing.

"You used to be a god," she said.

Just one more thing would make this perfect. She started tossing the contents of the dresser drawers.

He was talking again. Saying the same word over and over. She turned and he was standing behind her. The word he was saying. Familiar. Another impression. A name. Her name? Well, she supposed. All things belonged to her. Only a matter of time. He put his hands on her shoulders and that was not okay. *Insect*. He'd made his last mistake in thinking he could stop her from doing anything. The ambient bass in the air was so thick it was a wonder he could hear himself think.

He told her everything was going to be okay and she had to disagree.

She didn't waste any words on it, though. The show was about to start. There was just one thing missing. She spotted something white and shimmery behind his left ear, and strode toward it. He remained in front of her with his hands still on her shoulders. This did not stop her and her forward movement forced him back like a plow through muddy water. She brushed him aside like a fucking cobweb. He fell back on the bed as she pulled open the closet. There was as much real fear in his eyes as there was delight in her smile.

She took off her top and stepped into the big white dress. She could hear him about to call for help. A flick to the side of his head put a stop to that. Quit whining, didn't even hit you that hard.

"Relax," she said, "We're just having fun."

He stared at her, through her. Probably concussed.

He asked her if she was going out for a job interview.

She paused for one second. What did that mean?
He asked if the haircut was new.
"Yes," said Yakuza, "Thank you for noticing."
And that was the last thing she ever said to him.

Jacqueline stared at the undersides of her eyelids. Red, like intermission curtains. What she'd seen and heard and felt yesterday lingered like the rainbow shadows you got if you stared at bright lights and closed your eyes. These weren't fading, though. They pulsed. She ignored them.

She got up, kicking aside all her nocturnal sketches. They didn't matter anymore. Nothing did, not the faces, not the dreams and definitely not the hallucinations. The ghost images flickered around her apartment like holograms. She supposed she should be concerned. But really, she just didn't feel like it. Didn't feel much of anything, really. Numb to it. She shouldered through the images like snowfall. Jacqueline headed for the bathroom and took a really long shower. It had been a long yesterday, with very little time to relax. She felt like she deserved some. Outside the plastic curtain, a phantom's head came off. Jacqueline reminded herself to buy more shampoo.

She got out and looked at the squat rectangle covered in an extra towel, leaning in the corner. She looked at the bright spot in the paint. On the wall above the sink. No. She wasn't quite ready for that, yet.

She was ready to clean house, though. She left trails in puddles of phantasmal gore as she gathered up her garbage into a big black bag. Bloodless faces tried to catch her eye as she closed the drawstrings on them. She got dressed.

Pulling on her jacket made her realize how stiff her wrist still was. She put on the arm brace through hissing teeth. She thought about seeing a doctor and then immediately stopped thinking about it. The ethereal Doctor Folsom was convulsing in the corner, hands on his head, holding it together.

She picked up the pill bottle. Might be handy to have around in case Clara decided to check up on her. She cracked the seal on it. Took out the cotton plug that always made her think of spider eggs. The smell of pills filled her nostrils. An acrid yellow smell in little red and blue capsules. People shouldn't eat colors that bright. At least now she could prove to any casual voyeur she wasn't carrying around something she never intended to use. 32 capsules.

She looked up. Clear floor. Blank walls. A little humidity from the bathroom. Nothing more. She was alone. The ghosts of yesterday had vanished. She didn't wait up for them to come back.

This must be how normal people feel, Jacqueline thought. *Bad thoughts walled off in the back so they could get shit done.* Until now, she hadn't had a concept handy for "bad" thoughts. Just crushing uncertainty.

She felt like she'd survived a lightning strike. A war in her head between a reality where psychic demon women walked the streets tearing off faces, and one where they didn't. She'd take delusion over fantasy any day. The loser was clear.

She took a quick detour through the mid-morning fog, warmed by the cold sun down a side street to her favorite noodle stand. She liked Rico's food. It was cheap and well made. She liked Rico even more. He didn't ask questions and he didn't try to make conversation. She sat down on a stool next to an old man in a big overcoat, ducking under the little half-curtain that gave them some semblance of privacy while eating. He held up a newspaper so his face was covered, too. There was a wedding ring below one of his leathery knuckles. A simple silver band that was beginning to tarnish. Below that, he had a nice watch.

She hadn't needed to say anything to have a steaming bowl of vegetable soup placed in front of her. She cracked the balsa chopsticks out of their paper wrapper.

"Using chopsticks instead of a knife and fork can help prevent Alzheimer's later in life," she said in a mock cheery tone. The old man beside her turned the page. Rico transferred another empty dish from the sink to the drying rack. Jacqueline shook her head a little and looked back down at her food. She tucked in.

There was something different about the soup today. She couldn't quite place it. The broth looked the same. The vegetables looked the same. But there was definitely a new taste present. She'd never encountered it before. She'd remember. But it was giving her a sensation of familiar unease.

"Something wrong with the food?" asked Rico, "You're staring at me like you want me to die."

She had been staring. Again. But this time was worse. Confrontation. The bowl half empty. Sitting heavy in her stomach. Like Persephone, guilty of having taken food, but defiant to the end.

"Well? What is it?"

Looking away and saying nothing wouldn't fix this. She smacked her lips. Twice. Three times. Breathed in.

"This is the vegetarian bowl, right?" She asked, "Nothing new about it? No extra ingredient?"

He balked a little.

"Vegetarian? I mean, it has vegetables IN it..."

Jacqueline sat back. The twisting in her gut worsened.

"What is that supposed to mean?" she said icily.

He lightly bobbed his head back and forth, as if weighing several options floating above him.

"Well, you're right that there's a new ingredient. I changed up the mixture of the broth a little. Should fill you up longer. Good choice for breakfast," he said as if he was framing a compliment.

"That's not what I meant," she said, renewing her grip on the conversation.

"Then What DID you mean?"

"Why are you—are you fucking with me, Rico? Just tell me what you changed."

"Hey," he said at an offended pitch,

"Just because I'm wearing a nametag, that doesn't mean you get the right to say my name in that tone of voice, alright? Just calm down and eat your damn breakfast."

"WHAT THE FUCK DID YOU PUT IN MY FOOD," she said, standing up. The old man twitched his newspaper. There were clearly a few cracks in the wall he'd put up to get something done today, but it was still standing. Rico, on the other hand, was under siege.

"It's marrow, all right? I put bone marrow in the broth!" He shouted as quickly as he could. Word of mouth was a very large concern for his type of business. Especially at the volume she'd been using.

"How—how could you, Rico? You know I'm a vegetarian," she said, lowering the volume of her stutter.

"Lady, I don't know shit about you. All I know is you started coming here almost every day getting the same damn dish every time. This is the first time you opened your mouth and I didn't hear '#7,' and 'check please.' Have to say, not a fan," he snapped.

"Okay, try this on for size. Where are you getting your product?" she said evenly.

"What?" He frowned.

"Where are you getting bone stock from? You don't have nearly enough foot traffic for a commercial license. You haven't had a single health inspection in your Life. Who is selling prime KOBE Beef?" She pointed at the menu hanging over the bar between them, "To the man without a single SAIC sticker?"

"You're a fucking health inspector now? You need to lea—"

She slammed her badge on the counter.

"I know you sleep back there. I also know you're not zoned for both home and business in this space. Start talking, or I will."

He set his jaw. Buttoned his lip. She saw the word 'crazy' lurking behind it. She spoke up again in a flash of terrible inspiration.

"Where's The Beef from? WHERE'S—"

He held up his hands in incredulous surrender.

"Fong and Nunogawa! They bought out a bunch of slaughter houses. They give cut rates. Yeah obviously they do shady shit but that's none of my business! The meat passes the taste test. It's safe and it's clean. Now *please leave.*"

Gang enforcers. What were they doing buying up property? Moving up in the world or acting as middlemen for something worse...

Rico broke her out of her introspection.

"You can arrest me if you want. But I didn't rob nobody. Didn't kill anybody. I'll get out. And you ain't never eating here again."

She grimaced. She *could* bring him in, if she wanted. Could probably conflate the charges if she wanted. Close him down.

She looked down the bar. At the other people just waiting for their food. Looking at her. Waiting for her to finish. She picked up her badge.

"Check please," she spat.

She threw exact change down on the counter.

"Name?"

"Deirdre Watson."

Jacqueline tried not to stare at the old woman opposite her. She had one of those gazes that made you feel like a curse was coming your way. Quiet in here, at least.

"Please describe the assailant. Did they have any distinguishing features? Tattoos or piercings?"

Her pencil was poised over the paper. She was used to stuttering or reticence when it came to providing a description. She was not used to silence. Not unheard of, but it usually meant the worst for the victim. She forced herself to meet the auger gaze of the old woman. The way her lips were pinched spoke more of anger than fear.

"I came here to lodge a complaint. I'm not wasting my time providing any kind of description if I can't get a guarantee of punitive action."

Jacqueline tried to stop frowning. *What, was she just going to hold the information hostage? Did she not want them to catch the criminal? Was there even someone to catch?*

"We take all claims of illicit activity very seriously," she replied. Pointedly. The old woman did not take the hint.

"I mean it. I already called and you only caught one of them. What do I pay my taxes for?"

Roads and clean water, Jacqueline didn't say.

"We can't do anything without information about the culprit, ma'am," she said tiredly. She crossed her legs.

"Oh, very well. Lots of jewelry, that one. Not the proper kind, mind you. Spikes in the wrong places. That sort of thing."

Thok. A rubber ball bounced against Jacqueline's wall.

"Male or female," she said automatically.

"A woman. And one of those ghastly chains hanging across half her face. That can't be sanitary."

Thok. Kids with their stupid ball. Next it would be graffiti. And then carvings. And before you knew it the whole thing would come tumbling down. *Stop romanticizing your illness. This isn't healthy. Focus on your work.* She stuck her tongue out a bit, just a bit, as her pencil flew across the paper.

"And another thing. She absolutely reeked of *marijuana.*"

Mrs. Watson whispered this last bit, as if concerned that merely uttering such a word audibly might affect her reputation. The word 'reek' echoed in Jacqueline's head like a bat call. She could handle ignorance on the job.

Could even shut out the willful kind. But something about this woman's demeanor supremely aggravated her.

"Hair color, eye color?" she said, mouth still thankfully on autopilot. The old woman did not respond. Jacqueline looked back up. Deirdre was staring at her thoughtfully.

"Ma'am?" Jacqueline asked, extremely uncomfortable.

"She looked...just like you," said Deirdre.

Jacqueline licked her lips. They were very dry.

"I beg your pardon?"

"Her hair was cut a little different and she had all that junk on her face, but... "

"But what?" said Jacqueline, mystified.

"Well, I've nothing against your people, it's just that—oh dear, you're not going to make me say it, are you?" she said blithely.

Jacqueline's thoughts snagged, and she put down her pencil before looking back up. *What is that supposed to mean? Asian? That's half the city. Dark skin? Black hair?* She couldn't let it slide. *Your people?* It echoed around and around her brain. *Your people. What the fuck did you just say to me?*

"You know? I wasn't. Until just this very second."

Deirdre drew herself up, sitting more primly.

"I'm sorry. You can forgive me, can't you? But you all rather do look like one another. I must sound rather silly. As if a police woman would break into my home smelling of the reefer."

Jacqueline felt like a bandaid had torn off the little hairs on the back of her neck. There was one thing she really hated, and that was being forced to examine herself. Yes, she was Japanese. But that didn't mean anybody got to think about her in that way, as a category, as a checkbox. *Don't you touch me with your mind, you fat old crone.*

Several sentences crowded in front of each other trying to escape Jacqueline's mouth. The first one in line was:

"It's Detective." She chopped the tail off the sentence expertly before it could culminate in *motherfucker.*

Before Deirdre's gyroscope etiquette could right itself, Jacqueline gave it another shove.

"And uh, for the sake of completeness in my report, could you explain what you meant by 'your people'?"

Jacqueline's words had the same effect as someone cocking a shotgun in the near distance. Deirdre was likely beginning to realize she wasn't talking to the type of person who was content to merely listen. She leaned forward.

"I certainly hope any...offhand comments won't be reflected in your report, Officer."

Jacqueline knit her fingers together on the half-finished drawing in her lap. Her breath quickened as her anger overtook her manners again.

"It absolutely is already reflected in the report. You could see the look on your *face* in it, it's so reflected. At this juncture, I'm just giving you a chance to explain yourself. For the report." The air hummed.

She hoped Mrs. Watson couldn't see her gently swaying in her seat. Her bunched hands were acting as ballast so her lightheadedness wouldn't overtake her. She wasn't sure what it was about confrontation that always made her feel like this, but even sitting down it nearly took her breath away. Was standing up for herself that exhilarating?

"No, really," Deirdre insisted in the tones of one sinking in quicksand,

"She looked almost exactly like—like you!"

Thok.

Jacqueline took a deep breath. Her wall was still intact, and quicksand wasn't real. This woman deserved nothing more than court-appointed sympathy at this point.

"I'll be sure and make a note of that, ma'am. Since you've now provided an exact description, I'm confident we can catch the culprit."

Jacqueline had tried very hard not to condescend to the other woman, if only because doing so would be like admitting Deirdre's feelings were worthy of being spared.

This did not help.

"You have to believe me. I'm NOT crazy!"

Thok.

"Regardless, ma'am. We've done all we can at this point. Thank you for your time."

Deirdre balled up her fists.

"I am not—"

"Crazy. Yes. You mentioned. Now, unless you'd like such claims dismissed on the basis of having caused a scene, I suggest you collect your things and take your leave. Otherwise my, er, 'people' will have to escort you out of the building."

She put the sketch in her folder, got up and exited the interrogation room they'd repurposed for their privacy.

Jacqueline leaned back in her wooden swivel chair and tried to think of the name of the sitcom where someone sat in a chair like hers and threw pencils into the ceiling, before realizing she'd never actually seen one. That 'memory' was just sort of sitting around in her skull. Not much left to play with outside the wall the medicine had created. Cultural detritus and confusing impressions.

"I don't even watch TV," she said to herself quietly. She tried thinking about something else. She wasn't exactly fond of obsessing over past faux pas, but between Rico and actually trying to toss pencils into the ceiling (which was stupid) she didn't have much to occupy her mind while she worked. Had she been acting irrationally this morning? Was she wrong to get angry? He'd acted like she was a ghost to be exorcised.

"Or a parasite."

That was an ugly thought. Back behind the wall. Definitely not healthy, but she'd already admitted she was sick. What could you do?

"Officer Ueda?"

She looked back down. Put her feet on the floor.

The station chief was a slight man with the bearing of one who was very tall. He walked almost regally. When he stood, it was nearly at attention. His eyes crinkled around the edges. He had a very kind face. His owlish spectacles enhanced the flavor of his expressions. She wondered what he needed.

"It's um...Detective," she said.

"Detective, right! That's actually sort of what I wanted to talk about. If you could join me in my office for a moment?"

"Sure," she replied,

"Just let me wrap things up here."

He nodded. "Not a problem. Whenever you're ready."

He walked off to his office and she turned back to her computer.

WHAT THE FUCK.

Jacqueline was definitely having a panic attack. She typed gibberish on a blank screen. *Look busy. Buy time. Figure out what is happening.* Addressed in person by the chief. Unheard of. She hadn't even caught a glimpse of him since Pinkerton's retirement party. If he had an internal issue to resolve, even one that required facetime with an employee, he'd always send someone else to retrieve them. *That, or...* she took out her phone.

She closed her eyes. Visualized the wall in her mind. There was something behind there that she'd forgotten. Something she needed to remember. It flickered in front of her as another thought rippled across it.

This is stupid. Buying into visualizations like this would only weaken her ability to problem-solve without them. It started to fade.

NO, wait. We need information. What did I do to get myself noticed? The words echoed around her head. What did I do? *What did I do?*

Cracks formed in the wall as it grew brighter in her mind. A blinding Mobius strip distorting itself. She opened her eyes, but the wall, the light, the bandage were all she could see. The bandage was coming off. The wound beneath it bled information into space. The gash pulsed. Felt it at the center of her brain. A universe so small she could see the back of her own head.

You're a murderer, bled the wound.

You're a monster and you should die before you hurt anyone else. She could see herself through the hole inside her head. Shining through like a prism. Watch her limbs move robotically. Knock the pipe out of the wall. Kick and push over furniture in the coffee shop. Propel her like a missile through her psychiatrist's ground floor window. But not before discharging her weapon through it three times.

"Are you alright, Jacqueline?"

She stared at Clara through the keyhole in her mind. Stared into her kind eyes.

"No I'm not," she whispered. She couldn't tell if this was happening right now or if it was one of the many memories she'd taken for granted. A snapshot of an innocent bystander warmed by the fireball of the crash that was her life.

"I'm in trouble. Get me out of here."

Her tunnel vision led her out of her chair to her employer's office.

She wished the hallway was some Escher monstrosity. Wished her mind would twist it to give her more time to think. As it was, she was only a few steps away from opening the door at the end. She was surrounded by murmurs. All the terrors in the world were behind that door. She was about to knock.

"Come in," said seven or eight Doctor Folsoms from the other side. She shook her head. *Make it through this. Survive.* She opened the door.

All noise ceased, except for the ticking of an analog clock. It sat on the chief's desk. He sat behind his desk, writing, also analog. Wooden pencil. Wooden clock.

"Please, have a seat," he said without looking up. She began to move forward. "But, close the door, if you would."

No thunderclap of doom closing her mausoleum door. A quiet click and it was done. She sat down. He stayed silent for a few moments. Words like *the help you deserve* circled her head like vultures. She eyed the three other pencils lined up on his desk, She eyed his carotid artery.

"Detective," he enunciated carefully as he punctuated a sentence. "You've been calling yourself Detective, and we've been obliging you thus far."

She swallowed. This was it. Goodbye. Goodbye. Good—

"But you're rather more than that, aren't you?"

She was so thrown by this she'd have fallen if she weren't sitting. He looked up and steepled his fingers.

"Detective Specialist Second Class. Your work in putting together profiles has been nothing short of astonishing. You have an incredible mind. It would be ah, criminal, haha, to squander your talents."

She agreed with his assessment of her mind's credibility, but still wasn't convinced he'd brought her in here to blow smoke up her ass.

"To wit!" he tapped his pencil in a short drumroll, "I was thinking of giving you a promotion."

She searched his smile for the shoe, waited for it to drop.

"There's just one thing we need to take care of. A minor detail to attend to so we can put you in a position to really make a difference."

Through tunnel vision and swimmer's ear she watched and listened as he pulled open a drawer and withdrew a small manila folder, humming all the while.

He slapped it down on the desk. Not too hard, but the force of the drop made it the center of her world. She watched it send ripples through the air. They washed over her, and she couldn't see.

Is something wrong?

She rubbed at her eyes. "Just allergies." Pulled out

the pills, unscrewed the cap. Shook one out. Swallowed it dry.

Colored shapes came into focus in the darkness. She watched on VHS. Watched her hands and the rest of the room move at double speed to catch up to what she was seeing right now. Looked up out of the pill bottle. Swam back into her eyes. Held her breath, struggled for the surface.

Her ears popped. Her deep breath was deafening. Every little sound.

"QUITE ALRIGHT, QUITE ALRIGHT."

He'd been talking. She took his outstretched tissue. Rubbed at her eyes. Dropped the open bottle. *Shit.* Got down on her hands and knees.

"No, no. It's alright," she said. Picked them all up. 28 capsules. Sat back down.

"I'm so sorry," she said,

"What were you saying?"

"Think nothing of it," he replied, waving away her apologies.

"That's sort of what I meant, actually. We had no idea you had any allergies, for instance. Your file is...rather bare. We don't actually know much of anything about you. You were hired—"

He flipped open the file, "—on a provisional basis initially, and somewhere along the line your background check went missing. The boys downstairs were hard at work trying to recover it, but with what I had in mind for you, I thought a second run-through might be prudent. Likely just a filing error or some such. We certainly don't hold it against you..."

Was he letting that dangle or just drawing breath? What did he think she was hiding? *He knows you're crazy.*

She dabbed at her brow with the tissue he'd given her.

"As with any other opportunity like this, I'll need a bit more in-hand when I submit a formal request for your promotion. Where you went to school. Any psych evals you may have had. Things of that nature."

She nodded, and screamed as loud as she could inside her head. His kind face did not change, so it was likely he hadn't heard her.

"That's...great!" Jacqueline said with as much enthusiasm as she could scrounge up. She tried desperately to think of something tenable to say that would allow her to exit this room.

"Well, I'd better be going!"

Brilliant. She felt seasick as she got out of her chair.

"I went to Oxford, myself," he persisted. "Transferred to HKU in my final year to be closer to my mother. She'd taken ill. She's doing quite well now, though. And you?" he said to her back.

The conversation tugged her against her will, like a riptide, back into the room.

"Oh."

Think.

"Uh."

Say something and leave.

"I'm doing fine. Thank you."

The chief chuckled.

"I meant, where did you graduate?"

This is no good. The longer he keeps you talking, the more likely you are to give away just how far gone you really are. Do not engage.

"I, uh—"

DO NOT ENGAGE.

There was a knock on the door. *Oh thank god,* she may or may not have said out loud.

"Let me get that," she definitely said.

She spun around to open the door and quietly excuse herself at the same time. The chief said something but she didn't hear it as she came face to uncomfortably close face with Clara Pinkerton.

"Hey Chief," said Clara after a moment after a moment of meaningful eye contact. "I heard you might be in here," she said to Jacqueline with a wink.

"Can I borrow her for a second? We need some help putting together a composite."

She'd heard her. Heard her call for help. Jacqueline nearly sagged with relief.

"Is it...urgent?" asked the chief.

She felt the tug again. Froze up as she felt him digging for more. She couldn't look him in the eye. Her face was like an open book. Her gaze pleaded with Clara's. Clara nodded, putting on her serious expression.

"Oh, yes. Very. Extremely," she said.

"Very well. I look forward to picking this up another time, Detective Ueda. Try not to dally, though. Opportunities such as this tend not to wait on paperwork."

A multitude of sorries and thank yous bubbled on Jacqueline's tongue. She trailed in Clara's wake and tried to catch something to say. Clara, as per usual, already had.

"I did actually need your help with something. Lucky they came along when they did, I suppose."

Who though? Another variable.

Mrs. Watson's wizened face fixed Jacqueline's head with a death glare from the inside. Should have known the old bat wouldn't leave well enough alone. She'd likely returned to stir up trouble. Out of the fire, then... Jacqueline wanted to thank Clara for not using the word 'providence' at least, but was stopped cold. She was transfixed by the sight before her.

Another her—*the* other her, perhaps—sat at her desk. *Oh my god.* She'd straightened her hair, and wasn't wearing her big leather jacket, but it was *her*. Jacqueline was having an out of body experience. She had to be. There was no other explanation for what she was seeing. *No. Stop running, stop looking away. You know who that is. You know what that means.*

You're. Not. Crazy. Vindication filled her, overflowed her, drowned her. This changed everything. The world opened up before her, like a flower. Like a pair of hungry jaws. Like an oceanic abyss. The world became stranger and she, stranger still. What could she do now? *Now say it. Speak the truth. Say her name.*

"Yaqui," she breathed before she could stop herself. Yaqui started to turn. She started to turn, and Jacqueline's ears rang with a piercing tone that climbed towards a shriek. She started to turn, and Jacqueline's pulse slowed to a crawl. She started to turn and Jacqueline knew if their eyes met something terrible would happen. She ducked back around the corner. Clara followed and asked,

"What's wrong?"

Jacqueline shook her head.

"I can't tell you." She laughed.

It was Clara's turn to shake her head.

"Why not?"

Jacqueline rubbed her eyes. She felt like she hadn't slept in years.

"Because haha, because hahaha, you'll think I'm crazy."

Clara looked at her uncomprehendingly, but not without sympathy.

"I thought you were taking medicine for...that?"

Jacqueline swallowed. "I think that might be part of the problem. I think my um, situation might be more serious than I was prepared to deal with. I was just putting a bandaid on a head wound."

Clara nodded.

"You can take as much time as you need. I understand if you feel like high stress situations aren't what you need right now. That's why I pulled you out of there."

Jacqueline tried to keep her cool.

"It's not about how I 'feel,' Clara. It's something else."

Clara's hand twitched as though she were resisting putting it on Jacqueline's shoulder.

"That's fine. That's totally fine. I didn't agree to hear this woman's statement to put you in more stress. Go home. Rest."

Jacqueline took a sharp, bracing breath in through her nose.

"No. I have to be here. I have to hear what she has to say. I..."

How much should she say?

"...I know her. Please," she said as concern furrowed Clara's brow even further.

"Please. Just get her talking. I have to know if she's okay."

Clara didn't say anything. Desperation filled Jacqueline up, nearly tipped her over. Her skin tingled like she was waiting for a static shock. She took Clara's hand, placed it on her own shoulder. Rubbed it a little bit. People liked that, right?

"Please. I'll listen, on the other side of the glass in the interrogation room. You interview her. Help me."

Tears welled up in Clara's eyes.

"Oh, Jackie," she said. She embraced Jacqueline, who tried to keep herself from saying literally every word in her head.

"You're such a brave friend," said Clara.

"I am that," said Jacqueline, who half agreed.

Jacqueline sat at the control booth facing the two-way mirror. She felt like she was sitting in front of a backstage makeup station, ready for showtime. The edges of her vision flickered. She blinked hard, shook herself. Looked down at the only thing she'd brought.

The pill bottle in her lap rattled merrily as she shifted in her seat. She knew the ingredients well, if not intimately. Antipsychotic. There were 25 capsules left. She was hiding behind the rubble of her wall of denial. Hiding from the mounting terror that had taken a new form. She had less medicine now than when she came home yesterday. She'd been losing time. For how long, she did not know. An urge

BookSmart
421 Vineyard Town Center
Between Nob Hill Market and TJ MAXX
Morgan hill, CA 95037
(408) 778-6467

Transaction #:00052088
Station:2, 30005 Cle   TATION2
Saturday, October 12 2019   6:36 PM

SALES:
  1@   14.99 9781733347815   14.99
  Intrusive Thoughts
SUBTOTAL   14.99

TAX:
  Sales Tax   @9.0000%   1.35
TOTAL TAX   1.35

GRAND TOTAL   16.34

TENDER:
  Visa/master/disco.   16.34
TOTAL TENDER   16.34

CHANGE $0.00

*Special Orders Are Easy! Call -
408-778-6467 Email
brad@mybooksmart.com or on
the online at
www.mybooksmart.com*

00052088

to self-medicate gnawed inside her. Obvious, now. It had always been there. She wanted to correct all her internal mistakes. Her waking dreams, her paranoia, even her perfect memory seemed to be crystallizing around her, trapping her.

Resisting the urge seemed pointless. It seemed like the one part of her that had a good idea on how to solve or at least mitigate the problem of her waning sanity. Not like actually taking her medicine was the worst thing she could do. But back to the present. Back to Yaqui.

Up close, the resemblance was harder to see. Her hair had grown out longer than Jacqueline's, and her face was more haggard. Cheekbones and eyebrows just as striking, though. Same eye color.

Yaqui also wore a hooded sweatshirt that said 'SMILE' in white screen printed letters. The kind of boldface type that you'd buy still shrink-wrapped. She'd changed clothes hurriedly, then. Stopped at Burberry Street and picked up a new outfit on the way here. The jeans were probably bootlegged too. To say nothing of the sneakers with the misspelled brand name. The street vendors there only took cash. No cards meant no trail. Was she being followed?

A bandage on her right hand. Fresh gauze. No stain. Not a recent wound, but severe. Who'd hurt her and how were most pertinent. It might have been her captors, or maybe even Yakuza. Jacqueline shuddered. Difficult to conjure the image of something so fearful when it looked just like you. She hoped Yaqui hadn't come face to face with anything like that yet. Anything like what Jacqueline had had to face. She felt oddly protective, all of a sudden. As if she was looking at a long-lost sister.

Maybe you are.

Clara was still talking. If she'd seen the resemblance, she hadn't said anything yet. Ever the professional, she was trying to put Yaqui at ease with pleasantries. And pastries. Yaqui wasn't eating. Her face was drawn. A pair of cheap sunglasses, now sitting on the table, had hidden her dark circles. Jacqueline put a hand to her own face, feeling a phantom twinge of pain. Yaqui's face was pockmarked with old scars. Tiny ones, mostly. You'd have to know what was missing to recognize they were from her piercings.

A casual observer might mistake her haggard look and superficial wounds for the visual symptoms of withdrawal. But Jacqueline knew better, if not exactly how. They were both still self-medicating, it seemed. Yaqui had taken something for pain this morning, before she got here. After she'd taken off the nose chain and taken out the gauge in her earlobe, she'd replaced it with a little polished wooden plug. It would hold her body-heat better in winter than metal, keep the cold from damaging the thin tissue around the hole in her ear. Smart gift. Jimmy had bought it for her. Stupid of him. She had plenty of cash. She'd almost made him return it. But he'd insisted. Said he wanted her to have something to remember him by when he wasn't around.

Jacqueline wiped at her eyes. She felt like a voyeur.

"Why don't we start with the basics? Small details. Everything is important. Now, what is the nature of your visit today?" said Clara pleasantly.

Yaqui's voice was rough, a little deadpan. "Let me start by saying that I shouldn't be here. That this was a bad idea. I can already tell. But I'm trying this new thing where I don't bail on something the minute it gets tough."

Jacqueline realized she was jigging her leg because Yaqui was trying not to. She wondered if she was helping, by being so close. Her fascination was tempered by fear. She didn't understand the rules for whatever this connection was. Or if there were any. There weren't any notes she could refer to. Part of the reason she wasn't taking any now. The other part being that she was still unwilling to lend any more legitimacy to this than she had to. She definitely didn't want any evidence of this bizarre new thought process that could put her away.

"It's alright, Ms. Guzman," said Clara,

"I'd like you to feel like this is a safe place. Where you can share the truth without fear of repercussion...

Guzman, is that a family name? You might forgive me for asking, but are you...adopted? I have a friend who— well, she's Japanese. And you do look—" she tempted.

Yaqui sat up.

"Why would you ask that? Who have you been talking to?"

She stood.

Jacqueline broke out in a cold sweat. *Oh sure, Clara. Lock yourself in this room with this stranger who could be anybody.* One terrifying thought ate another, like a food chain diagram. What if she wasn't just a street junkie who'd turned up in Jacqueline's hallucinations, but someone else entirely? Someone she'd been dreaming about. Someone with a knack for impersonation.

"Clara!" she shouted, as she shot to her feet, images of choking Yakuza to death clouding her vision. Neither woman in the other room seemed to hear. Jacqueline forestalled her vengeful dash for the door as Yaqui sat back, looking pained and sick. She rubbed her temples as Jacqueline began to let her guard down a few inches. Clara was unperturbed. She'd dealt with worse.

Yaqui said, "You got a file on me?"

Clara put her composition notebook and pencil down on the table between them. The signal to begin recording audio for Jacqueline, in this case. She flipped the switch.

"Not at all," said Clara, "And there doesn't need to be one," she lied. A little too easily, Jacqueline thought.

"Just start at the beginning. What brings you here today? Are you in any danger? Is there someone you're worried about?" said Clara.

"Kind of...the opposite," said Yaqui, squeezing the words around her headache.

"The beginning. I didn't have a shitty childhood, or anything. I mean, maybe I don't remember a lot of it. From before I was adopted."

Clara interrupted her, "Ms. Guzman. I am absolutely here to provide you with a safe space to speak your mind, but I'm not your psychiatrist,"

Jacqueline grimaced a little at this, somewhat guiltily.

"If we're going to get you the help you need, we've got to get to the heart of the matter. If you could just tell me why—"

"—Look, could I just get one of your cigarettes? I can't fucking think straight."

Clara's next words fused into a lump.

"My—"

Her stutter was evidence of her struggle to process this.

"The ones in your purse. Behind the pocket where you keep your credit cards."

Rather than react to how Yaqui could have gleaned this information, Clara appeared to jump to the next available impulse.

"You can't smoke in here," she said desperately. She looked like she didn't even want to address how this woman knew such a thing about her. No need and just as well. Jacqueline would do the irrational thinking for the both of them. Yaqui knew about the cigarettes off hand, probably didn't even know how she knew, but Jacqueline could guess. Would guess. Would happily make the leap in logic to her death. Yaqui knew it because Jacqueline knew it.

Information was bleeding between them. The most important question now was how much, and starting when? "Why" and "how" were also strong contenders, but if Yaqui knew too much about Jacqueline, she risked outing both of them. Either as headcases, or as missing persons with no official resting place. Apart from a black site dissection table.

Despite everything that had happened, faced with an unsolvable conundrum Jacqueline's instinct was to solve it. The mystery she'd been faced with opened like the face of a clock, all its pieces ticking into place around her. Fascination didn't even begin to describe it. Her brain was working overtime to absorb this new intel. Convert it into solid ground to stand on.

Yaqui looked like her body was working overtime just to stay upright. Occasionally she would sway lightly in time with a deep breath and a bloodshot eye roll.

"How did you know that?" Clara managed finally. Yaqui shook her head. Stared at the floor.

"Lucky fucking guess. Now please give me a cigarette. Until then, I don't know anything. I mean that. Help me out."

Jacqueline was glad that Clara's most driving force, the desire to help those in pain, overrode her compunction to enforce little rules. She reached into her purse and pulled out a battered cardboard packet. Yaqui greedily took the cigarettes and fumbled one out. She lit it with a matchstick. The book it came out of had a stencil drawing of a crimson fish.

The match stayed lit for a few extra seconds while Yaqui took a rejuvenating drag. She pushed another cig out of the pack and pointed it at Clara, who waved it away with a 'god no' under her breath and a half-hearted chuckle.

"You look stressed," said Yaqui, more brightly.

"No thank you," said Clara firmly, regaining control of the conversation.

The match went out.

"Are you feeling ill?" probed Clara.

"Ever since I got here," said Yaqui,

"But that's neither here nor there."

"Quite right," said Clara,

"Now that you've got...what you need, you can tell me what you'd like to report."

"A murder," said Yaqui.

Jacqueline had been steadily fading into the background of her own thoughts. She had been worried about being subsumed in the narrative of Yaqui's life again, but this snapped her wide awake.

"I think Meredith framed me for it. I know that sounds crazy, but it gets her what she wants. She was the only witness."

Clara picked her black marble composition notebook

back up and started to scribble.

"Those are...very serious allegations. I don't even know where to...who was murdered?" said Clara.

"My boyfriend," said Yaqui.

Jacqueline searched for emotion in her voice, but it was long absent. Numb.

"When was the body discovered?" asked Clara.

"Two weeks ago," Yaqui replied.

Clara flared her nostrils as her handwriting became more exaggerated, telltale signs for Jacqueline that her friend was reeling. Jacqueline, on the other hand was zeroing in on the details of Yaqui's face. Hunting for any telltale signs of a lie. There was nothing there. Great waves of pain and sadness had stripped it all away. Eroded everything but that look in her eyes. Floating above the dry tides of salt like ancient suns. She—

She'd been talking. And Jacqueline had been losing herself again. She hurriedly refocused. In this darkened room where the only light came from these other people with far greater presence, she could almost forget she existed.

"That's the worst part. I'm not even being accused. They've hushed it all up," said Yaqui, "Even Jimmy's parents went along with it. I don't even know how much of Daddy's money it took, but they cooked up some story about how he moved away. It's not like people are lining up to go look for him, anyway. His parents won't talk to me. They think I did it. They think I'm some rich sociopath who can get away with anything. Hard to convince them otherwise with no case, no body."

Clara leaned forward.

"Where *is* the body?"

Yaqui shook her head. "I don't know. They took it away. Men. Wearing—"

She choked a tiny bit.

"—hazmat suits. Took him away. Tore up the carpet in my room. The floor. They wouldn't let me see. The past few days, they locked me up in a spare bedroom upstairs. They're going to send me away, I think. Not to prison. Too public. But I've heard them talking. Arguing. I keep hearing 'send her back' as the subject of discussion. Considering I'm quite literally a charity case, not hard to figure that one out."

Then how did she escape? Jacqueline thought.

"Then how did you escape?" said Clara.

Yaqui fiddled with her fingers. "I jumped out the window."

"Aah!" Jacqueline exclaimed suddenly.

"They'd put a guard on my door," Yaqui said blankly. There'd been disbelief in her tone once, but it had been replaced by resignation.

Jacqueline clutched at her ankle. It felt swollen. Tender.

"He'd give me meals three times a day. Like clockwork. I left right after dinner so I'd have more time before they checked on me."

Jacqueline gritted her teeth.

"Did you *have* to jump?" Jacqueline asked, in great discomfort.

At least now she knew why Yaqui had taken those pain meds.

Her head thumped against the window as she tried to will the phantom sprain away. Clara glanced in her direction before continuing with her questions.

"Why wasn't any of this reported?"

Yaqui shook her head. "Same reason I was being quietly sent away to god knows where instead of right to prison. Literally the only thing dad can't afford is scandal."

This isn't happening. This isn't happening this isn't happening this...

Something twinged and snapped inside of Jacqueline. She blinked and and and—

The ugly bruise was gone.

"What the fuck," she breathed. Yaqui reached down and rubbed at her own ankle, wincing. This was dangerous. She couldn't stay near her for too much longer. Who knew what else might happen? At the same time, she NEEDED her close. Or at least somewhere safe until she could get to the bottom of this mess.

"I think I'd like to be placed into protective custody," said Yaqui.

Perfect. Jacqueline smiled in spite of herself.

"You read my mind," Jacqueline said to herself, and laughed at her own little joke. She stopped immediately. Coughed. Clara took a few more notes.

"That is...something I'd like very much like to be able to do for you," Clara said hesitantly.

Yaqui and Jacqueline made the same wary face, like they'd both stumbled over a tripwire.

"Why," said Jacqueline in bloody disbelief.

"What does that mean?" said Yaqui stonily.

Clara closed the book.

"By your own admission, we've got no body. It could be anywhere—"

"He," interrupted Yaqui.

Clara took a deep breath and lowered her expectations ever so slightly.

"He could be anywhere," she said gently, "What's more, you're talking about accusing your own mother of murder with no hard evidence—"

"Meredith is not my mother," said Yaqui firmly. She crossed her arms, looked away.

Clara changed tactics. "That's right. I'm sorry, you mentioned. She's your adopted mother?"

Probing again, Jacqueline thought. *What's the angle here?*

"Yeah," said Yaqui.

"I'm adopted, like I said. That's what I meant by charity case. I found out when I turned ten. But I feel like I knew for a while before that...listen, I really need this from you guys. I don't feel safe out there. They want to shut me up. But somebody needs, no,everyone needs to know what really happened."

Clara opened the book again. Turned the page.

"You said your adopted mother was the only witness.

Was she the one who discovered the body?"

Yaqui shifted in her seat. "No. That was me."

Her eyes retreated into the past.

"...He was in two pieces," she said, finally. "His eyes were open. They were so big. He always had real pretty eyes. The smell...overpowering. I just...I dunno. Um." She faltered.

"Please," said Clara, "I know this is difficult. But for his sake, we need to know everything. Like I said. Every detail is important."

Yaqui didn't say anything for a moment.

"I just held him for a while. I was covered in him when they pulled me off. Red everywhere."

She chewed her lip.

"They burned my clothes. I just wanted to hold him. I said I was sorry. They hosed me off. Like an animal."

Jacqueline would have been speechless, but Clara forged ahead with a cold vigor she found admirable. "Where did they burn the evidence?" she asked.

Yaqui looked up, rubbed at her eyes with her sleeve. "There's a furnace downstairs. Big one. Old one. The smell—" She shook her head. "Couldn't smell anything else for days."

Jacqueline nodded as Clara scribbled. That ruled out one avenue of attack. The disposal had been entirely internal. Well, not entirely. There might not be any charnel smoke in the sky, but she doubted the Guzman family had a private stable of "cleaners" waiting in the wings, however rich they might be. Which led to the next thought: who had they hired? They certainly had enough money to retain the most discreet services in that field. Then again, however discreet you might be there was always a money trail to follow, if not a paper trail. She licked her lips.

In fact, she could think of one business specializing in waste disposal that had recently spent a lot of money on new property. She made a mental note to pay a visit to Fong and Nunogawa later.

"What did you mean earlier when you said your

adopted mother was the only witness? What exactly did she see?" Clara asked.

"Me. Being the last one to go upstairs before they found—Jimmy," Yaqui said with only a slight hitch in her voice.

"I see, and your childhood. Tell me a little bit more about that."

What? thought Jacqueline.

"What?" said Yaqui.

"Humor me," said Clara,

"You were very keen to talk about it earlier. Why is that?"

Yaqui shook her head warily. "I wasn't thinking straight. Tired. What does this have to do with—"

"And—" interrupted Clara

"—how much time would you say you typically spend like that? In that state of mind?"

Jacqueline was unsure of where Clara was going with this, but Yaqui looked like she knew...and by her frown, she wasn't happy about it.

"I haven't been sleeping well. So a lot of time, I suppose. I've been very tired for quite some time," she said icily.

"And if you didn't kill your boyfriend, and weren't there to see it, where were you really?" Clara added on.

"I...I don't," Yaqui stuttered.

"Do you have an alibi?" Clara prompted.

Yaqui rubbed her temples. Jacqueline could see her pulse quicken.

"There're...gaps. I've been tired—very tired, like I said. Some things aren't clear. But I wasn't home that day. I was... "

She fell silent, but Jacqueline watched the scene balloon into living color above Yaqui's head. She'd been *walking, looking for a place to smoke. And then she'd been set upon, chased by a bald man with a gun. And then, yes, there was a* gap. Worst of all, Jacqueline had been the one who put it there. Naive to assume that piggybacking along in her vision yesterday hadn't had any effect on Yaqui's situation. None of this helped her. Jacqueline glanced at her reflection, ghostly in the dark glass. *Guilty.* No wonder Yaqui was having doubts.

"Where were they going to send you?" asked Clara without looking up.

A fog of terror was creeping into Yaqui's gaze. Of all the ways this could have gone, she probably hadn't expected anything like what she was hearing.

"What is this about? Can you actually help me?" she asked bluntly.

Clara didn't answer her.

"Hey!" she said angrily, trying to grab Clara's attention. No response. Yaqui sat back. A look of horror beginning to dawn on her face.

"You think I did it," she said, her voice rising shrilly.

"It's in your best interest to answer all of our questions, Miss Guzman," said Clara quietly into her busy book.

Yaqui swallowed.

"...I never got an answer on where they were sending me. But they waved this phony doctor's note in my face. They paid some private quack to diagnose me without ever seeing me. Said they'd only use it if I made a fuss. Send me to an asylum. Otherwise, my life would be very comfortable. Fuck knows what that means. Happy?" she said.

Clara tsked softly.

"I suspect you know exactly what that means. You took a big risk in coming here. One you probably wouldn't have taken unless you were sure it would pay off," said Clara.

Yaqui was speechless.

Jacqueline pressed her lips together as she saw what Clara was doing. Clever. She'd probably have done it herself if the idea of sharing a room with Yaqui wasn't existentially terrifying.

"How long have you had substance abuse problems, Miss Guzman?" Clara asked.

Yaqui didn't answer. Just stared daggers back.

"What I'm hearing is this—you never had a good relationship with your adopted mother. In fact, you were concerned you wouldn't be included in your adopted father's substantial will because of your status as an adoptee. In your mind, there was only one way to claim what was rightfully yours. More than that, to keep her from getting any. You framed yourself for murder, knowing your father's discretion would cause him to dispose of all damning evidence. You made sure your adopted mother was the accuser. That way when you came here to build a case, there wouldn't be any contradictions. With her having done something so heinous as frame you for murder in the public eye, she'd be out in the cold. And you'd have all the pill money you could ask for," said Clara.

"What the fuck is wrong with you?" Yaqui asked.

"Nothing putting you behind bars won't solve," replied Clara. She waved a hand, signaling Jacqueline to stop recording. Then, she leaned forward, dropping the act.

"I am so, so sorry I had to say all those horrible things to you. But it was the only way to get you the help you need," Clara apologized frantically. She leaned back as Yaqui continued to look at her like she was crazy.

"…How?" She asked, still a little dazed by this turn of events. Clara closed her notebook.

"This isn't a hotel. The only way we can keep you here is if you become a person of interest in an unsolved case. This way, we don't have to release your sign-in today, and your presence is now part of an investigation. A file closed off to all but Detective Ueda and myself."

Yaqui blinked.

"Who?"

Clara lightly scoffed and rolled her eyes at herself.

"Silly me. Of course, Detective Ueda was bearing witness to our little interview over there."

She gestured at the two-way mirror.

"Oh," said Yaqui, "Hey."

She gave a little half-hearted wave at her reflection. In spite of herself, Jacqueline reflexively lifted her hand to throw a little wave back. She cleared her throat and straightened up as she shook off the impulse. Whatever connection they shared, it wasn't active now. Yaqui displayed no reaction.

"There's just one more bit of info we need from you before we can get started," said Clara.

"Name it," said Yaqui.

"Do you remember the name of the doctor from the letter? The one you said you'd never seen?"

Yaqui sucked in air through her teeth as she started thinking.

"I didn't get a good look at it. I think it started with an F?"

Jacqueline's eyes widened.

"Oh no," she said.

"Might've been a J..." Added Yaqui.

"Anything that might help," said Clara.

"No, no," Jacqueline almost whined as the inevitable connection reared its ugly head.

Yaqui snapped her fingers.

"Folsom! Jonathan Folsom. Fucking spineless bastard. Hope you guys nail him to the wall."

"Fuck," said Jacqueline hopelessly. Until now, all she'd had to worry about was interrogating two criminal psychopaths for this case. Now she'd have to track down her doctor again.

Outside, Clara was signing Yaqui's booking papers when Jacqueline approached her, JANE DOE.

"So," Jacqueline attempted after an awkward silence,

"That seemed like a lot to take in. Are you, um—"

She struggled to find the words.

"Thank you," she said suddenly, after remembering Clara had taken the interview as a favor to her.

"It's nothing," said Clara as she initialed here, there, and there.

Jacqueline found the words she needed.

"Her story was really something. Do you think she's telling the truth?" she asked.

Clara closed up the file and locked it in her desk. "I trust her. I don't know what it is about her, but I believe her story."

Truly an amazing police officer, Jacqueline thought only half-sarcastically. As she sat down, she wondered offhand what it was that had given Clara such a forgiving attitude toward Yaqui's outlandish claims. She avoided her own gaze from the reflection in the window behind Clara's head.

It was Jacqueline herself. Of course Clara believed her, good old Jackie vouched for the story. Jacqueline could entertain every insane theory regarding her doppelganger till the cows came home, but each was useless without concrete proof. It might be prudent to get Yaqui's blood tested though. Just in case Jacqueline really did have a sister.

If Clara had noticed the resemblance beyond superficial features, she hadn't said as much. She might be in the same book club as Deirdre Watson for all Jacqueline knew, but Clara would never be so crass as to say that Jacqueline and Yaqui looked almost exactly alike. It would be unbecoming of her to even present the appearance of such willful ignorance. She'd sound more than a little foolish if she outright said that Yaqui and Jacqueline were related.

She thought back to how Yaqui had looked in the interrogation room. Recreated the scene using her perfect memory. Yaqui looked haggard, certainly. But also smaller somehow. Reduced. As if the pain she'd suffered had robbed her of strength. Jacqueline spooled forward, out of the two-way mirror booth. Looked at the memory of the form Clara had filled out. Hmm. Yaqui was five years younger than Jacqueline. If you didn't know what to look for, if you couldn't see past all the little scars, you'd never in a million years think "that's the same exact person sitting there." *Thank god Clara didn't look too close.*

Clara calmly withdrew a small Tupperware container from the bag beneath her desk.

"So tell me. How come Ms. Guzman didn't know your last name?" Clara asked.

Jacqueline froze. She swore the sweat beading on her forehead turned to ice too. Her mouth was definitely closed for the winter. Clara withdrew a fried hash brown and took a bite. Chewed. Swallowed.

"You said you were friends, right? She didn't react to your name at all back there."

Jacqueline swallowed. The high she'd been riding during the interview was cresting. Crashing. She grasped at something, anything on her way down.

"We're on a first name basis."

Still looking at her, Clara took another bite and handed her more silence to fill.

"We go to...the same meetings."

Bingo. Clara's look immediately softened. Jacqueline pressed her advantage.

"AA meetings. Alcoholics Anonymous. That's how I know her."

"I see," said Clara kindly.

"And you don't use your last name at AA...which is why she didn't know it."

"Gotcha," said Clara tolerantly.

Jacqueline shut up.

Clara continued eating her breakfast while Jacqueline mentally perused the intel she'd collected on Yaqui's case thus far. In the back of her mind, she tried not to think about lying to Clara like that. But would the truth have been of any use to her? Jacqueline didn't want to think about what the truth might entail. A tireless monster, a gentle spiral into madness, a murderous obsession eating her like cancer. No way of knowing. Not anymore. Not since her dreams had started crossing over into reality.

There was a lot going on in the back of her mind she didn't want to think about. That little dark store room was overflowing brackish water into her perfect library. Scattering her thoughts. She put her head down on her desk. These visualizations were becoming increasingly annoying. Metaphor and simile wouldn't help solve her case. She wished she could cut them out of her brain. Like tumors.

She sat up. Closed her eyes. Shook her head. *Focus on the leads. The points where all this bullshit intersects with reality.* Her lip curled as she reviewed her options.

"Not a lot to go on, is it?" Jacqueline said, half to herself.

"I'd start with the doctor," said Clara, wiping her mouth with a paper napkin. Jacqueline grimaced openly. Shit. She'd wanted to hold off on another confrontation if she could. She could handle crooks, they thought in straight lines. Predictable. The doctor was mad, that was clear. Beyond irrational. Living in a fantasy land *he* was sure she'd deported him to. She might have believed him initially. Now however, she had a little more evidence to the contrary.

No you don't, she thought. *You can't trust anything you see. You deliberately kept yourself out of the interrogation room. The better to hallucinate a narrative that would reupholster your delusions. You could have been staring at static on a TV screen for all the good it would have done.*

"No," she whispered.

"I have proof. A witness. A recording. On record."

You are infected with a disease of your own making. It can color-correct any red flags you see. The notes are blank. The only person of interest is you. This is something you made up to finally put yourself at the center of something important.

"Clara."

Her call for help was almost inaudible. The other woman had gotten up to throw away her trash. Put her back to Jacqueline.

It's Clara you can trust least of all. There's no way she doesn't know what's really going on with you. Playing along with your game of pretend out of pity. She's in on it. She's going to put you away once she finds out how far gone you really are. You've got to beat her to it.

"Hh-"

She'd almost asked 'how.'

Talking to yourself is never good. Show her how far gone you really are. Make sure it's the last thing she ever sees.

Her thoughts fell silent as she stared at Clara's back. All she could hear was the bustle of the office as she watched her friend make coffee. She looked around at her co-workers. Their family photos. Overdue paperwork. She looked back at her friend. Yes, her friend. Jacqueline clenched her fists.

No, she thought. And it was her thinking it, definitely. *I saw her. Clara saw her. Yaqui's real. She's a real person who needs my help. Would I go back to that horrible place if I thought for a second I was wrong? Would I put myself in danger—*

—visions of Folsom's fearsome face drifted by like ghostly fish,

if I thought I could run or hide? No. I've got a case to close.

She was gone before Clara got back.

4792LLL. It had been an easy plate number to memorize and Jacqueline had done it ages ago. She didn't see it anywhere now. Where the fuck was her car? She was certain she'd parked it in a side street by her home. Admittedly, it had been a few days, but still. Which was more likely: it had been stolen, or she'd forgotten where it really was? She bit her tongue. At this point, she'd prefer if it had been stolen. She looked over the little horizon of her neighborhood. Back at the looming shadow of the precinct. A sane person would **return** to the station. Report the car stolen. Treat the case they were working on with slow, methodical care. It wasn't THAT important.

Jacqueline thought back to Yaqui sitting there like a prize fighter with nobody in her corner. Beat to hell by life, alone. *No. Not alone. She's got me...she's got me and I've got no more excuses to waste time helping her.* This was a test, whoever or whatever was behind it. She headed for the muni railcar station.

Jacqueline's muni ride was a blur. She got off on Imperial Avenue. Without a car, she'd have to go the rest of the way through the outskirts on foot. The walk to the medical center was taking way too long. She was walking as fast she could without running. Trying to outpace whatever unpleasant thought might assault her next. No way of knowing when another situation would occur. She never stopped. Didn't want to attract too much attention. She took in every little detail. Watched for people watching her. There weren't any.

Not a lot of people on the streets this time of day. There was the coffee shop. All clean, no sign of the trouble she'd caused the other day. Maybe three people in there. Five if you counted the clerks. They were all staring dutifully ahead at their futures, which largely contained coffee. None of them were looking her way. A fear bubbled up that they had been, until the very second she'd looked. That everyone was doing that. Ridiculous. Irrational. But she couldn't get the image out of her head. She quickened her pace. She saw movement in the corner of her eye and started jogging. *Don't look back.* A laugh track burbled to life in the distance. Impossible to place. She might be running toward it.

Running. Flat out running now. This might be worse than the waking dreams. No longer operating on dream logic but unable to ignore the irrational impulses. There was the coffee shop again. She hadn't taken any turns. Yet here she was, running in circles. She ran faster. The edges of her vision were turning black. She knew that blackness was everything behind her. Had swallowed everything. There was the coffee shop. The people inside looked scared. Frozen with fear. They couldn't move. Looking at nothing. She was nothing. The blackness had swallowed her entirely. A pair of blue stars overhead were all that was left of the sky. She heard a distant rumble that might have been thunder and might have been a growl. Many strange beasts prowled around every corner, a hint of a tail or a wing or a flash of needle teeth. She was surrounded by a horde of the things, or merely stalked by one that didn't obey the laws of physics. She was in a very bad place. The shadows gave way to pitch black and everything fell away except for the coffee shop.

The people inside couldn't move. And she couldn't stop moving. Hurtling towards them like a meteor. The people inside were different. Not the ones she'd just seen. No, these were...

No. Stop. *I don't want to see this again.*

She tried to stop running, but she didn't have legs anymore. These were the people who'd been in the shop when she'd awakened after escaping from the doctor's office. Witness to her episode. Her yesterday was happening in reverse. Headed towards the doctor's office instead of running away, forced back into the shop she'd ended up in. Someone was trying to show her a scene she'd missed.

No, I DON'T WANT TO SEE THIS, she tried to say, but she didn't have a mouth anymore. The moment approached too fast. She screamed as the door opened and the little bell over it jangled. The shop was filled with blinding light, which engulfed her.

She blinked in the sunlight. She was alone with the sound of her breathing. It looked like she'd gotten her wish. She was standing outside somebody's house. Nowhere near where she needed to be. She looked around for a sign. Glacier Street.

Regular old fear flooded her system. Why? She turned at a noise from behind her. The door to the nearby home was ajar. A string of curses floated her way on the breeze. She sniffed, and wrinkled her nose. She wasn't a beat cop, so she'd never seen weed outside of an evidence locker. She'd definitely never used any either. But you'd have to be colorblind to not smell how green this was.

"Ugh," she said. It was all over her. She looked down at her arms. She frowned. Thick, heavy black leather.

"This isn't my jacket," she said.

The cursing intensified and she turned to face it directly. Through the door, an old woman was struggling to her feet in chunky plastic heels.

"Ms. Watson?" She said. There was no coherent answer forthcoming.

Movement in the corner of her eye jerked Jacqueline's head around. She jingled ever so slightly as she moved. Events began to crystallize around her. Two policemen leaned against their squad car. Their hood was up. Blocking the dash cam. A bald-headed man, no—

THE bald-headed man was talking with them. Laughing. He reached into his jacket and handed a thick yellow envelope to one of them. The other shook hands with him.

The bald-headed man. From her dreams of Yaqui, from the pretzel shop, and more importantly from their most recent one of being chased. Of Yaqui being chased. Worst of all, he still had his gun. The police hadn't taken it from him, let alone arrested him. *Dirty*. She looked down at her hands. No, not her hands. She knew where she was, who she was.

"Yaqui," she said before she could stop herself.

There should have been a drum roll. Something deep and ominous, with a bit of bass to it. There should have been a spotlight. He turned to look at her. The stage players stood poised to play their parts. Their expressions began to change. Jacqueline felt as if she was moving through molasses. She was already turning to run. Her mind worked overtime while her body tried to catch up. How to even begin to make sense of this? This was the same dream. Or a continuation of it, somehow. Like she'd left a bookmark there. But this time, she was in control. No longer behind glass, struggling for influence like before.

She gritted her teeth against whatever invisible force was holding her back. If the same basic rules applied, all her dreams were replays of things that had already happened to Yaqui or Yakuza. Assuming they were actually real...

No. *Focus.* If there were any facts remaining after the hurricane of bullshit she'd been through, the most self-evident one was that She, the She that she thought of as her own consciousness, had come unmoored from any kind of tangible reality. And if you knew you were in a dream, the only logical action you could take would be to wake up. If she stopped to question every little thing, she'd quite literally be killed for it. The footfalls of the bald gunman fell behind her like a sleeping heartbeat.

Still running. Taking forever. She was already tired of this rerun. She knew how it ended. Yaqui escaped, and days later was sitting in an interrogation booth. She could see the path of the dream before her. A mirror gallery of ghostly blue after-images. Fore-images? Ready for her to step into. A dark thought crossed her mind. What if Yaqui didn't escape today? Could she actually change history? Or did dying in your dreams really just wake you up? She stared again at the fairy trail leading to the end of this story. Bright blue. It threw everything else into sharp relief. Everything in this memory was tinged blue. She was seeing, thinking faster than everything else. Blue shifting.

I'm here for a reason. These people already had their chance to say something interesting. It's my turn now. Her glacial trajectory had taken her around all of two corners while she'd been thinking. As hard as it had been to follow someone else's footsteps, turning to face her own demons was surprisingly easy. Like moving through water instead of boring through rock. Her pursuer had a path too. A translucent worm of frozen strides bleeding into each other.

His motives were less clear, but not invisible. She could literally see him coming a mile away. She squared up to receive him. A scrap of garbage paper that had been hanging in the air blew away. Time was speeding back up. That made sense. Dreams happened at a different pace than real life right? This wasn't a dream anymore. This was a story she was telling. The wind-up was particularly satisfying. Almost as much as the delivery. A double-handed hammerfist from overhead. The blue haze exploded in a fountain of red as she punched his fucking clock. His nose caved in. He clutched at his face and choked as he fell to his knees. There was so much blood. She just watched it for a little while. Niagara.

Hit him again.

He put a hand on the alley brickwork to steady himself and she aimed a kick at his wrist. *Love these boots.* Heavy. Steel toe? *Really comfy.* Another kick to the jaw jerked his head back. Probably concussed by this point. He looked up. Shaky.

Definitely concussed. One pupil was bigger than the other. She could see herself in it. She could see—

She was smiling.

Take a step back.

What was she really seeing? Was this her? She'd wanted to hurt him. Really enjoyed it, too.

To her, this man was a phantom. She didn't owe him anything, not even a beating. She'd liked to have questioned him, but now he was in no fit state to say much of anything. How close was she to this other life? Too close wouldn't even begin to describe it, but 'compromised' was a good start. That smile didn't belong to her. It was too wide. She blinked. Became aware of her own breathing. Out of sync with this body's. She was breaking up. Not a great time. She hadn't seen him draw the gun.

She'd heard the shot. And now she was staring at her reflection again. The bullet was spinning slowly.

Looked like a tiny cement mixer. She could see herself in it. It wasn't her face, but at least it was her expression. She brushed at Yaqui's nose chain. Would Yaqui remember any of this? Would this change anything?

Probably not. They were both still alive. She moved around the bullet. It whistled as it caught up with its momentum. Hit the wall behind her. She leaned in close to her assailant. Studied his face. Memorized every detail. Bald, of course. No piercings. No tattoos. Unusually blue eyes. She mentally erased the bruises and the blood. Got a clean picture in her mind.

He could barely hold his gun aloft. She easily pushed it away. She wasn't sure if he could hear her, if she could really affect this dream, but she was damn well going to try.

"This was a warning. If I see you again, it'll be the last time."

He swallowed. Sputtered and choked lightly. Still bleeding.

"Muh. Mm—"

She grimaced. He might be too out of it to hear anything she was saying, regardless of how real it was. A funny thought crossed her mind in the opposite direction. Maybe his brain was damaged enough to be on the same wavelength. She shook her head. No crazy talk. There were limits to what she'd accept.

"For now," she said darkly.

The air jingled behind her, again. She turned. There was the coffee shop. She moved slowly. Off kilter. Her time had run out. She was becoming herself again. Could feel her shell of being dissolving in this hostile environment. She put her hand on the door handle and walked into the coffee shop. The facade was two dimensional, nothing beyond it but the void. The awakening. The return to reality.

Jacqueline stood alone in the field of wildflowers. She could see the road from here. The air was hot, and reassuringly real on her skin. No people looking at her. Flat land meant nobody could sneak up on her. She knew this road. She realized where she was, the little field that ran alongside the connecting road between downtown and the pavilion. The place where her doctor worked.

Had worked; she'd be extremely surprised if he'd stayed. She'd be so surprised she just might forget to slap him in cuffs for a second. Just one.

And that was just the start. She'd round things out by nailing those bastards who had the gall to call themselves cops to the fucking wall. It would take a little longer to get to them. She'd have to cross-reference every detail she could recall about their involvement—the sun's position in the sky, a statement from Yaqui about the incident, and any instances of interference in auto-surveillance. In the meantime, she knew their faces. Every pore. She had time now to puzzle it all together. She started walking.

··

When Jacqueline arrived at the medical pavilion, she was tired and sweaty. This, in itself, was refreshing. Like the cold rain, it made her feel alive. She made a beeline for the water fountain. Splashed a little on her face too. Didn't care how she looked. Avoided using the bathroom sink, though it would have made more sense. It certainly didn't make sense to hide from your reflection, but she was done with trying to make sense of any of this. That and looking in the mirror were two things that had done her no good thus far. She looked up, out the sliding glass door and across the parking lot at the psych building. She was in the pharmacy right now. She knew it well too. The art on the walls and the carpeting on the floor were ugly and cheap. Muted sea green and lilac met somewhere in the middle for a uniform fuzzy grey.

Nobody she knew behind the counter today. Just

as well. She might be tempted to re-up one of her many prescriptions by a familiar face. She needed a clear head for this.

Bright sunlight, fading but still strong. Her thoughts were silent as she watched the neurology clinic approach and get larger. She didn't want to say "something's wrong," because there was nobody else with her there and she had decided talking to herself was a bad thing to do. She also didn't want to draw any parallels between now and the nightmare she'd just escaped from. More silence. A blast of cool air brushed her hair back as the doors slid open. A wall of noise followed after, bursting like a bubble.

There were a lot more people here than usual, and the waiting room was usually quite full. Desperation was one thing you'd never find in short supply. One thing you wouldn't see was all these people standing up. If there was anyone who deserved a rest, it was the families of the children who couldn't do anything but sit.

One of the people standing up broke away from the group he was talking to and approached her.

"Detective Ueda? I'm officer Jameson. Desk Sergeant Pinkerton said you'd be coming by, but not when. Can I assume you've been briefed?"

She stared at his face. He was standing there in front of her, *but also leaning against his squad car, laughing as he watched her run like she was prize game.* No, not her. *Yaqui.* He was supposed to be an officer of the law, and a couple billfolds later he'd never heard of her—of Yaqui. It was that same dirty cop from the vision. Hate consumed her. Her first thought, her very first one, was: *Don't kill him. Not right away.*

"...Detective Ueda?"

His face was very different now. He wore an expression he probably wasn't used to. Fear. For him, life must have been good. The deals he'd cut with criminals ensured his job was easy.

She wondered what her expression looked like, and discovered that she didn't care. She didn't care that she'd probably been making a weird face while she was looking at him.

"Officer, Jameson, was it? I'm going to need you to give me your full 'briefing' on what I was given to understand was a classified investigation."

"I was just following up on a report filed yesterday. Shots fired. Initial canvas turned up nothing." Him doing the stammering was a nice change of pace.

This time, Jacqueline's face betrayed nothing. She was already thinking ahead. In her mind, she stood in the little garden between buildings outside Dr. Folsom's office, looking for the bullet holes from her escape. Digging into the plaster for the slugs. Looking around, looking up— SHIT.

Her perfect memory painted a security camera there. It would have seen her. Would have seen her yesterday. Jacqueline would have to account for every detail. She'd need to hit the security office first. Steal the tape. *Tape?* They'd have switched to a digital format ages ago. Wipe the drives. Then get the spent shells out of the office. Scene of the crime. *Amazing,* she thought bitterly. She was the one who'd been assaulted but now she was working to cover it up. All because the alternative would be too hard to explain.

"...Detective?"

He faded back into focus. His face was hard to read now. He was looking at her arm. She waved hello, playing at Slightly Exasperated.

"Anything else?"

A background process caught up with her and she spoke over him a little.

"Anyth—oh, sorry. Hahaha," she laughed.

"Haha," he laughed too, automatically.

Her arm didn't hurt nearly as much. Should have ditched the arm brace. She could see the question welling up behind his eyes.

"Detective. Can I ask how you sustained that injury?"

Far too formal. Fishing for something. *Nice try.*

"I slipped. And fell...down the stairs."

Neither said anything for the longest second Jacqueline had ever experienced. She waited to see if he would question her further. She was already lining up the next few relevant details. Shuffle the cue cards together. Tap them on the desk. Tap. Tap. Tap.

Just a light sprain. Won't keep me off the job. I live on the bottom floor of my building. The stairwell is a little dark. Yesterday. Yesterday night. The elevator's out.

"I'm sorry to hear that," Jameson said finally. He reached out and grabbed a clipboard from a passing orderly.

"That roster you wanted to see, Officer," she said.

Good. Willing to drop it. Smart. *Maybe too smart.* Waiting for a better opportunity to expose her. Exploit her. *Not again.*

He pored over the list in his fingers, heedless of her piercing gaze.

Relax. He knows nothing. He doesn't know you. He didn't even get a clear look at Yaqui...did he?

A shutter speed zoetrope flickered backwards over her field of sight. Jameson was a little further away now. She watched him take the envelope and laugh. Watched the bald man turn toward her and start to run. Jameson's eyes lit over her for the barest second before turning to his partner and saying something funny. 60% chance it would have been workplace inappropriate. Did dash cams have sound? Another detail to cross-reference. A hand gave her a clipboard as the bald man closed the gap on the street. He disappeared as she scanned the names in front of her.

"What am I missing here?" she said to herself.

"Not what, who," replied Jameson.

He seemed pretty proud of his snappy little reply. His nose followed his eyebrows up whenever he thought he was being smart. She elected not to pick up on any of that. She'd already picked up on the fact that Doctor Jonathan Folsom did not appear to exist, nor had he ever. According to this form, he might as well have diagnosed himself as one of her neuroses. *'On the run,'* Folsom echoed in her head as she scrolled down the list.

"This guy, this Doctor Folsom's like a ghost," said Jameson.

"A ghost would at least have a gravestone," she mused as she memorized all the details on the page.

"Hand-to-hands confirm he was here yesterday and for some time before that. Quiet, kept to himself. Almost like one of those dramatic reenactment specials. And you know what that means," said Jameson.

Jacqueline frowned, processing several thoughts.

"A hand-to-hand is an op for exposing street dealers. That doesn't make sense unless you were using drug deals for info—"

She looked up. Jameson smiled and jingled a little pill bottle of just-below-the-counter pain meds.

"I get headaches," he chuckled.

Jacqueline stared at him, then blinked. "Ah. A joke. That's one of your regular prescriptions."

His smile dipped a little as she explained his joke. "Yeah," he said hesitantly.

"And you picked it up on the way here."

He nodded, eyes like a man trapped in a very small box.

"That's right."

Few things worse than a joke that doesn't land. *I should know,* she thought unsympathetically.

"So, our friend the missing doctor is a person of interest? Have you combed his office?" she asked.

"Yes. And no," he said.

Her sigh of relief was inaudible. Nothing on her. Nothing. No trace. She'd make sure. "I'll take it from here, Officer Jameson."

The plaque on his door was missing.

Jacqueline was immediately surprised by how quiet

it was. The wind blew through the shattered window, rustling the torn pages of Folsom's notes like forlorn flags. She ducked under the police tape.

It felt almost peaceful here. Much of the furniture was still overturned, but it had been moved around the edges of the disheveled room so forensics could do their work.

That reminded her—Jameson claimed the initial search had turned up nothing. 'Nothing' wasn't very descriptive, but Jacqueline could bet that if they'd found any evidence she'd been here, she wouldn't have spent the night in her own bed.

She sniffed. *Alcohol. Bleach.* Sharp and just as telling as blood. She looked up from the indentations in the carpet where furniture had stood. The desk was upright again, in the far corner. The doctor had an intercom phone, and it was still plugged in on top there. The current time glowed green on the little display by the receiver.

Shots fired. She patted her gun absentmindedly. *Three shots fired.* Difficult to tell exactitudes given the state she'd been in, but no more than a few minutes could have passed between the time she'd stepped into his abyssal trap and the time she'd escaped. The office seemed a lot smaller and less existentially threatening now that it was brighter, but she felt like she could still piece together the sequence of events.

Shots fired. After which, she had made her exit, going god knows where but ending up at the Imperial Coffee by the muni railcar station. He wasn't here now; the logic of self-preservation dictated he needed to leave the premises. He also needed to clean up, but not too much. *Eyewitnesses would confirm he'd been here, obviously.* And he couldn't kill all of them. He'd taken his plaque, but that probably had more to do with his hubris. The chemicals and the system wipe had to have a less obvious motive, then.

She looked around suspiciously. HAD he killed anyone? You didn't need bleach to cover up a small scuffle. More likely someone had stumbled on his lair after hearing gunfire and he'd silenced them. But he was just one man, and unathletic besides. Now, who did she know that disposed of bodies for the discerning customer? She made a mental note, linking Fong and Nunogawa to the case by another thin but strong thread.

But why go to all that trouble? What did he have to gain?

The phone rang in the present. Her eyes widened slightly. Her heartbeat quickened. She felt sick as the realization hit her. The phone kept ringing. Unknown number.

Folsom was covering for Jacqueline. He couldn't completely erase that he'd been here, but bleaching the DNA evidence on the door and in the carpet would erase her. He wouldn't keep the cops off her unless he had a good reason. She'd balk at his possessive nature being "good," but it tracked. If, to him, she was some monstrous foe, then only *he* could defeat her. He wouldn't let anyone else take a shot. His obsession with control wouldn't permit it.

The phone kept ringing. She found herself drawn to it through a perverse sense of inevitability. She picked it up, knowing who she'd hear.

Silence. Only her own breathing.

"Hello?" She said with shaky defiance. Her voice echoed in her ear.

When he spoke, it wasn't the frightening cacophony she'd been bracing for. "Hello again, Ms. Ueda," Dr. Folsom whispered. He was still the loudest thing in the room. Her ears rung from the silence. Little sounds were huge.

"I'm so glad we got a chance to speak one more time before my sabbatical."

Too many questions jockeyed for the position of most pertinent. She opted for the one that would theoretically let her get her hands on him to ask more questions.

"Where are you?" she said tersely, failing to keep the anger out of her voice.

"Now now," he condescended, "Ordinarily I'd be happy to indulge you, but I'm afraid our time today is short. We'll need to focus on questions for you, specifically the question of your willingness to change."

Her subconscious caught up with her as she listened to Folsom's sotto voce wheedling. She looked wildly around, hoping to spot him somewhere, perhaps peering out a window or behind a corner.

He cleared his throat like his office hours were still in effect and she was burning his daylight.

"I regard myself as a professional. As such, I've always tried to remove my own bias as much as is possible from the instructive portion of our sessions."

He could see her, somehow. Knew she'd be here. A camera? Nowhere to hide it in here. She looked out the window. What was missing, what was changed?

The realization hit her so hard she nearly fell as she ducked. There was a bit of scenery that had been present for all of her previous visits, even in the most recent and dire of circumstances.

It simply wouldn't do to have a camera looking into a psychiatrist's office during his private visits. That was why the curtains had always been drawn.

Having ducked behind the doctor's traditionalist couch, she peeked over and tried to see if she could spot the courtyard camera from there.

"But I'm afraid I'll have to be frank with you. I've sacrificed a great deal for the sake of your mental health. My own, for starters," he said, and laughed.

As details began to fit into place, Jacqueline found herself slightly more at ease. If he was watching her on camera, that meant he was in the security office. She knew this place inside and out. If he was in the office, she knew all the routes in and out of there and how long it would take to travel them.

"Which is why I think it's only fair that you try and meet me halfway. For your sake as much as mine. I really only want one thing from you. A promise."

Indulge him. Keep him talking.

"No," she said to herself, aloud.

It would have been out of character for her to start taking his advice now. More suspicious than anything to suddenly capitulate. She started timing her interception of his escape instead. She'd meet him halfway, alright. His voice quavered like he was trying to keep from laughing.

"Really now, Ms. Ueda. It's no insurmountable task I'm asking of you. I just want you to focus on the things we've talked about."

"You're wanted for questioning in an official investigation, Mister Folsom. You're really not in any position to be making demands," she replied.

If he followed the quickest turns out of the office to the nearest exit, he'd be gone in ten minutes. She could catch him in five if she didn't stop. On the phone, he'd noticed that she no longer considered him as a doctor. His tone sharpened.

"As if you'd be particularly overjoyed for your colleagues to hear anything I've got to say. Let us not forget how lucky you are that I've decided to respect our doctor-patient confidentiality. It's very important to me that our hard work pays off. I know how much of a flight risk you are. I'd hate for you to relapse and disappear before I got another chance to see you again. And I can promise you, we will see each other again," he hissed.

A threat, then. Another power play haunted by the specter of ownership. Trying to exert control over her, weaken her resolve and inflame her paranoia even as he fled. Likely out of the country.

In her mind, she continued toward him. Right turn. Left. Left. Right—no, straight. That utility closet opened into two hallways. She might even be able to surprise him there if he was moving as fast as she thought he was. Too early, and he'd turn heel and run back the other way. But he'd be flat footed. If he was wearing the same shoes he always wore, an old pair of penny loafers, he might even slip.

She'd be the wolf in the kitchen, then. A devil in a special hell consisting of eight magic seconds where she would chase him, and he would run and be caught. She wasn't going to lie; she was looking forward to the chasing almost as much as the catching. It was time for him to be afraid.

"Sooner than you think," Jacqueline said darkly. She dropped the cordless phone on her desk and turned to go. Faintly, she caught his reply as she laid eyes on a very unwelcome sight.

"Going somewhere?" the receiver said as two heavy set men approached cautiously down the hallway to Folsom's office. The urge to run intensified as they got closer. She recognized their name tags from the roster she'd memorized earlier. They weren't supposed to be on this floor today. The wind and the sound of their footsteps was muted. All she could hear was his voice.

"I conferred with an old friend of yours about your appointment. I was surprised (as I'm sure you are) to learn you had such conscientious family. So concerned was I for your well being, I must confess I rather hurried over the paperwork. If there's been any sort of error, mistaken identity, false accusation, that sort of thing, we can sort it out after these nice men have checked you in."

A setup.

The walls didn't close in. Her reality stayed right where it was. Even as her very worst fear came to pass, her mind did not wander or flee into madness as it had before. She became aware of her own breathing. This was it. The worst thing that could possibly happen was happening.

She'd be trapped, forgotten inside her own head. Sedated in a padded room. She stepped back, bumping into the desk. She couldn't take her eyes off of her approaching doom. The wind rustled her hair, beckoning through the broken window.

Run.

No.

Fight.

No. This is what he wanted, what he'd wanted all along. For her to seal her own fate. And it would be her own doing this time. No vision to blame it on this time. *Go quietly into the night.* They were coming through the door. One at a time. Hands up, palms out like she was an animal. Apt, considering she only had two real options left that would reinforce that notion. What would it be: run and prove them right, or fight and prove him right? Her eyes darted to the window. Sharp glass there. One pair of their eyes followed hers.

"Don't—" he started to say.

Fuck it, she thought, had already done it once, and dove through the broken window. The wind whistled by her ears as she sailed through. Didn't even get nicked. She rolled once she hit the courtyard grass. Sprung to her feet and into a sprint. Shouts from behind her and the sound of breaking glass as her would-be jailers kicked out more of the window to give chase.

Left. The door was automatic, starting to close as another orderly with a rolling cart finished passing by its sensor in the hallway beyond. Not slowing down, she very nearly sashayed through the narrowing gap. Turned sideways to avoid touching the sides. It was an older model that had to close all the way before it would open again, buying her precious seconds while she made good her escape.

Left. Drew a few stares as she dashed through the hallway intersection. A doctor with a stern face and a sallow patient closed the door to their little room. The orderly with the rolling cart stopped ahead of her and looked like he was going to say something. Jacqueline kicked the cart over and kept running as the shouts behind her bloomed and multiplied.

Right—no, straight. Having tripped one of the pursuing orderlies by using the fallen cart, she juked the other one. Wall-stepped off a corner and made a beeline for the utility closet she'd chosen as a shortcut. Her closest pursuer crashed into the wall behind her, his attempt at a running tackle paying back painful dividends. She slammed into the closet door foot-first, leaving a dent right by the handle as it was forced open. Kicking aside a mop and bucket, she shouldered aside a surprised scream that resolved into a janitor. The opposite door was already open. She panted and scanned the hallway. Empty. She kicked the closet closed behind her. There was a click. More shouting and pounding on the door. Was she too early? Too late? She'd had to alter her course somewhat to intercept the doctor, but he should still be here if he was taking the quickest path out.

Movement caught her eye. Another large window, this one taking up most of the wall opposite. The sun shone down through a skylight on another lobby, a spiral staircase in brushed steel, and the doctor trit-trotting down it.

No.

Baseball cap pulled low over his stupid comb over. A pair of aviators to obscure his unmistakable face. Plainclothes. No, a security uniform. Stolen, likely. Its owner just as likely dead. He'd been in the camera bay, after all. Bleach wafted under her nose in her memory. No. No, no. He was getting away.

No. How was he getting away? He'd taken a slower path that she was now effectively cut off from. That bastard. The bastard had taken a suboptimal turn! He stopped. Looked up. Smiled and waved. As if to say: I know you. I own you.

So predictable. Thinking in straight lines. Like a TV show. The end.

Was what she was seeing even real, here? She couldn't stop picturing the floor to ceiling window as a movie screen. It flickered with static. More lies. More uncertainty. No.

"No."

She backed up a step. Legs tensed like steel as she kicked off against the wall behind her.

"NO!"

Breaking through the window was like jumping into a pool. Falling so slow. She relished the look on his face. He was staggering into a run.

Yaqui sailed through the open night air and hit the lawn below her mansion's balcony at an angle, twisting her ankle. The green courtyard swam in front of Yaqui's vision and became—

—The doctor's foyer jingled with falling glass.

Jacqueline pushed herself up off the linoleum and gritted her teeth against the pain. *Stupid.* No way she could catch him like this. He was already throwing himself into a little blue hatchback outside. *Catch the plate number. Now.*

She limped forward, caught herself against an unattended check-in counter. 3 L B C -

Gone. Memorized the make and model of the car as it sped away. *I'll find you. I'll find you, you fucker.*

Footsteps from behind her. The vise started to tighten. Caught in the bear trap the moment she set foot in this place. She turned, with some difficulty. There were three of them now. One of them had grabbed a little syringe. *That was a bit dramatic,* she reflected dryly. She looked back up at the hole she'd made as the men spread out to encircle her. There again, perhaps they were right to be afraid. They had, after all, put themselves in a very dangerous position—in her way.

These men weren't bad. It wasn't their intention to hurt her. She felt eerily calm as they drew closer to dooming her. She was kind of at a loss as to what to do with them.

What does anyone do with corpses they don't need? asked a thought that didn't feel like hers. She almost laughed. Sure. Kill them. Seal the deal and show everyone they were right about her. Disappear if she was lucky. Get put on display if she wasn't. What kind of choice was that? She couldn't take her eyes off that syringe. Felt her hand reach into her jacket. Brushed against her gun. Her fingers closed around metal. There was a high-pitched buzzing noise in her ears. It grew higher when she withdrew her hand. Her foes had stopped by this point. This might be the last time she saw them. She studied their faces. They were sweating. They'd probably run all the way here. She was not unkind. They wouldn't need to run anymore.

She held up her badge.

When she spoke, her words felt like bleached driftwood as the waves receded. These men would bear witness. Like her, their resolve would be tested. This time, it would not be found wanting.

Obstruction of justice was a scary combination of words. After Jacqueline had explained to the men very slowly and carefully what those words meant, they were extremely receptive. That was before Jameson had arrived. Although she outranked him, she thought it prudent to stick around and explain the situation. That was turning out to be about as difficult as she'd anticipated.

"I mean, it doesn't look good."

Jameson kicked at some of the glass on the ground. Jacqueline leaned against the vacant check-in counter in the lobby. More police tape on the exit door. On the wrong side of it again. Where did she go wrong?

She looked up at the cannonball splash-sized hole in the glass.

Where did she *first* go wrong, she self-corrected.

Let the bad guy get away.

"What am I supposed to tell HQ on this?" Jameson asked.

She'd love it if he could tell them the truth, because it would mean she could too. What she was stuck with now was far less desirable. As it was, she'd need to find evidence of wrongdoing that wasn't hers. She'd be doing that right now if she wasn't—

Jacqueline grimaced as she shifted her injured leg. Wasn't nearly as bad she'd thought, thank god. That said, she wasn't hobbling anywhere fast. Jameson would have to do the walking and talking for her.

"Did you check the camera room?" Jacqueline asked

impatiently.

Jameson broke eye contact with her and resumed scuffing the floor.

"Yes. I told you already. First thing I told you. If you remember."

She narrowed her eyes. Couldn't see his. Sure he was lying, though. Not necessarily that he and his men hadn't checked, but that he'd briefed her already. She blinked.

No, he definitely hadn't. What a strange, small thing to lie about. Her disgust for him mounted as he kept his back to her. He put two fingers to an ear. Was he even really listening to an earpiece? Or was he just stalling? He'd already told HQ, hadn't he? They were coming to cart her off now, weren't they? They wouldn't have to take her far.

Why else would he gaslight her, lie to her, shut her out of her own investigation? Unless he knew she was compromised. She had to act first. Escape wasn't an option. Not while he was still around.

"Yeah, so, like I said. Nothing in the office. Nothing in the security room. Smelled funny, though."

Jacqueline took her hand out of her jacket.

"What kind of smell?" she asked, as if she didn't already know the answer.

"...like bleach. Smelled like bleach in the camera room," he confirmed after conferring with his earpiece.

Dead end. Nothing left here that could save her. Folsom had thought of everything. Covered everything, including his tracks. She was the only thing left. Holding the bag.

She looked around like she was thinking. She was the one stalling now. Only a matter of time before they arrived at the same conclusion. Nothing to see here except her. Nothing here... She was looking at the jagged silhouette she'd made. Couldn't deny the parallel that was forming in her mind. She was on the wrong side of the crime scene again. Like before, her vantage kept her from seeing a crucial detail. Nothing here...

Jacqueline closed her eyes. Fell backwards into

her perfect memory. Up through the air like Alice in wonderland. She looked out through the window, yet to be broken. What wasn't missing yet? She frowned, and smashed through the glass.

Stop.

She hung in the air over the doctor, mid-scramble. And there was his getaway vehicle. No, not his. She would have recognized his. Stolen, then. Another lead. He wouldn't leave more loose ends untied than he needed to. Wouldn't source an escape car from someone else who might blab. Not if he already had a dead body to loot. No, this car belonged to the security guard who apparently dissolved into bleach. But no body didn't mean no blood. She just needed to follow the trail. The car would have the answers she needed.

3LBC072.

She opened her eyes.

"Where's that car I told you to search for? The blue hatchback."

Jameson turned back around.

"What car? You never—"

"It's the first thing I told you," she interrupted pointedly, using his own brand of white lie against him, "Blue hatchback. Plate number 3LBC072. Our, scratch that—my person of interest has just been upgraded to suspect after he was spotted fleeing the scene of the crime in that car. He disobeyed calls to halt from an officer of the law. Innocent people don't run. Not wearing stolen uniforms. Further, double checking the roster revealed a second missing person. A security guard. All this, combined with circumstantial evidence I gleaned from a crime scene you didn't even visit led me to believe YOUR suspect in MY case may have committed murder in the first degree."

Jameson was pale and speechless, so she steamrolled right over him.

"Patterns of behavior and the evidence of a coverup YOU noted—the bleach," she added helpfully as he mouthed the last two words along with her,

"—point to a violent and unstable individual in possession of a stolen vehicle which is now getting farther and farther away from us—" she nearly shouted.

Jacqueline visually translated her fake exasperation into fake resignation. "I mean, this doesn't look good. What am I supposed to tell HQ?"

"What was that plate number?" Jameson asked hurriedly, fear and self-preservation overtaking him.

"It was the first thing I told you," she said, this time truthfully.

Jacqueline faded into the background as Jameson scrambled to find the car. She wouldn't lie, she felt exhilarated and not at all bad to have told so many lies. Turnabout was fair play. In truth, she'd only guessed the guard was missing. But Jameson didn't need to know that.

"They found the car," he said, interrupting her thoughts.

"Where?" She snapped hungrily. She couldn't hide her satisfaction and didn't care. Folsom would be caught. HE'D be discredited, HE'D be silenced. HE'D be the crazy one.

"Abandoned by the airport highway. Some…"

He listened to his earpiece for a few more seconds.

"Some discarded items and other evidence point to signs of a struggle," he finished.

"What evidence?" Said Jacqueline, in freefall. Her eyes followed the corners of her mouth downward. Her stomach turned sour and tried to eat itself and her heart along with it.

"Blood on several of the seats of the abandoned car. Skid marks and superficial damage to the chassis also suggest the car was involved in a collision."

She realized her smile had been falling. She dropped it the rest of the way. *The bad guy gets away. I'm not a hero and the bad guy gets away.*

"This clinches it. That doctor's certifiable. I'm…sorry I doubted you," said Jameson, but she didn't hear him. His approval, something she'd never needed, was cold comfort.

"We'll put out an APB For his arrest."

Waste of time. He's already gone. And with two bodies on him, no less. At least.

She heaved herself into a painful stand, which became a painful walk.

"I'm going back to his office. There may be something I missed when I was...interrupted."

"Hey, do you want—" Jameson began, eyes darting to her limp.

"NO," said Jacqueline.

Where the hell was it? Jacqueline pawed through the contents of Folsom's desk. Plenty of old papers. Client lists. Theoretical notes. Murderous illegible scrawl. Those last ones seemed more recent. Nothing useful or telling in any of it. Least of all, the letter she needed to prove Yaqui had been falsely diagnosed. After four hours of searching and categorizing, she was certain she hadn't missed anything. That meant someone else had disposed of it. Either before she got here or...

She looked out the broken window.

...after. The doctor's distraction. It was suspicious how quickly he'd managed to Section 8 her. But, he'd been all the way across the complex...That meant an accomplice. What was it he'd said? A family member had supposedly tried to check her in. She very much doubted that. More likely, it was whoever made off with the letter.

A footstep from behind her. She didn't turn right away. Unlikely the accomplice was still here. Movement in her periphery made her tense up. *Relax. Just Jameson.*

The feeling didn't go away as she finished turning to look at him.

Was Jameson...just Jameson?

She forced the emotion out of her face as she unpacked that thought. He'd been here before she arrived. Had been conveniently absent while she was being chased.

To say nothing of Folsom hiding in the camera bay and then escaping so easily. Most telling of all, Jameson could be bought. If he'd take money from a criminal on the street, why not from a doctor in an office? She heard his pills rattle in the bottle in his pocket. Maybe he'd been paid in scrips, as well. A hand-to-hand, indeed.

Jameson was holding a sheaf of papers in one hand. The bald man's handoff superimposed itself over him for a moment. He offered the envelope of money to her as it turned back into the test results she'd requested. What she wouldn't give for THAT bit of leverage against him. This leech would have to wait, though. She had bigger fish to fry.

"What's all this?" The leech said. He gestured at the little maze of paper stacks she'd created. She ignored the question.

"Officer Jameson. Are those the test results I requested?"

She took them from him and flipped to the most relevant paragraph. He began to tell her what she already knew.

"Hospital was more than happy to cooperate after everything that happened. They practically set a record. This basically connects all the dots. Blood belongs to our missing guard."

Jacqueline closed the folder and connected her own dots. Folsom couldn't have escaped on foot after abandoning the stolen car. Evidence of a collision pointed to another car theft, with the possibility of a second body for the doctor to dispose of.

More and more roads were leading to the slaughterhouses as his case wore on. The thought of so many people disappearing into the maw of that place sickened her. Especially since it seemed to be such a public secret. It was obvious that Fong and Nunogawa were responsible, guilty. Yet, in all likelihood they'd never face justice...

Jameson adjusted his gun belt as he knelt to paw

through one of her carefully organized stacks, as though trying to look busy, useful. She eyed the gun thoughtfully.

"...Maybe not in a courtroom," she said, completing the thought.

"What?" Jameson said, craning his neck.

Jacqueline cleared her throat. "Nothing. Just—"

She turned away, faced the window.

"Distracted," she finished lamely.

The window had now been broken so thoroughly that only a jagged quarter of it remained in the bottom right of the frame. It reflected her from the neck down. She stared at her absence of face. The green backdrop, out of focus.

Sure, she could kill the gangsters. There might even be a safe outlet for all of...whatever this was if she did. *Kill bad people. Keep good people safe...*

"...From me."

Jameson made a noise but didn't say anything. Jacqueline didn't look around. Kept staring at the headless her.

No. No, no, no. There was only one real foe. All of this: the doctor, the cleaners, the crooked cops...it was all because of Her. Yakuza. She was the one who'd killed Jimmy and countless others, who'd driven the doctor insane. And she'd done it all for Jacqueline.

"Or *to* me," she said aloud.

"You've gotta know how that sounds," said Jameson.

"I—" she flushed, and swallowed the sentence, "I'm thinking out loud. Sorry if that bothers you."

Go away. Go away. Go away.

He stood up.

"Well. While you're doing that, I'm gonna go sort out that APB."

She allowed her frown to deepen as he left. His tone had been noticeably sour. Like she'd missed picking up on something he'd been putting down.

She snorted. Not important. Another distraction. Like so many others. All, paling in comparison to one person. She looked back at her headless reflection. Her hand twitched for a second before she drew the curtains back over the broken window.

Why? What drove Yakuza to do what she was doing? Loathsome as they were to touch, the memories of those crimson escapades were all still there. Ready to peruse in perfect gory detail at any time. But as close as she'd been to the act, Jacqueline still couldn't read the script. Yakuza might be predictable when it came to self interest and preservation, but Jacqueline had never seen anything she would call logical in her monstrous actions.

"Lights! Camera!" Jameson said as he returned, startling her. "Your close-up, milady," he added, handing her a photo.

Every second you talk is pain. "Thanks," she said out loud.

She fell silent again as she stared at the little black and white face in her hands.

"Had it faxed to the next office over. Knew you'd want to see it right away," Jameson said proudly. Jacqueline didn't answer. She just stared at Folsom's face. His perfect, unmarred face. Smiling up at her like a cat. FILE PHOTO. That dry little smirk that used to peer at her over a blank notebook. Folsom would pretend to write in it at key moments during their sessions to upset and confuse her. That had all stopped when she'd caught a glimpse of its empty pages during an unscheduled early visit. Its power over her gone, she'd begun to practice faking her micro-expressions whenever he tried to throw her off. She'd won that battle, but now it seemed a fluke had cost her the war.

"Useless," she hissed, as the tension in her hands crumpled the BOLO mockup.

"Hey, what gives?" Jameson huffed, as if he'd been personally slighted.

"He—"

She straightened the paper. Forcing the anger out of her voice.

"He has a scar on his face. A big one. It's new. This

photo is...it's useless."

Jameson shrugged.

"Well, that's no big deal. You're...aces at faces," he said jovially, after a moment. He probably thought that was funny. She bet all his friends would, too. She had to get rid of him.

"Yeah. Fine, sure. I'll have a composite ready in time for the morning news," she said blankly.

Folsom would be long gone by then. All the things he'd said, at their last meeting and on the phone painted a very ugly picture. Killing at random, running from the police...it was like he'd become a copycat of his diagnosis of her. Perhaps the only silver lining there was that he'd soon go to ground. Wouldn't go out of his way to hurt anyone else.

Anyone but her.

"It's getting dark. Let me take you home," Jameson said, cutting into her thoughts with his annoyingly persistent voice.

She focused back in on him. Was he still here?

"No. It's fine. I'm fine."

She began to limp forward.

He tsked.

"C'mon. Don't be stupid. You can barely—"

He tried to grab her under an arm.

"NO—" she said, trying to pull away.

"Swallow your pride here, let me—" he continued in that conciliatory tone.

"Don't FUCKING TOUCH ME, YOU LITTLE SHIT," she shouted, shouldering away from him. The look in his eyes. Like a dog who'd been kicked. A genuine lack of understanding.

It all clicked. The tone in his voice. Nice, kind. And now, possessive.

What, because she'd held a conversation with him without trying to cut his balls off? Because she could stand to talk to him for more than five minutes? Because in his mind, affection and politeness were the same thing?

Because in the story in his head, he was the hero and she was the prize. Well, there'd be no more of that. This wolf would be sorry she'd ever opened the door. He was still speechless. She'd help there, too. After everything that had happened, conveying how she really felt was easy.

"Get out. GET THE FUCK OUT," she said as calmly as she could.

The garbage took itself out, and she was alone again. Blessedly alone. She was shaking with anger.

Her phone rang and she almost threw it against the wall. She gripped it tight and closed her eyes. Tried to get control of her breathing. The phone vibrated out of sync with her heartbeat.

Babum. Mmm. Babum. Mmm.

She tapped the receiver and held it to her ear. She hadn't looked to see who it was. She awaited a voice in silence. In darkness.

"...Hello?" said Clara hesitantly.

"Clara," said Jacqueline, anchoring herself to the image of the other woman.

"You told me to call you if anything came up," said Clara, the notes in her voice a concerto of helpful and hopeful.

"I didn't actually say that," Jacqueline said before she could stop herself. "...but I appreciate the thought, of course," she added.

She swallowed, "What's up?"

Clara lowered her voice to a conspiratorial whisper that could probably carry to the rafters.

"It's about our 'mutual friend.' I should probably tell you in person. Something seriously fishy is going on down here."

Jacqueline's stomach dropped out of the known universe. Something had happened to Yaqui. Her only concrete lead in all of this.

"Is she...alright?" she said, a little less heartlessly.

"I don't know," said Clara, "That depends on what you can tell me about the people who took her."

Jacqueline had already started walking forward, heedless of any pain.

"I'll be right there."

Back at the station, nothing was any clearer.

"Rewind, please," said Jacqueline.

She didn't look away from the screen as Clara dutifully rotated the dial on the console in front of her. Jacqueline didn't say anything as she watched the group of figures approach the bullpen with an official-looking document again. Clara coughed lightly as the group waited for Yaqui to be brought out again.

"So, did you get back okay? No traffic?"

"Commandeered a police vehicle," said Jacqueline dryly as the leader of the group on screen presented the document to the captain when he emerged from his office. Jacqueline studied the faces of the hired muscle as the captain studied the document he'd been handed. They kept adjusting their footing. Fidgeting against the lining of their suits as though unused to wearing them. Jacqueline was getting closer to reading their script. The goons' leader, a woman, stepped forward into better light and Jacqueline raised a hand.

"Stop," she said, and then again louder when Clara didn't reciprocate right away. Clara had started to say something when Jacqueline had spoken over her. Jacqueline didn't notice Clara's reaction as she stared at the clearest view of the ringleader's face she was going to get.

Ballsy. She'd walked right into a police station without blinking. Literally. Jacqueline had been through the whole scene multiple times, and the woman never batted her eyes. Perhaps that shouldn't have been surprising. An ordinary killer might have shaken and buckled under the weight of such a role, but Yakuza had never seemed to fear anything. Obviously it had worked. Amazing how much a costume could accomplish in the right context. Her hair was drawn back into a bun. Couldn't be sure of the color. Footage was in black and white.

"Her hair was black, right?" Jacqueline asked Clara.

Clara stuttered, "I, I don't—"

Jacqueline pointed at the tiny Clara on the screen. "There you are. You were there. What color was her hair?"

"Jacqueline," Clara said gently, "We've been at this for... hours! And I still don't have any idea what connections you're looking for. It's getting late. Very late. Why don't we—"

Jacqueline pointed at the screen again. "These people said they were lawyers."

She moved her finger slightly. Pointing at a different set of pixels. "What self-respecting lawyer wears a suit with the tag still on it?"

Clara slowly shook her head, mouth slightly agape.

"I don't see—"

Jacqueline intended to say 'you were there' again, but even though she didn't want to admit it she was just as tired as Clara.

"She was there!" she said angrily.

Clara closed her mouth, as though locking away all the things she suddenly wanted to say.

Here they were again—Jacqueline unable to say what she really meant, what she really needed. Clara unable to help her or ask what was really going on, for fear of getting too close. Too involved.

"Clara must have been wondering who she meant. Jacqueline had to be the one to say something. They couldn't keep pretending nothing was happening here. Jacqueline swiveled to face Clara.

"Are you afraid of me?" she said slowly.

If she wasn't before, Clara was having an impossible time hiding just how afraid she was. Breathing through the nose, twitchy fingers, pupils dilated. She couldn't escape from Jacqueline's gaze. It compelled her to fill the silence.

She smiled weakly and said, "I'm afraid...for you."

This was most telling of all, and basically summed up their entire working relationship. Jacqueline, unwilling to ask for help or reveal the truth. Clara, unwilling to say anything that might hurt too much.

Fine.

"You're right, Clara. It is pretty late. Why don't you go home and get some rest?"

Clara was tight-lipped, and remained so as she stood and headed for the door. She paused there. Almost turned around. Almost said something. Didn't.

Alone again. Jacqueline laughed to herself.

Of course. Just tell her everything. Tell her you've got mountains of evidence that would only be admissible if you were using it to prove you were crazy. As close as Clara had been to stepping in something she was not prepared to deal with, Jacqueline had been even closer to breaking down and laying it all out for her. *Stupid. Stupid!*

She bit her lip. To the point of pain.

Yes, Clara. She was there. Who is she? Why, that's Yakuza. She lives in my head and kills people.

She stood up, light-headed with embarrassment. Waved it away like a cloud of smoke. *Get back to work.*

Jacqueline walked over to Clara's chair and sat down. Still warm. *Focus. New angle.* Sitting further back, she tried to reassess what she was looking at.

The whole thing was a snow job, that much was clear. She looked at Yakuza's face. Rewound the footage and watched it all the way through. Blank, and impassive. Was this her playing a role, or was she genuinely incapable of expressing emotion?

No. She'd smiled, alright. But only when her prey appeared.

Here came Yaqui again. Trudging head down, sedate. *Maybe sedated?* Wouldn't have been that hard to slip something into her food. Clara had been careful, but all it would have taken was a lone pair of eyes where they shouldn't have been. Someone could have recognized Yaqui when she came here for help. There must have been a rat somewhere. How were they tied to Yakuza? Jameson reappeared in her mind, took the money from the thug in the road. If anyone qualified as "rat," it was him. The thread on the photo board in her mind bent taut around two more pins. Jameson, connected to the thug, connected to Yaqui, connected to Yakuza.

Thinking about all this, Jacqueline almost missed Yakuza's face light up. Her smile was really something. Her teeth were perfect. And sharp. On went the mask again. She didn't even touch Yaqui as her goon squad led them out.

Rewind.

Jacqueline watched her smile again. The crescent scar on her cheek crinkled into its own little grin, then gone. So quick only electronic eyes could catch it.

Jacqueline put her head in her hands. *Pointless.* The facts were self-evident and unilaterally pointed to a zero-sum outcome. Yakuza had outplayed her at every turn. She'd even gotten documentation from Folsom's office to get Yaqui released into her care. Who knew what she'd do to…

Wait.

That didn't make any sense. Folsom believed Jacqueline was Yakuza's doppelganger, the monster who'd disfigured him. He'd never have worked with her willingly. Especially if he knew the truth. To say nothing of believing such an insane story.

Go back. She froze on the first stage direction in the act. Yakuza presenting her official document to the captain. She'd been struck by how odd it was to see him out of his office interacting with a civilian. So struck, in fact, that she hadn't really paid very close attention to the document itself the first few times around. She zoomed in as far as she was able.

And didn't take her hand off the dial. She didn't move for five whole seconds. And then lightning quick she pulled back. Rewound the clip again and again. Stopping it every few seconds to take close looks at the paper.

That's all it was, a blank piece of paper. She watched

it wave back and forth, dance from hand to hand. She was literally looking at a prop.

Back to the beginning. Watched each of the players in turn. Were they all in on it? Clara, in the corner. Trying not to look up when the troupe came in, but unable to look away as they led Yaqui out. Clara glanced guiltily toward the camera.

Jacqueline froze on a frame of the room after everyone had made their exits. Closed her eyes and rubbed them. She'd been watching a farce. There was no way Yakuza could have bent an entire room full of policemen around her finger like that.

"You're asking me to believe at least eight people saw a blank sheet of paper and treated it like holy writ," she said to the dead air.

"Clara, how could you—"

She looked back up, and yelped at Yakuza's manic animal grin filling the screen.

"There's one way," said Yakuza's image without moving its lips.

Jacqueline was mashing the power button on the old control pad in front of her.

This isn't really happening. I'm not really seeing this.

"Wouldn't be the first time."

Her laughter was—

Can't think—

So loud—

Jacqueline fell to the floor, covered her ears. Couldn't block the laughter out. Ahead, under the console through watery eyes she saw the screen's power plug.

She crawled forward, noise assaulting her from every angle.

Grabbed the cord. It writhed in her hand. A vein full of parasitic worms. She yanked it out of the wall and sparks flew. The vacuum of space sucked at her ears and she couldn't breathe. Howling wind tore her brains out through a hole in her head. She was screaming so loud that nobody could hear her.

She finally blinked and everything went quiet. Alone in the ordinary room. Lights out but shapes were easily recognizable. She sat up. Came face to face with her reflection in the black mirror of the screen. Didn't look away. Eyes darting back and forth with each other. Heart rate slowing down.

She pricked her ears forward for any movement outside the door. She didn't dare move. No one was coming. If she had been screaming, it wasn't out loud.

She didn't want to be in this room for one more second. Her mind was sacred. Fractured as her thoughts were, she didn't want to share them with anyone else. But her foe wasn't here. Or maybe she just couldn't see her. Fear gave way to cleansing anger. Time to get going. Form a plan of attack.

Her reflection blinked.

Jacqueline sat in her chair, alone once more. Alone, but surrounded by people. The night shift clattered around her. It'd be the day shift soon. She looked out the window. Utterly black out there. She might have believed the building was just hanging in a featureless abyss. This thought didn't feel dissociative or even frightening. If anything it was comforting to think that at any time she could get up, walk over to the window and disappear. No more impossible problems to solve. No more anonymous faces staring lifelessly out of her dreams.

Dawn broke, shattering her illusion. She was still feverish from the...afterglow, or was it fallout, of Yakuza's attack. She felt in her jacket for the little orange pill bottle while she watched the sunrise. Took it out and held it up to block the light. Shook it gently.

Empty.

Who knew for how long? If she was losing time to a dissociative identity, then this other person might have been throwing them in the trash or down the toilet. She certainly wasn't ingesting them if her visions were any indication.

It might have been Yakuza. Obviously their connection was deep enough for the monstrous woman to have begun expertly flaying crucial parts from Jacqueline's life. She'd transformed her (their?) psychiatrist into an antagonist in her story. Dedicated now to either killing her or working the program in reverse and driving her mad.

She'd also attacked Yaqui more directly, again removing a source of information about their plight. And now, if it couldn't be said she'd been doing it before, Yakuza had violated Jacqueline's mind as close to face-to-face as she'd come yet. Distinct. Telegraphed. A wind-up punch meant to leave her dazed and fearful. Deliberate. Calculated. Jacqueline looked back at the door to the station's security office. Jacqueline had been onto something when Yakuza's presence threw her off. Jacqueline's eyes narrowed and her jaw set.

"It's you who's afraid," she whispered.

Those men who'd been with Yakuza. Hired toughs, obviously. But from where? What detail was she missing? She could go back and watch the footage again but, ahaha, now she was supposed to be scared of that room. Jacqueline looked around at her fellow officers. What about Clara, and the chief, and every cop who'd seen the paper? Were they in on it? Or maybe Yakuza had *made* them see an official document, the same way she'd made Jacqueline see a heart attack's worth of funhouse horror in her own head. What couldn't she do?

How close was she watching? *Does she know everything I'm thinking?*

In either case it made the most sense to act predictably. An enemy that thought it had the upper hand would always strike first. Jacqueline would see it coming this time. Besides, she didn't need camera footage when she had the next best thing.

She sat back and spooled through her own perfect memory. Watched herself watch the screen. This was far more efficient. Stopping and focusing on a given detail was so much easier like this. One by one, she collected the faces of the thugs at the forefront of her mind. Ready to match features to mug shots.

She caught herself avoiding the tail end of her viewing sessions. No telling how a perfect replay of a hallucination would affect her. What traps it might trigger. She bit her lip. No. If she couldn't be certain her mind was secure at her most lucid, might as well pack it all in now.

She bravely forged ahead. Her hands shook as the phantom face appeared. Didn't appear. Jacqueline watched herself watch a screen showing an empty room. Watched it turn off and stay off as her past self mashed the power button in a panic. Now she was lying down. Reaching out methodically. Pulling the plug in one swift motion.

Sparks.

And then just lying there.

And then just lying there.

Something was wrong. She wasn't moving. Fast forward. On and on. The image didn't change. Try as she might, the other her never left that room. Never got up. She tried to move her arm in the present. Where there should have been empty air, she felt the cold and pitted linoleum of the footage bay. Two sets of sensations tried to superimpose themselves over each other. She drew a sharp breath as shock set in. Felt four lungs fill up. Out of sync. One of her staggered to her feet, and the other one writhed on the floor.

This was it. This was her trap. A virus in the code. Yakuza had trapped her in a dream. *Where am I really? When am I?* Jacqueline's co-workers didn't have faces, and they just kept walking back and forth, occasionally clipping through either wall. She bashed her knees against the ground as she tried to rise from a standing position. Vertigo from lying down in reality while standing in a dream.

Have to sync up. Break this.

She lay down in what she'd wrongly thought was the present. People walked over her like spotlights across a stage. Once she was in roughly the same position in both places, she started to push. Muscles felt like tar. Her busted ankle screamed and her wrist added to the chorus as she put exactly the wrong kind of stress on joints that were supposed to be healing. She was dreaming in one eye and awake in the other. Sleep paralysis didn't even begin to describe it.

Her hearts pumped with fear. She'd never been able to break free of a dream before it was finished with her. Raised her head like it was on pulleys. Looked toward the door that was a window that was a door. No, the window. She needed the window. She let go. Let the memory that was her waking reality fade. Staggered to her feet. Made for the window as her pulse slowed. Just a few more agonizing feet.

How were you supposed to wake up from a dream you didn't want to be in?

Look for the correlation. How did all of her other dreams end?

She leaned heavily against the sill. With a death.

She opened the window and the cityscape slid up with it. Gone.

Only blackness remained, lit by two blue stars. Perfect. Just as she'd envisioned it. She stuck her head outside. The rest of the building wasn't even there. The void had no smell. It wasn't even especially cold. She could detect only the absence of these things. Behind her, the ghosts of her coworkers were all standing still. Watching her. She heard heavy breathing fill the room, claws scratch against the floor. She didn't dare turn around. Jacqueline put one leg up on the sill. Swallowed.

Did she really want to do this? Haha. For the second time in as many days she'd wished for death and then almost immediately been confronted with a reasonable facsimile thereof. She was breathing heavily, but there wasn't any air out here. It hurt to think about. Trying to comprehend death, trying to comprehend the sensation of incomprehension was paralyzing. That, and the—

Yes, the fear.

The fear of death.

"I'm afraid to die," she tried to say out loud. But no air meant no sound. She looked behind her. The imaginary room had begun to degrade. Its phantom occupants as dim and flickering as the lights. The ground still looked solid though. She could step back, consider her options. Not die.

She looked back out at the void. It might not kill her. It...

She waved her hand in front of her face. The other one too. She looked up in horror. The window was shrinking into the distance. No sensation without reality. Hadn't even felt herself leave the perch. No horizon to pinpoint distance from. Just a vanishing square of light. And, was that a face leaning out of it? Couldn't feel anything, hear anything. No way to tell if she'd been pushed. And by who? This was her head. Or a metaphor for a small part of it that was dying. She tried to summon her memories again. At least to get a closer look at that face. Images surrounded her for a moment, then blew away, and up. Like washing off a line in a high wind. Watched them disappear above her. She tried to see them again, but this time nothing happened. She had no past. There was nothing left here. This universe had no time and no space. It was shrinking around her. She couldn't do anything more because she didn't have a future here. The timeline had run out. She was out of questions, but at least there was one obvious answer. Who else wished her ill and was known to vacation in her head?

"Yakuza," she somehow said as the last of her breath left her body as flame—she was the only object with 3D space left. The universe disappeared and she was the last of the universe. She was crushed under her own weight. She closed her eyes to see red instead of black for a moment, but there was no light. No fear either. No more time. Her universe was one second long, and it ended. She died. The last neuron fired as she became impossible.

Jacqueline was unbelievably cold. She tried to move, and her muscles ached. So stiff. She rolled over on her back and tried to sit up. Her core creaked like a suspension bridge. All other pain suddenly paled in comparison as she smacked her head on the underside of the desk that the footage monitor rested on. She curled up into a little ball of agony on the cold linoleum. Clutched her forehead. Forced a few words out.

"Fuck! Fucking—"

Clenched her teeth.

Definitely alive, or real, at least. She opened her bleary eyes. Sat up carefully this time. The room smelled like ozone. Her mouth tasted coppery. An electrical short, from when she'd pulled out the cord. She shook her head. Enough solipsism. And enough of this room. Time for action. A counterattack.

She remained focused on her goal as she exited the footage bay. Remove the enemy's support structure. Return the favor. Should have been obvious from the start. Yakuza had been killing people, and these weren't murder cases because the bodies were being destroyed or buried by Fong and Nunogawa. They were her cat's paw. How had Yakuza come to control them so utterly?

She arrived at her desk and pulled her private drawer open, snapping the flimsy lock apart easily.

It didn't matter. She'd just ask them herself. They'd better hope they had answers she liked. There was no going back now. Time for a data purge. The sun came up. She turned to face it, folder in hand. Reality set in. Ordinarily a troubling statement, but in this instance very comforting. After lying on a cold floor unconscious for who knew how long, the sun's rays were warm and soft on her aching bones. Reality set in, and her sense of urgency began to fade. Reality set in, and she realized how tired she was. She should go home and rest. It wouldn't be the first time she'd gone to sleep with the sun.

She looked down at all the little faces in her hands. She suddenly became very angry. Mostly with herself. She'd been THIS CLOSE to giving up on them. Going back to sleep, in a metaphorical sense. Tomorrow, she'd be able to rationalize away all her errant manias and waking dreams as the effects of stress and trauma. *Go home?*

No. There was only one place she needed to be. She walked over to the copy machine and dragged back the little black trash can with the device on top. With the shredder next to her, she sat down and set to work.

"I'm protecting you," she told the faces as she shredded them.

This was her high noon moment. If she was really going to set out for the slaughterhouse district based on the legally admissible equivalent of a hunch, she wasn't going to be coming back. Another face gone, then another, and another.

Can't risk them finding all of you. Asking too many questions. Especially after what I'm going to do.

What are you going to do?

Her hand slowed for a moment. She kept going. Jacqueline could tell herself she was just going to lean on thugs she'd seen for info, but this would be a study in denial. She was going to find Yakuza. Kill her. And everyone in the way.

One face in the middle of the pile gave her pause.

"Jimmy," she said to him. She couldn't seem to move her hand enough to throw him away. Not just yet.

"I never knew you. But, I'm sorry for…"

She just looked at him for a while.

"I can't pretend I'm protecting you, can I?"

No response. Her guilt and imagination were silent. *Thank god.*

"So…we'll say you're protecting me. This'll be a clean break. Once I'm done taking out the trash, there'll be nobody left who remembers what really happened.

Nobody else will get hurt."

She fed him into the shredder.

The flames of the furnace consumed the red remains of his body, turning the white light blue.

"So long, Jimmy. We'll all go down together."

It was a long commute to the slaughterhouse district. Outskirts of the city. If Jacqueline's life were some sort of fairy tale, this would be the part with the dark tower. She stepped off the muni railcar onto the landing platform, below the highway but above the street. This was the most well-maintained civic structure she was likely to see. The stone platform itself and the stone steps leading down and the stone walls of the sheltered divider were all practically white. Nobody came here. She turned her head as she caught the first scent of blood on the wind. That, or nobody who came here ever left.

She trip-trapped down the steps as the muni railcar pulled away. The mournful wail of its whistle serving as a warning unheeded. *Lots of warehouses here.* High, hemming her in. Down by the road, there was a concrete aqueduct. Set lower than street level. It didn't look very deep—but she couldn't see the bottom. As she watched, an underwater tributary bubbled forth. It briefly turned a stretch of green current red. She held her nose. Gagged. Shook her head to clear it as she started walking. Perhaps that was how you left a place like this—through a pipe one tenth your original size. The smell of blood was overpowering. So much so that even her acute senses couldn't sort out the source from the offal and the chemical muck. It might just be animal blood. *Might be.* No reason to get too worked up, right? She watched the red phantom disappear down the concrete stream.

She didn't see any people. Nobody walking the streets. No lights on in the buildings. No busy silhouettes. This place was a necropolis. With the thrum of water through sewer chambers below her feet, and the highway and railway honeycombing a sky lined with too many tall buildings, she felt immensely claustrophobic. Surrounded. It was so arid here. Hard to breathe. *Tough it out. Not far now.* Just another block's worth of trudging through this crypt.

There. The sign, weathered and rusty, read Fong and Nunogawa Holdings, LLC. Several cars parked out front by the barbed wire fence. Three out of four were beat-up old pickup trucks. She approached the fourth, a red convertible. Much newer make than the others. A sports car was an ostentatious choice. Not a lot of room to go fast and far in the city. A status symbol. She approached it like a predator. Placed her hand on the hood. Still warm. Arrived no earlier than half an hour ago, she guessed. She looked down. A well-worn trail of skid marks besides this car's. She knelt. Tread pattern matched the tires of the sports car. *Matching cars? Touching.*

Standing closer, she saw a fifth car parked a block down, in an alleyway. A tired sedan, too boxy to be modern but not enough chrome to be classic. Familiar to her. An extra in a background shot. Where had she seen it? Her memory offered her a card: *Temple Street.*

Maybe it wasn't Jacqueline who had seen it, then. Another connection from the bald headed man to that night that confirmed she was in the right place.

Jacqueline looked back up at the sign. The "Fong" in "Fong and Nunogawa" had suffered the worst of the wind and weather, being closer to the top. And...something else. She looked again. Damage she'd thought was just superficial turned out to be a bullet hole. No. three bullet holes that she could see. She bet if she could climb a little higher, she could make out the boring that would give away the caliber. Her eyes traced imaginary lines through the holes, to and fro.

There.

Tiny impact crater in the opposite sidewalk. At least one broken window that she could see inside the fence.

She approached the little crack in the sidewalk and started digging at it with her fingernails.

Paydirt.

She held up the little silvery slug. Shots fired from inside the building.

"Looks like probable cause to me," she said with satisfaction. She probed Yaqui's memory of that night at the shop. He'd had a gun, the bald man. But she bet he didn't have a permit.

She stood up and crept to the gate. Heavy padlock on it, but the gap was just wide enough to admit her if she went through sideways. She coughed. Sucking in a bit of air allowed her to fit all the way through and out the other side. She coughed again. The smell of blood was strongest here. This must be their main base of operations. Funny how one could claim to be a pillar of the community even as your business choked out all the life around it. Every other building here was empty and run-down. Just how they liked it, she bet. Less eyes around meant less chance of being seen. Less ears meant less chance of screams being heard. Jacqueline listened carefully for any signs of life within. Nothing. She stalked forward. Now, how did she want to play this?

Ahead of her, a phantom Jacqueline drew her gun, braced it on her other forearm and began firing silent shots. Imaginary thugs walked and then fell through the steel door in the side of the building. Bottlenecked there, she took out three of them with relative ease. A fourth went down before the probable Jacqueline took a hit in the shoulder and then three more in the chest.

The real Jacqueline looked up. An imaginary Kalashnikov disappeared from the broken window it had been poking out of upstairs. The target dummies phased out. Jacqueline pursed her lips. The violent approach wouldn't get her the answers she needed. Likewise, she didn't trust in her ability to shoot her way out if she was caught sneaking around. She could try bluffing her way in. With one of the men in charge absent, according to his parking space, she might have a better chance at providing the only viewpoint the administrative remainder really needed.

"Knock and talk it is, then," she said. She tumbled the spent slug in her fingers as she closed the distance to the imposing steel door.

Clutched it tight as the door opened before she could even touch it. She'd been expecting one or many hulking scar faces, she admitted. She was surprised, therefore to see a very diminutive man behind the portal. He wasn't even armed.

"There you are. Right this way," he said in a nasally gravel.

Any bloodlust she might've had left vanished, eaten by her curiosity, a much larger beast. Her feet carried her forward as he dipped his head in a low bow to let her pass.

What was happening? She kept one eye on him as he shut the door and began to lead the way deeper into the facility. He kept fiddling with his ponytail and stealing sidelong glances at her over his shoulder. Fiddling, fiddling, scratching at his balding scalp. The fear on his face became more apparent as her eyes adjusted to the dim interior. No, something worse than fear. *Recognition.*

"Here, uh, here are the new handling facilities," he stammered, gesturing at a loading bay as they left the cramped hallway.

There were only two men working the cuts of meat there, dressed for the arctic as they hooked the frozen sides of beef. Lifting them as easily as fathers lift their children. There was a lot of empty space here, a serious lack of bustle. They'd had to scale back their operation substantially, and recently, too. This little man certainly wasn't hoisting fifty pound slabs all day. *What happened to this place?*

Jacqueline caught the doorman staring intently at her the way a mouse does a cat.

She'd happened to it. Yakuza had wrapped these men around her finger, and who knew how far she'd spread the other digits. Back to the present. He thought she was Yakuza. They looked almost exactly alike, after all. Right down to the scar on her cheek. Jacqueline's pulse quickened as she realized all this meant the doorman was expecting Yakuza to speak when Jacqueline opened her mouth. *What would Yakuza say?*

"You've managed well. But I didn't come here to speak to you."

No emotion. Level tone. Perfect. He broke eye contact. Yakuza wouldn't care what Yakuza *should* say. She rarely talked, if ever. Actions spoke louder than words, after all. Ideally, next she'd brush past this insect, find Fong or Nunogawa and squeeze them for info. But while Yakuza likely knew the layout, Jacqueline was lost. She needed to find any traces of Yaqui. Nowhere to hide her up here. She couldn't stop to ask for directions.

The doorman looked ready to speak, if tentatively. Better to not give him the chance. Taciturn as she was, Yakuza didn't like waiting to talk. Jacqueline had to stay in character.

"Take me to the man in charge. Now."

In an instant, he was back to bowing and scraping. "Right away miss—ma'am! Right away ma'am."

He was sweating bullets and the caliber was night terror. It flecked off him as he literally genuflected out of murder range.

He veritably power walked down a connecting hallway and Jacqueline stalked after him. One could only wonder what shock and awe Yakuza had got up to with these people. It had obviously left a lasting impression on this man, at the very least. For a butcher, he seemed easily cowed.

These hallways felt so fragile. Jacqueline could see a hole in the ceiling ahead. Very small, in a corner. But definitely there. Something dripping out of it. This place had been sucked dry. Like a plum pit with a bit of skin still on. No maintenance had been done here in quite some time, she guessed. She passed by a leopard pattern of black mold surrounding a window choked with dust. Faint as it was, it was the last sun she'd see.

Down one flight of stairs and then another after a short connecting hallway, doors hissed shut pneumatically. The air down here didn't stir. It got colder. These spiraling steps put her in mind of a nautilus shell. This was helped by the sound of the ocean, muted but close. On the other side of the wall. She traced a hand along the concrete chute they were striding down. Came away damp. *The artificial river.* Must be deep underground by now if she could hear a sewer main.

Hit bottom, finally. The ground here felt the most stable it had since she got off the muni railcar. The foundation of the catacomb. Colder here than anywhere she'd ever been. Misty breath plumed above the doorman's bald head. He was short enough that she almost walked into it. It smelled like blood and stomach acid. Nerves must have been eating him alive. She put her foot in something wet one second after hearing her guide's footfalls turn to gentle splashing. The sound of an ocean gave way to whiter water. Very dim here, but ahead she could see a great crack in one wall. A waterfall in miniature cascading out of it. Must have been a drain nearby because the water hadn't reached her ankles just yet. Still extremely troubling. Like walking into a house and being greeted by eighteen cats. Often indicative of far more serious wrack and ruin.

"How long has that been there?" she asked.

The doorman turned to look at her. Only the murky blue light of a little viewing window on a heavy steel door remained down here. Even so, his expression was unmistakable. It matched the tone of confusion in his voice when he said, "What are you talking about?"

Did he really not see...?

Pressed by her gaze, he laughed nervously.

"Very—very funny, ma'am!"

His laughter took on a manic tint. Of course he knew what she was talking about. They were standing in it.

That only left the why. She looked around, measured the dimensions of the bottom floor landing. Not enough room for any kind of battering ram to build up enough speed. Fracturing inconsistent with multiple blows, so that ruled out a team of men with sledge hammers. Too big of an impact crater for a gunshot.

A single blow, from a standing start, with enough force to crack what must have been a foot's width of concrete... she drew her gaze back to her guide. His eyes had followed hers to the hole, and met for a moment before lowering in fear. *Yakuza.*

Obvious in hindsight. She'd already made the leap in believing Yakuza capable of feats of gore and psychic imagery. The question was, how strong did Jacqueline really want her to be?

Fear was Jacqueline's motivator too, now. Hers and this little man's. Fear fed her denial. She didn't want to believe that Yakuza could invade minds and break concrete. As if thinking too much of Yakuza would give her that power. What then could stop her from breaking down Jacqueline's door one night? But, come on. Who else did she know that—

"Ma'am?"

He was lightly shifting back and forth, back and forth. Nervously jigging. This was the last place he wanted to be, she could tell. Least of all alone with her. Wouldn't do to keep him waiting. Yakuza wouldn't be keen to waste any time, either. That said, she also wouldn't be given to any kindness or consideration.

"Move. Haven't got all day."

He seemed only too happy to comply. Curiosity was likely a worthless commodity to him. He worked for Yakuza, after all. Jacqueline bet the turnover was insane.

He made for the door at the far end of the landing, the only one giving off light. There were a few stray objects in his way. He kicked one aside. It made a loud clang as it hit the wall. Eyes adjusted as she followed behind him. Tools of some sort, and there was their box in the corner.

The wall wasn't fixed but someone had made a go of it. She made note of the crowbar, pipe wrench and claw hammer in case she needed to make injurious close-range use of them on her way out. She stared at the back of her guide's head. Ponytail like a tasseled target. The rest of his head shiny with sweat. Three knocks echoed through the basement, breaking her focus. Perhaps for the best.

No obvious lock that she could see, yet he knocked. Their kingdom might be in ruins, but Fong and Nunogawa still commanded respect. The door swung outward. The room beyond was bare. No hooks or shelves in this freezer unit, but a blast of frigid air confirmed it was still in working order. A man sat with his back to them. Heavy coat. High fur collar. Slick Ivy League haircut. Opposite his chair was an oblong shape under a sheet. About the same size. The new man didn't look around as the door opened. Three empty bottles of Steeplejack whiskey lay scattered at his feet. The inch of low tide Jacqueline had let in tugged at them, lightly.

"Close...th' fucking door. Haven't you done 'nough?" the man said wretchedly.

Right. Drunk as he was, he had a point. Water would freeze in here, maybe trap them if it got on the door. She moved past her guide, his job done. She turned to thank him or bid him farewell before remembering that Yakuza would not bother with the latter and seemed incapable of the former. However, it was a good thing Jacqueline was a stickler for both. Otherwise, she would not have noticed his horrified gaze until it was too late. He was staring fixedly at the back of her windbreaker. At the word emblazoned there, in yellow. Why would Yakuza be wearing a "Police" jacket? Maybe as a joke. Maybe as a grisly trophy. She wouldn't bother to explain herself, either way. Unfortunately, Jacqueline didn't have Yakuza's stony face or her killer instinct. She did, however, have enough reflexes on hand to slam the door in his face. He began pounding on the outside. Thankfully, the door was so thick his voice was muffled entirely. She looked down at the latch. Recently modified. Would only open from inside. The pounding continued as she looked over her shoulder at what remained of Fong or Nunogawa. She knew them through reputation alone. The first act in this play would need to include an introduction, somehow. Whoever he was, he still hadn't moved. He just kept staring at the shape under the sheet as he spoke.

"What's with the fuckin' racket?" he asked.

Good that paranoia had gotten the better of her host before she arrived. She needed privacy. The more limiting factors, the better. Now, what would Yakuza say to keep it that way? Something rude, probably.

"He wants to feel important."

Very convincing. Especially since this cold was eating her alive. Her windbreaker did nothing to keep it out. She realized she was shivering and forced herself to stop.

"Yeah...I don't want them too close to this. They're good men. Loyal. They deserve clean noses. I'm a good person. Or at least I like to think so."

He sat up straighter.

"You wanna drink?"

He held his remaining whiskey aloft so she could see it.

"I'd say it'd warm you up, but you don't get cold, do you?"

He lowered the bottle.

"Do you even drink? I mean, I've seen you eat."

He chuckled darkly.

She was about to ask what he meant when a loud noise made her flinch. Good thing, too. Yakuza would already know.

The man in the chair had a long ice pick in hand and was stabbing at the new layer of frost on the drain at his feet.

"Is this a new game? I have to guess what you want without any words now?"

He tossed the pick to the side as the water she'd brought with her drained away. "I know. I know, I know."

He hung his head and then looked back up at the thing under the sheet.

"You are my god now," he said to her.

She didn't know how to respond to that. Mildly horrified that Yakuza would. He answered over her silence.

"I should learn to expect that by now. You here to finish the job?" He looked meaningfully at the ice pick. "Third time's the charm."

The context was impossible to miss. "No. I need you alive," she said, finally. Just barely kept the shiver out of her voice.

He gestured wildly. "What for? What's left? We did everything you asked! As inefficient as it, as...as costly as it was." He faltered.

"We spread ourselves so thin. You know how much it took to buy out, muscle out all our competition in distribution and butchery? We're fucking bankrupt." He gestured at the sheet.

"And when Fong had the gall to ask WHY, to ask why it was so important to cast such an insanely wide net, to make sure everyone ate the—"

Nunogawa put his head in his hands. "I shouldn't be saying this, I know. You'll kill me. Like you did him. Maybe I don't care anymore. There's nothing left. There's nothing left of me."

Jacqueline couldn't take her eyes off the sheet, now that she knew what was under it. She almost missed Nunogawa stand up.

"Do it, then. FUCKING DO IT YOU—"

He stared at her. His occluded blue eyes were glassy from drink, red rimmed from lack of sleep and twitchy from existential dread. His face was drawn, pale. But none of it mattered. It was all falling away in the face of his discovery.

"You." He pointed a shaking finger at her. Started to laugh. "I know you. She told me you'd be coming. Told me what to look for. Everything, your clothes, even that dumb look on your face."

He pitched his voice a little lower, flat monotone, imitating Yakuza. "This is my final task for you. Show our guest the utmost courtesy." She was almost relieved to have her cover blown, even as her pulse rocketed skyward. She started moving one hand toward her gun. Every little movement stung her bare skin.

Nunogawa spoke as himself again. "She made it sound like you were in charge. Like this was all for you."

Jacqueline was shaking her head but the drink and the misery and maybe even a little hypothermia of his own had incensed him beyond any reason.

"Look," he said mock-excitedly. "Look what you did!"

He yanked the sheet off in a shower of frost. The sudden movement made her pull her gun, but her trigger discipline stayed her hand. Jacqueline wanted to look away, but the dead man's gaze pulled her in. Eyes askew, staring at nothing. Shriveled. One pupil still larger than the other from when she'd rung his bell. Light brown skin drawn tight over his skull. Frostbite and rot had begun to turn the contours of his face checkerboard black and white.

The bald man from the pretzel shop. Fong. Nunogawa thought Yakuza had killed him, but he was only half-right.

"Where did you find him?" she asked. Couldn't be sure of the timeline. Had to know. Her gun had slowed Nunogawa down, at least.

"Dead in the street. Where you and your freak left him after you were done beating him to death."

She wanted to shake her head, tell him no. But for once she couldn't give all the credit to Yakuza. Jacqueline had been puppeting Yaqui in that dream about defending herself. But that smile...that hadn't been Jacqueline's. Had Yakuza just been watching, or had she lent her own helping hand? He couldn't know that.

"What makes you think it was her?" she said.

He was moving slow. He must have thought she didn't notice him edging toward the ice pick. Kept her sights trained on him. Her breath obscured the crosshair.

"He was angry. She'd killed three of our guys right in front of him. Working too slow, she said. He went looking for trouble after that. Looks like he found it."

Having Fong uncovered seemed about as distressing for Nunogawa as it did for Jacqueline, if not more so. His knees were shaking. Survival kept his eyes on her, but he couldn't keep himself from shooting glances at his dead business partner.

The blood rushed out of her head and into the hand holding her gun. Bile licked at the bottom of her heart. It was the last of the heat in her body and her anger consumed it. This was the same song she'd danced with Folsom. A setup by Yakuza to get Jacqueline killed by someone who'd be an excellent witness otherwise. It was perfect. Stretched to the breaking point by Yakuza's maddening labor, all his anger was redirected to Jacqueline at the last moment. And now she was alone in a locked room with him and two murder weapons.

"How long have the two of you been planning this?" he asked, "You been watching me? Us?"

Jacqueline shook her head, forced herself to speak. "I had no part in this It's a setup It's a FUCKING setup."

Had to fight not to slur her words. Early symptoms of hypothermia. Her extremities were going numb. Fine motor control shot. Maintaining her death grip on the gun was easy but pulling the trigger might prove challenging. The chance that she'd hit what she was aiming at had shrunk. Couldn't give that away. No way she could accurately shoot to wound. It had all lined up perfectly. She'd have to kill him to make it out of here alive. Cruel, perhaps, but she had to get as much information out of him as possible before then. *Keep him talking.*

"How did you know him? What's your connection?" she said.

He raised his eyebrows at this. Genuine surprise. And then laughter. Bitter notes in it like bad wine or good beer.

"We came up in the same foster home. Too many kids in that house. Never enough food to go around. Even less money for toys, clothes that fit, shit like that. We had to look out for each other from day one. It's always been that way."

He waved his hands as if to say 'anyway.' "Your freaky doppelgänger knew all this. Knew everything. Knew every string to pull, every button to push, every wedge to drive deeper and where." He shook his head. "I'm surprised, given your relationship to her that you didn't know all this."

His fake smile was more like an animal grimace. "Kinda don't believe it, actually." Now he was crying.

"And now you're here to arrest me. Should've figured. Should've figured from the start. I think Fong did. Probably why you killed him, huh?"

Jacqueline felt it then. A wave of revulsion in her gut. She was freezing to death, but still warm somehow. Surrounded, enveloped by Yakuza. Drowning in a great black ocean she hadn't noticed was there until it had filled her lungs. Yakuza had done all this for her. Jacqueline could feel it. Pulsing out of the part of her mind where she kept thoughts about Yakuza. The wound in space. A switch triggered by their thoughts lining up somehow. These men, criminals maybe, gift wrapped for Jacqueline to—

Rrnk

Took her a moment to translate the noise back into something recognizable. An instinct to act on. Metal sliding along the ground. She renewed her grip on her gun. Sharp intake of painful breath. Ready to blow a hole in his fucking head.

Nunogawa dropped the ice pick. Slowly raised his hands as he straightened up. Locked eyes.

"You know, she meditates sometimes too. I see her go away. There's not much in her eyes to start with but sometimes they go somewhere else. When she comes back she always seems to know a little more than she should."

Jacqueline put both hands on her gun to steady her aim. "Like what? What does she know?"

Nunogawa ignored her. "Tough to get the drop on

her, too. Even when she's resting her eyes like that. God knows I tried."

He was moving closer. "What are you to her? If you don't mind me asking. Sister? I can definitely see the resemblance," Nunogawa mused.

Jacqueline thumbed back the hammer, "Sit your ass back down."

"S-s-sit down," he mocked, "Yeah. You ain't her. Honestly had my doubts but she's got something you don't. Or maybe the other way around?"

"For the last time! Back away!" She shouted, cursing the chatter in her teeth.

"I just," he waved his hands, as if massaging the words out, "I'm just tired of being the least important person in my own life, you know? I'm not sure exactly when it happened, but I'd like it to stop now. Right now."

His conversational demeanor vanished as he took one last step closer. Like parting a curtain. She tensed the same time he did. His tackle was in slow motion. Her shot went wild, grazing his left shoulder in a spray of blood and a shower of down feathers. The word 'Tinnitus' appeared at the forefront of her mind as the thunderclap from her gun in this enclosed echoey space sent a piercing shriek through her eardrums.

Nunogawa's momentum carried him forward. His arms grasped her middle. She brought her hands down, tried to hit the back of his head with the butt of her gun. Missed as the two of them hit the ground. Joints weren't cooperating in this cold. Seizing up. Struck the soft flesh between his shoulder blade and spine. He stank. Likely hadn't gone home in days.

"Right now!" he finished saying as time caught up with her senses. He struggled to stay on top of her. Establish a position from which to strike.

En garde. She wrapped her legs around his middle. Knit her ankles.

"I don't care," he breathed heavily, "I don't care what she wants anymore."

Crossed her arms behind his head. He'd have to deadlift her to get anywhere now. Clear he wasn't skilled in close-quarters combat. Dehydrated and malnourished besides, he posed about as much threat as a wild animal. Maintaining a grip on him might prove difficult with numb extremities, however. He rolled over, which was a mistake. She sat exactly where he'd wanted to be. Able to put her hips into her strikes, she laid into him. Weakly, he tried to defend his face as she pistol whipped him. Broke his nose.

"Stupid."

Blacked an eye.

"Stupid, worthless—" Contempt dripped from her mouth.

Boxed an ear. Blood trickled out of it. She dropped her gun and wrapped her hands around his throat. Brought her legs up, held down his arms with her knees. Leaned back. Something welled up inside her. Indescribable. A buoyant feeling that filled every part of her. Endorphins fizzing in her brain like champagne bubbles.

"No," she heard herself say. But distantly, over the roar of an ocean. Blood from Nunogawa's shoulder was pooling around his head. His breathless red pallor complimented it nicely. Cherry in chocolate sauce. So fucking tasty. *Pluck it.*

"No. Stop it. Let go, please let go," Jacqueline said, but Yakuza wasn't listening.

Pain had given way to numbness, which had given way to all-encompassing warmth. Right next to his head, crystallizing in the pool of blood as it froze, there was another face. It was hers. She didn't recognize it. The smile was way too big. Way too happy. Jacqueline took a deep gasping breath as she fell back off Nunogawa's body.

Couldn't get the air in fast enough. Felt like she'd been holding it for hours. She breathed fire, razors. She was dying, she realized. She had to get out of here. Her legs barely worked. She shakily stood. Bent to retrieve her gun. She looked at Nunogawa, lying there motionless.

"...'bye," she slurred at him and made for the door.

No response. She pushed at the door's special handle once, twice. *Stuck?* She took a look at the bottom of it. Sure enough, a patina of ice had formed there from the water she'd let in. At least that crony had stopped his incessant banging. She pushed again. Almost no give. Maybe if she used the—

Ice pick thudded into her shoulder. Felt it scrape her collar bone. Out it came and all the heat seemed to leave her body through the hole. Dripped off her shoulder in a cape of red warmth. The wound steamed like a fresh plate of food. Her vision swam as she staggered back. Nunogawa's hand on her other shoulder spun her around. Couldn't feel anything. Watched her arm come up of its own accord, block his next strike. Just under the wrist with the edge of her palm. Other hand delivered a swift chop to his trachea. Easily disarmed as his grip loosened to massage and protect his abused windpipe.

Armed now. Opponent weakened, off balance.

She raised up the pick and stabbed at the ice at her feet. With one good shove, she left Nunogawa gasping inside.

"No!" he choked out as the door slammed on him. Thinking quickly, she jammed the ice pick under the bottom lip of the door. Nunogawa slammed against the other side, to no avail. His muffled obscenities followed her as she ran for the stairs.

"There!"

She looked up, and caught sight of her tour guide from earlier. He was bug-eyed. Transfixed. She remembered she was covered in blood.

"She killed him! She fucking killed him!" He shrieked. His next words were drowned out by gunshots as the two men he'd brought with him opened fire. Bullets whizzed by her head as she ducked back down the hallway. She was starting to thaw out, but still had the shakes. Walked on thousands of pins as she splashed back towards the dead end. No way out. She was a sitting duck if she tried to go up. No way she could accurately shoot to kill all three before blood loss finished her. To say nothing of any more holes she might suffer. Evidently the good will Yakuza had achieved through force extended only so far. If they even thought it was still her. If they cared.

The gash in the wall caught her eye. *If it's leaking down here, that means it leads up, right?* She had one good arm. The other hand kept pressure on her stab wound. Her free hand picked up a crowbar. The gunfire had ceased and given way to a rhythmic tapping. *Raindrops?* No, footsteps. *Focus.* They were coming down to clean out their rat trap.

She wedged the crowbar as deep into the crack in the wall as she could. Gritted her teeth as she asked her whole body to heave at it and her whole body revolted. She felt a crack and thought: *bones.*

Then she felt the pitter patter of rain on her face. The gap was widening. Pressurized mist and new rivulets escaping. Out of the corner of her eye, she saw a booted foot step into view down the stairs. She focused back in on the hole. Making it wider. She felt light-headed. A gun appeared down the way, but Jacqueline couldn't take her eyes off her work. There was something behind the wall. White fingers and milky eyes and bloody, busy teeth peeking through eagerly. All the coagulated death was hidden behind here. The wall groaned, and she heard men scream as the vein burst and blood filled the hallway.

She was knocked backward, and hit the opposite wall like a thrown toy. Her lungs were fit to burst. It was a wonder the water hadn't rushed into her all at once. Disintegrated her. With aching muscles, she kicked off the wall, swam toward light.

Wrong way. Nunogawa's face on the other side of the little window of his new submarine. Didn't look angry anymore. Almost resigned. He stepped back. Turned around. Sat back down with his brother. She pushed away and made for the stairwell. Below her, the toolbox had been upended by the current and pulled to the middle of the floor. Blocking the drain. Water and pressure would keep it stuck there. Just like Nunogawa.

Almost there. She bumped against the ceiling on her way. *No air pockets.* She kicked faster. Her head broke water, but her gasp turned to a shout of surprise at the gun barrel on the flight above her. Two others joined it and the cavernous stairwell turned their volley into booming thunder.

With one last deep breath, she kicked off the bottom step and dove back into the grotto she'd created. Bullets rained down around her, leaving thick trails of superheated bubbles. Slow enough to dodge. The current had weakened. Enough for her to get close to the hole in the wall. Much wider now. *Wide enough to fit through?* Survival had narrowed her options somewhat. Certain death awaited her back there, down here. Uncertain death awaited beyond the wall. And darkness. Darkness waited there, ready to fill her mind before the water filled her lungs. No time to feel any fear, but she burned precious seconds hesitating. She put her hands behind either edge. Twisted sideways to fit through. Wall almost gone. Big hole in the pipe. Big enough to hold a person. She squeezed in. The water was warm, the current strong. She almost had to climb her way up. Kicking her legs was nearly useless. Almost immediately, she realized she'd made a mistake. Wordless fear clutched at her from every side. Panic drummed a beat on her mind. It twanged a screaming tune in the key of momento mori. Every human instinct howled at her *you're going to die,* over and over again. Pitch black. The only real sound was the rush of water all around her. Sensory deprivation was about to set in when the pipe began to narrow. Harder to move her limbs. Less space. Pushed her back against the wall of the pipe and her feet opposite. Hands on either side. Spidered her way up. How long had she been going? Should have suffocated by now.

What if she already had? Nothing else seemed to exist except for her and this tiny space. Only the five points of contact where her body met the pipe defined that she actually WAS anywhere. Darkness. White noise. Already gone. Brain's electrical signal fading, broadcasting one last dream.

Blessedly, her lungs chimed in. Stabbing pain. She needed to breathe. Her lungs seized up with the pain. She relished it. She couldn't be dead if she still needed to die. *Wouldn't want to miss out.* The current weakened. She could see her hands in front of her face. Survival propelled her muscles. She looked up. A dirty coin shined through the silt above her. Resolved into a streetlight. The sun was gone. But... outside, she was outside! She reached up for a new handhold, and her foot slipped. Algae or something. She lost at least two feet of progress. *No. No! No!*

She scrabbled at the slick walls of the pipe. *Refuse to die. Refuse.* She threw her hand up and caught the lip of something. Felt concrete. Her fingers pulled her up. Inch by inch. A second hand. And just like that, she was free. Still under water, but the current bore her along instead of crushing her down one of the causeways she'd seen earlier.

The light began to dim. *Blackout?* She tried to swim towards the surface. Her limbs wouldn't move. The only thing she could feel was her heartbeat now. Beating like crazy, out of control. The light continued to dim. Her, not the lamp, she realized. All the lights were going out as her body reached its limit. One last thought froze solid on its way between her synapses.

Yaqui, I'm sorry.

Hands surrounded her. Dozens of white faces opened their mouths and bit into her flesh. Pulled her into darkness.

SHE DROVE WITH THE lights off. She didn't need them. Hadn't for some time. It had taken a while to make it out of the sprawl and infill to the kind of road she was looking for. A seaside highway. The top was down. The car wasn't a convertible but a few minutes work with her hands and now she had the wind in her hair. The sun was on the horizon. Was it rising or setting?

"Sunset," she said matter-of-factly. The wind howled around her ears and the old roadster she'd ruined. The sun flickered, and found itself in the west. Dipped into the sea. Another car appeared ahead of her in the oncoming lane, where she'd been cruising. They leaned on the horn and swerved their sports car in a wide curve around her. The sound curved, too. She followed it through the air with her nose. Tasted its emotion.

"You're right. That was an unsatisfying conclusion."

She lazily switched lanes with one hand. With the other, she snapped her fingers and said,

"Crash."

Behind her, the tail of sound culminated in a comet as the other car skidded into the railing and then flipped over. Nothing between it and the ocean except sheer cliffs. Not that she cared. Plenty of other scenery she wanted to sink her teeth into.

Things were so much better now. Ever since she'd taken the brat and reeducated her, there was nothing she hadn't been able to do. Limits were gone. Sense and reason and fear were dead. No need for them now. Pathetic human things. All that was left was the Experience Uninhibited. Beauty everywhere she looked. Especially in the—

She glanced at her rear-view mirror and did a double-take.

"Oh, shit."

She grabbed it, pulled it closer. Off its hinges, actually.

"Hey, baby," said Yakuza.

She laughed, and let her laughter die away. Tasted it in her mouth like wine.

"You okay?"

She stared intently at the mirror. Something about it was bothering her. Might have been that the face there didn't quite match hers. It looked like the Other One had stepped a little too far out of bounds. Her frown deepened. Her jaw set. She took a deep breath.

"Hang on."

Yakuza veered right and plowed her car through the sparse brush on the side of the road. Back toward the city.

Red.

It took Jacqueline a second to recognize the underside of her eyelids coming back online. Hot. itchy. *So dry.* Every breath a reminder she didn't have enough water in her body. Her muscles stirred. She opened her eyes. Still couldn't see her hand in front of her face. Managed to guide one of them there despite this. Sensations made sense of each other as she draped her fingers across her brow and felt cloth. Pulled off the blindfold, no, sleep mask. Kitsch, with big eyes drawn on it. Room came into focus. Blue light covered everything in silver. *Take in every detail.* Big window to the left. No, sliding door. Straight ahead of her, a dresser with a...

...with a mirror on it. She looked herself in the eye, warily. She was propped up on a soft queen sized bed. Big, heavy blanket on top of her, paisley. She'd been tucked in. She tugged the blanket off with some difficulty. Every inch of her was sore. Open air made her feel raw, bandage fresh. She gingerly stood. Carpet was old and coarse between her toes. She was wearing red silk pajama bottoms and a matching robe. Her bra was missing. It had been replaced by a large section of gauze, also wrapped around her shoulder. A phantom twinge of pain reminded her she'd been stabbed. She draped one of the robe's shoulders down to the crook of her elbow. A dark red blot gave testament to the wound she'd suffered. It itched, but didn't hurt. She looked out the window. Full moon. Brain still waking up. Shifting shadows outside in blue, white and black made her head hurt. How long had she been out? And where was she now?

Two doors to the right. One of them ajar, *bathroom*. Sea green tile. Matching shower curtain. She tugged it aside right away. Unable to banish visions of an assassin lying in wait. She also opened the medicine cabinet. It had a mirror built into it. Two toothbrushes. Purple and green. Aside from the usual toiletries, there was a little orange bottle. The label had been torn off, leaving a reef of white adhesive. She still managed to recognize the caliber of the sleep meds inside.

"Hello, old friends," she said dryly.

Jacqueline splashed some water on her face from the sink. Took a long draught. A black wicker hamper stood by the toilet. A small, crumpled garbage bag sat on top. She peered inside, and was rewarded with the foul cocktail of old blood and sewage. Her clothes from yesterday.

The urgency of her situation became more apparent as Jacqueline woke up to the fact that she was now at the mercy of whoever had "rescued" her. Whoever they were, they knew far too much about her and Jacqueline knew next to nothing. Her heart sped up as she dove back in the bag and pawed through it. *No badge. No gun.* Her pill bottle gone. Phone gone. Wallet, gone.

She ran back into the bedroom and tried the other door. Surprisingly, it popped open right away. She stood there holding it for a second before closing the door again. Reassuring that she wasn't a prisoner. *Not in the immediate sense, at least.* Less reassuring that this door wasn't secure. She walked over to the left side of the dresser and started to push. A moment of scraping later and the heavy dresser now blocked the door sideways. She glanced sidelong at the sliding glass door to the left. An avenue of escape, yes, easily. But also a vector of attack. She stepped closer.

It let out into a small fenced-in yard. No obvious exits. Manicured lawn. Concrete patio. Two wooden chairs and an umbrella table. *Picturesque.* So much so that she felt it would tear apart if she opened the door, like a magazine page. She turned back toward the center of the room. If she were going outside or anywhere, she'd need to be properly dressed.

The dresser wasn't packed. Mostly slacks and dress shirts. A single drawer held women's underwear. A shallow divot of a closet had a few sun dresses hanging there, but nothing in her size. Not that she was in the mood for dresses. Or ever had been. She selected a pair of dark brown slacks and a white button up shirt. Black socks. She took them into the restroom to change.

She was rolling up the shirt sleeves when she heard the bedroom door open. A soft clunk as it hit the dresser she'd left in the way. She stood perfectly still, holding her breath. The other person must have been doing the same. Jacqueline didn't hear a thing until the door closed again. She looked around the bathroom. Should she arm herself? If so, what with? *Shatter the mirror?* They'd hear that. Maybe barge in before she was ready. Looked up at the shower curtain rod. Wasn't built into the wall, like the one in her apartment and other older buildings. Store bought, collapsible, held in place by suction or something. She rapped it with her knuckles. *Hollow.* Would bend after one strike. Useless in a prolonged fight. Glanced at the toilet. She lifted the square lid off the tank. Hefted it experimentally. Stood on the digital scale with it, without. About five pounds. Swung horizontally, its edge could cave in a skull without putting too much pressure on the ceramic.

Back in the bedroom, Jacqueline leaned her makeshift club against the wall for a moment and moved the dresser back a foot or so. The hallway outside was empty. Same sea green as the tile in the bathroom. Single picture frame on the right wall. A black and white drawing of a vase with some sunflowers inside. She recognized it as one of the default pictures that came with the frames you could buy at the drugstore. She must've passed them dozens of times on the way to the pharmacy. Decorator in a hurry? Or was it another purposeful touch? A manufactured environment for her to wake up in?

Ahead of her, dust motes danced in a blue spotlight. Skylight in the ceiling. Moon directly overhead. The clouds had all beat feet, finally. She walked toward the dust and light, ears pricked. Silence pressed in on the sides of her head like a giant pair of fingers ready to pinch. Someone else had been here, and recently. The dust might have been stirred by the wind, and wind might have opened her door, but to close it again? The air here was still. Warm and close. Baked by the sun during the day but untouched by the outside world since then.

She'd almost missed it since the moonlight had cast everything else in shadow; as she drew level with the skylight, she caught sight of three other doors. She listened at the first one on the left. No sound. Set the tank lid down. Flattened herself against the wall on the far side, by the knob. Further down the hallway, she stood fully illuminated in the moon's spotlight. She knew if she overthought it any longer, the sun would come up. Click click click. She eased the door open. Her heart leapt as her imagination shot a hand out of the darkness within to grab her wrist. She shook her head. Peered inside. A closet. Five or six heavy coats and one very familiar windbreaker.

"What kind of sick fuck..." she whispered incredulously as she brushed a hand over the yellow lettering on the back. 'Police.' She took it off the hanger and its weight immediately made her realize her mistake. Heavier than hers. One or two sizes larger. A look at the tag confirmed this. Another cop, then. *Jameson?*

She picked the lid back up. He'd be sorry if it was. If he'd taken her, maybe conspired with one of her foes, maybe been bought off...she didn't have long. Reconnoiter. Gather evidence. *Find some shoes.* Wouldn't get far without those.

Of her other foes, Nunogawa came to mind. He'd been the closest. Who else was in the wind? Immediately, she couldn't stop imagining the doors before her populated with the ghoulish faces of Doctor Folsom peering around each corner. Wide milky eyes. Grins crooked. She forcibly shut her own eyes and willed the awful vision away. Unlikely it was him, although he had means and motive at his disposal. He wouldn't be ready to do anything but run for his life for some time. Nunogawa would have just killed her if she'd been discovered by his crew.

Jameson continued to lurk on the periphery of her suspicion. Could it really have been him? Her gut said fuck yes it could have. He was dirty. Not above taking money to see people hurt. The doctor might not have kidnapped her directly, but if he'd approached Jameson as a go-between...paid him off? Supplied him with narcotics?

She crept to the next door on the left as silently as she could. That's what the pills in the bathroom must have been for. To subdue her long enough to be delivered as a prize. *A hand-to-hand.* Her theory also explained why the label had been missing from the bottle in the bathroom.

A clatter like a rattlesnake spun her around. Jameson's phantom hand holding the pills he'd said were for headaches. Floating there, faded away into the moonlight. *Seeing* and *hearing things now.* She pinched herself, hard. Not still dreaming, at least. She kept a wary eye opposite her as she tried the door on the left. One on the right, slightly ajar.

Last door on the left was locked. Cheap wood. Probably hollow. Most suburban homes were like ticky-tacky. She could break it down, but not quietly. And her housemate was still up and about. What's more, he knew she was too. She turned away. Ahead there was a tiny window, high up in the little room across from her. It was illuminating another bathroom. More spacious, with—

What was that?

A shadow of movement. Corner of her eye. Sharp

intake of breath as she raised the lid to attack. Nothing there. She didn't move. Waited.

There. Ahead, at the end of the hallway. A living room. Two windows let into it, facing her on the opposite wall and from the left. Another shadow moved. She entered the room, hugging the wall and then the corner. A coffee table garnished with a copy of *Little House On The Prairie*, flanked by two couches. A kitchen off to the right, cast in darkness. And the big window. The source of the movement. She followed its shaft of light to the left. The other one just showed some shrubs. The left one had a suburban street, curving off to the right. Some trees planted here and there. Houses were old enough that they didn't all look exactly alike. Yaqui materialized mid-sprint in the middle of the road and vanished again as she turned the corner. Jacqueline watched, mesmerized as the VHS ghost ran on repeat several more times. Followed the footsteps to the street sign on the corner with her eyes.

Glacier street.

Too many connections. A flash of red added itself to the paint swirl of blue in her periphery. Car lights. Locked itself. The front door clicked as she spun back around. Too slow to react. The car lit up briefly, burned into her immediate memory. The boxy little sedan from the butcher's road, and Temple Street before that. And now here. In the den of the beast. The front door opened. The shade who'd opened it was tall and thin. The cool night breeze he'd brought with him smelled of walnut and spruce. The trees outside.

"Well, this is awkward. We're wearing the same outfit," said Mr. Pinkerton as he stepped into the light.

He'd made tea. He'd made Jacqueline tea. He'd made himself a martini. He was avoiding saying something. As he'd mentioned, they were wearing much the same in the way of clothing. He had a light jacket on to ward off the midnight dew. And shoes of course. Would have been nice if he'd had some of those lying around for her to borrow. She'd already be gone and he'd have spared the both of them this awkward encounter. She followed the nose of his hawkish profile as it bobbed back and forth. Pacing. *Good sign,* she thought sarcastically. Pomade in his grey hair pulled it back in silver. Bronze skin. Only just starting to wrinkle in earnest. He'd likely have a few more after tonight.

Any nerves were belied by the skill with which he mixed his drink. He caught her watching his hands.

"The important thing is the rhythm." He smiled. His voice wasn't nearly as nasally as his nose would suggest. More cello than flute. They had never interacted much before he left the force. No context to work backwards from. The look in his eyes was doubly unfamiliar. *Fear.* He masked it well, but Jacqueline's business was composite profiling—his poker face didn't stand a chance when the game was rigged from the start.

Since he'd come in, he might as well have been silent. Or repeating the same sentence over and over. Nothing he'd said had any substance. He'd kept the conversation as dry and flavorless as the drink in his hand. She offered an olive.

"Why am I here?"

He almost dropped his glass. "Well it's, kind of a long story."

Jacqueline shook her head. "I'm sorry. I have...zero interest in, in any of this. No small talk. No pleasantries. Definitely no stalling. If that's all you've got to offer, I'll be leaving."

Pinkerton moved to block the door. "I have a very compelling reason why you don't want to do that."

The fear in his eyes was unmistakable now. Fear of her? Silvered with an edge of defiance.

"Several, actually," he added, sinking the words into the pool of silence that had precipitated between them. His eyes darted downward, and she followed them. Without realizing, she'd picked up the heavy ceramic lid in one hand. She dropped it with a hollow thud and cleared her throat.

"Does one of them include what you did with my gun?" She asked evenly.

"As a matter of fact, yes. Please, relax and drink your tea. This will take some explaining."

She looked down at her china cup.

"I'm not thirsty. Where's Clara? Does your wife know I'm here?"

He stepped away from the door. "She's working late. Looking for her best friend. Who went missing three days ago."

Jacqueline's eyes widened as Pinkerton sat down on the couch opposite hers.

"Clara hasn't been home for two days. I discovered you a few hours ago. The night of your disappearance, I Watched you enter the butchery and later heard some commotion...but I didn't see you again until I revisited the ruins and fished you out of a storm drain. Odd place for a swim, I thought."

She remembered seeing his car there now, the old sedan, but... *Three days? Not possible.* Even if she hadn't almost drowned, three days without food would spell certain death. She was missing something. Or Pinkerton was hiding something from her. She blinked.

"You didn't answer my question."

Pinkerton took a sip of his martini. "No, I haven't yet informed her that you're here. I thought it prudent to apprise you of the situation you've found yourself in first. But before that," He set down his drink on the coffee table and held out a hand, "Would you mind terribly if we put that back in the restroom?"

He indicated the toilet tank lid. "I'm not sure Clara would approve of its use as a conversation piece. The room's already rather tied together."

Jacqueline pursed her lips, nodded. "Funny. How about a trade? You give me back my gun, and I won't charge you with obstruction of justice," she said flatly.

He didn't reply right away. Couldn't keep the tremor out of his hand as he reached for his drink again.

"It's very difficult...to do that kind of paperwork when you've been slapped with a section eight. I should know."

He took a sip. Jacqueline blanched, realized she was holding her breath. Pinkerton swirled his drink, followed the curve with his eyes.

"The higher-ups tried to serve Clara with one of those not long after we had Elaine. It was post-partum depression, you know. They tried again after Elaine passed away. Surprised they'd wait twelve years to try the same thing twice."

The hitch in his voice was barely detectable.

"I care deeply about Clara. And it's clear she cares deeply about you. So, I'm asking—" He rubbed his mouth. "I'm begging you, for one thing, to not beat me to death—"

Once spoken aloud, the option of assaulting Mr. Pinkerton evaporated in her mind. Unthinkable. Yet impossible to deny she'd been thinking about it.

"—because I don't think I could stop you."

Jacqueline swallowed. "And the other thing?"

He waved a hand. "Just, hear everything I've got to say. Trust that if I've put your gun somewhere safe, it's because I've got the same goal in mind for you."

To keep her safe? Maybe. Couldn't ignore the oblique threat of a section eight, though. Once the police decided you were crazy, there weren't many who'd argue with them. He knew too much. Maybe everything. Enough to get her fired, or worse, put away. *Somewhere safe.*

She met his gaze. He'd shored it up. Impossible to read. Leaving this room would introduce new variables though, maybe even give her a chance to glean what he knew. And *silence him.*

She winced. Pushed the thought back down.

"Okay. Lead the way, then."

They stood and Jacqueline made sure he left the room first. She kept him in her sights as they went back down the hallway. Less intimidating with the lights on. The oppressive heat of fear had given way to icy pinpricks of annoyance, and she was working on keeping it from blossoming into anger. She needed all her wits about her, even if she had to pantomime her way through this transparent power play bullshit. She stood reluctantly at the door to the bedroom. Handed him the lid.

He smiled. "A simple show of trust."

He brought it back into the restroom, and she took the opportunity to rifle through the dresser again. Maybe there was something she'd missed. Maybe he'd hidden one of her personal artifacts here. Had to rule it out.

"Say, what's that man doing in my drawers?" said Pinkerton from behind her.

She stopped, took a deep breath. "Another joke? I'm glad you're enjoying this. I'm just looking for some shoes. The one part of your outfit I've yet to replicate."

Pinkerton shuffled his feet. "Sorry. From behind, you know, for a moment you looked like another me."

"I'm flattered," said Jacqueline, "Are you ever going to tell me exactly why I'm still here? Or did you have any other chores to take care of?"

Pinkerton shrugged. "Well, since you mention it."

He walked over and started to make the bed.

"Oh," said Jacqueline.

What is he doing? Her pulse quickened. Suddenly, she couldn't deny the strangeness of the moment. They were no longer colleagues in the same house, they were a man and woman alone in a bedroom. With one of them touching up the sheets. The moment of panic settled as she realized the gesture likely wasn't...sexual. Made her skin crawl to think of it but he'd already had the opportunity while she slept. If she wasn't a detective her instincts would have told her to fight. He really was just...making the bed for some asinine reason. Her pulse slowed.

What a quirky sense of humor, she thought sarcastically. She watched his attention to detail when it came to folding the sheets and blankets so exactly. She remembered she'd been tucked in when she awoke. *He must have been a sterling father.* Jacqueline's paranoia interrupted her sarcasm for a moment. Why was he making the bed, putting back the things she'd moved? Why was it so important to do those things first? Unless he was erasing the evidence that she'd been here.

He'd moved on to folding the clothes she'd disturbed back into their drawers. She looked around. No ornamentation. No bedside tables for Clara or her husband. *A guest room.* She remembered the dust in the air. A room long undisturbed. Not good for any follow up investigation from Clara, should her friend Jackie go missing much longer.

Something caught her eye on the wall. An absence. Square sections of plaster that were lighter than the rest. *A sterling father, indeed.* This used to be his daughter's room. Was it worth reminding him of that, trying to appeal to his better nature?

He wouldn't really kill her, would he? He'd already had ample opportunity. It didn't make sense. He was a cop, besides.

So was Jameson. So are you.

"You're mumbling," said Pinkerton as he closed the drawer.

Shit.

"Where'd all your photos go?" she said, for something to say.

He stood up and turned around. "I'm not sure what you mean."

She gestured at the wall. "This room used to be covered in them. The only one I've seen in your house is that drugstore frame in the hallway."

His facade dropped for a moment, and she glimpsed the baleful gaze of a man who had gone without proper sleep for many, many years. A weak spot. A chance to reveal the real him. Make him give away too much.

"Is this actually your house? It's kind of bare," she baited.

"Yes. This is my house," he said slowly. "Our house," he corrected himself.

He seemed to realize he wasn't doing the best job of portraying himself as the loving husband he'd made himself out to be, and started down the slippery slope of negotiating against himself.

"After Elaine passed away, Clara was devastated. Nobody had fought harder to keep our daughter alive and well. In the months following the funeral, she became despondent. Almost unresponsive. We needed to be able to move on. We had to take steps to make that happen."

Jacqueline raised an eyebrow.

"We?" She said.

Pinkerton's jaw set. "I'm not made of stone. Leaving behind the memories of Elaine was the single most painful thing I've ever done."

"You seem fine now," said Jacqueline, "You're really comfortable erasing your daughter like that?"

"My daughter is dead, Ms. Ueda. But my wife is alive. And the memory of our daughter was killing her."

He dipped his head and spread out an arm towards the door. "If you're quite finished, I think it's high time we concluded our discussion."

"After you," said Jacqueline coldly, not willing to let him out of her sight any more than she had to. He closed his eyes and shrugged before proceeding. In the hall, he stopped at the closet for a moment.

"Here. A gesture of goodwill."

He withdrew a heavy-looking black case. A gun safe.

"As soon as we're done talking, I'll tell you the combination. I've stored your most important personal effects inside. Safe, as promised," he said.

"And my shoes?" Said Jacqueline off hand, unsure of the box's inner dimensions.

"Those are outside. They're wet," said Pinkerton, slightly distastefully.

"Mm. Thanks again for undressing me. Wouldn't have wanted to ruin the good sheets," she replied.

"You had a stab wound. Prone to infection those, and your clothing was filthy. Would you prefer I'd taken you to a hospital?"

Ordinarily such a pointed question would have been rhetorical. It still was, but in an entirely different context. Hospitals meant questions. Where she'd been. Who'd stabbed her. Where *they* were now. The fact that Pinkerton had presented it as a threat meant she'd exasperated him. *Good.* Anger was the strongest lever she had. It was clear given his intimations of a section eight that some sort of blackmail was in store. He had no other reason for avoiding official channels. Even less for not involving his wife. *His wife...* Something clicked. She walked quickly to catch up. He was already back in the living room.

"How much did Clara tell you?" Asked Jacqueline as she set her new box on the coffee table and sat down.

"Everything," said Pinkerton.

Jacqueline felt her face drain of color.

"We tell each other everything as a matter of course, and this was no different. The thing I heard that concerned me most was news of your little fugue states and the property damage that follows."

Her face grew hot.

"I almost feel sorry for the chief, but that's what he gets for being so stingy with regular maintenance and repairs."

A million thoughts clambered over each other in an unruly dog pile that threatened to bury her.

How could...

Traitor...

Everything...

"Now, when I say everything, I don't necessarily mean *everything* everything. Given how much she cares for you, I'm only getting a given value of *everything* at any one time. But she told me enough that I was able to put the pieces together after some reconnaissance and deduction. I am now more than certain that I am in possession of enough facts to qualify this information as everything," he exposited.

Jacqueline was barely listening. Head bowed under the weight of over-stimulation. She held it up with her hands.

"Please calm down," said Pinkerton as he picked up where he'd left off with his drink. "I understand if you're... embarrassed of what I've heard about, but that's not what need concern you here."

Jacqueline remained closed to him.

"Clara is still very much your friend. Everything she told me was out of direct concern for you. The most important takeaway for you is that there's no grand conspiracy at work here."

No response. He pointed at the teacup, which had only just stopped steaming.

"Clara has her own garden. She planted it not long ago but it's growing like gangbusters. Those are her tea leaves."

Jacqueline's eyes focused in on the bottom of her cup. Wanted to believe that there was still a way out of this. Wanted to believe she could catch those responsible. More than anything wanted to believe she still had a friend. Her eyes felt hot. Welling up. Throat prickly. She took the cup in both hands and tipped it back. Empty. Tasted like relief. He'd added something sweet. *Pomegranate?*

Pinkerton smiled gently.

"1934."

She regained eye contact, set the cup down.

"Mh?"

"The combination to the safe," he replied.

She wasted no time in clicking the digits into place. It was all there—wallet, with wet cash fused into a lump; Phone, screen dark forever more; Gun, with only one good shot left before the flooded chamber jammed it. She'd never been happier to see garbage. The high didn't last long. She still wasn't going anywhere. Constrained.

"Better?" said Pinkerton.

"What exactly did she say to you? I want details," said Jacqueline.

"That's not important right now. Our time is limited, so I'll be concise—"

Our time is limited. That phrase buzzed in her mind. Folsom liked to use it. It put the onus of shame for wasting time on her. Her frustration mounted. She gripped her temples.

"What the fuck is with this nonsense? Why are you wasting my time with all this back and forth? There's..."

He hadn't moved. He merely sat, watching her intently.

She piled on. "If she told you everything, then you know there's a fucking murderer on the loose!"

She felt light-headed. He tapped a finger idly on the table and then sat forward.

"The murderer...is right in this room," he said gravely.

She became acutely aware of the silence in the house. No cars drove by. No insects chirped. The wind did not rustle the trees. She certainly felt as if there wasn't enough air left in here. She couldn't take her eyes off of his. She didn't dare. Her eyes felt so big no movement could escape. Faced with men who'd wanted to lock her in a padded room or stab her to death, she'd only been as afraid as circumstances required. Haunted by a specter wearing her face to a new crime scene every night, she'd been resolute, logical. Confronted it head on.

Faced with Pinkerton now, and his unblinking gaze, she felt the primal urge to run, scream. The familiar becoming unfamiliar. The scent of betrayal unmistakable, impossible to wash off since she got here. She'd known she wasn't safe here. Like skipping to the end of a book, an inevitable knife twist. The butler did it. All the little clues amounting to no more than a warning shot, fired too late.

Inserting himself into the investigation. Preying on his wife's trust. Was she in on it too? No grand conspiracy indeed. His features were alien, suddenly. Shadows blending with the actual contours of his face. Perched across from her like a gargoyle. *The murderer is in this room.* She jumped as he put a hand on the table.

"Jacqueline."

The silence in the house rang.

She could hear all the little noises of it settling. The spell, broken.

"It's you," he said.

"What?" She barely heard herself.

He looked down, slid his glass along the table idly. "You are the one you've been looking for."

She shook her head, even as everything she'd been tacitly ignoring began to click into place around her. Paralyzing her. She almost said 'What do you mean?' But even without speaking, he was happy to oblige her.

"Was it luck that this went unnoticed for so long, that it happened right under our noses? Was it luck? No, we just weren't paying attention," he said half to himself. He brought his full attention to bear on her once again,

"The last time I saw my wife, she couldn't tell me where you'd gone. Couldn't or wouldn't. Thankfully, I already had some idea. I'd watched you jump to that particular conclusion several days ago. A good thing we happened to breakfast at the same spot that morning."

Reeling, Jacqueline grabbed for a detail. "Th— you've been spying on me?"

Pinkerton ignored that. "You took issue with Rico's recipe, rather loudly as I recall. When he mentioned where he was getting his product, I could almost see the connection form. A habit for you, I've noticed."

The old man at the counter. Hiding behind a newspaper of all things. Of course. No coincidences allowed, not anymore.

"I can see it happening now," he added pointedly, leaning in, "A pattern arises of mistaking correlation for causation. Of slight for attack."

He leaned back. "The girl, the heiress. Yaqui Guzman. A striking resemblance."

"What does that have to do with—"

He interrupted her, "Another mistake. Seeing a connection where there is none."

"There is a connection! I saw—" she said frantically.

"Where?" he said flatly, "The evidence you claim to have been acting on. Where did you see it?"

No answer.

"Up here?" He tapped his temple.

She kept her mouth shut. Glared at him. He thought about it for a moment and then took another swig of his drink.

"I got a chance to speak to Ms. Guzman myself some weeks ago. I was driving down Temple Street at the time."

Jacqueline blinked. The memory of the car. Not her memory. A second-hand glimpse of Pinkerton's concerned face as he stepped into the rain.

"Retirement has its good days but I still miss my old patrol car. Sometimes I go on a nighttime drive to steady my nerves. In any case, I discovered her in some distress in the middle of the road. I was able to get her name and a shortlist of her troubles before her well-meaning friends hustled her away. An interesting encounter, but I didn't dare think anything of it until some time later when I was informed she'd checked into the care of my old station. Funny, that."

Jacqueline looked up and for a moment, behind Pinkerton's head a monochrome image floated. Yakuza and her thugs taking Yaqui away. Her eyes narrowed.

"...You," she spat.

"Me?" Asked Pinkerton, trying to follow her gaze.

"Yaqui was abducted from police custody. Now I think I know how," she said.

"I had nothing to do with that, and again, not what you should be concerned about," He finished his drink, "I'm detecting a worryingly possessive tone when talking about Ms. Guzman. Clara told me, as I'm sure she told you, that Ms. Guzman was taken lawfully into the care of her legal guardians. All the paperwork was in order—"

"What she told me was that something about the pickup didn't sit right with her," said Jacqueline.

"Which no doubt prompted you to investigate. Clara

did mention you spent all night in the camera room. What did you find?"

Silence. She certainly couldn't tell him a fucking vision had given her the answer she'd been looking for.

"I can safely assume you found something, since your very next stop was the slaughterhouse district."

Jacqueline realized she was tapping her foot, but didn't stop. "Is that what this is? You gaslight me until you've got real leverage, and then what?"

Pinkerton appeared to change track, rubbing his temples as if his frustration was giving him a headache. "What this is—do you know why I stopped for Yaqui that night? It's because for a moment I thought it was you. I can almost see why you did what you did. All the little resemblances and coincidences must have been maddening. And it's because if I thought for even a moment that you were in trouble, I'd want to help you. Which is what I'm doing now."

Burying the lede. She was not buying his crocodile tears.

"I'm sorry, what exactly did I do?" she said incredulously.

Thankfully, it seemed he was done avoiding her questions.

"When I happened upon Miss Yaqui that night, there was one word she kept saying over and over: Jacqueline. Jacqueline, Jacqueline."

Her eyes widened as he unraveled her story.

"You'd already begun stalking her by that point, hadn't you? She was clearly traumatized when I found her."

"No, no!" she shouted.

"Then, what?" He said simply," What's the connection?"

"We—"

She couldn't say it.

"The two of you have something special in common? A link of some kind?" he asked rhetorically. His conciliatory tone was really beginning to grate. But she couldn't say anything. How could she make him understand what she'd been seeing? He derailed her train of thought.

"I'm not hearing any disagreement. So you do think there's something there beyond what the rest of us can see. Particularly Ms. Guzman."

He steepled his fingers.

"Can we examine that statement for a moment? You've been chasing leads, apprehending suspects, and making extremely dangerous snap decisions based on...what? Psychic impressions? Prophetic dreams? Invisible voices?"

He leaned forward. "Here are some facts. Based on the report Clara recorded, the eye witness to the murder of Jimmy Frame claimed it was Yaqui, or someone who looked just like her."

Finally out in the open, the accusation had the same effect as a gun to the head. It focused all the attention on the task at hand.

"I didn't kill him," she said, terrified. Everything was falling away from her. Stripped bare to the bones.

"No? But another witness, my wife, can attest by your own admission that there's time you can't account for in your busy schedule. I'm not necessarily saying this was malicious, planned. Maybe you really did think there was someone else doing these things. Maybe you chased them to the slaughterhouse. Maybe that's why the place is now in shambles."

He raised an eyebrow. She stared back, numb.

"Old foundations. No bodies so far. In any case, from where I'm sitting it seems more likely that trip was meant to erase evidence. It certainly accomplished that rather neatly. However, in either scenario we are presented with a tangibly clear and present danger to and from yourself."

Jacqueline shook her head. Her panic dashed against the dam of her frigid exterior. It made her insides feel fizzy, ready to explode. "You just admitted you don't have any solid evidence against me," she said coldly.

"I'm not a cop anymore," Pinkerton replied brightly, "Further, you've already admitted to on-the-job delusions that have affected your judgment in the execution of your duties."

"You need to stop putting words in my mouth right fucking now," she growled.

"I've done nothing of the sort," he retorted calmly,

"I'm merely showing you how an unbiased view of your head state can benefit you. In fact, if you'd allowed yourself a visit to a mental health facility, none of this would have happened. I was trying to help you then and I'm trying to help you now."

Her jaw dropped as the realization hit her. She was absorbing this new paradigm at lightning speed.

"Holy shit. *You* called those goons on me. You and Folsom. He said a concerned family member wrote me in, but I didn't think anyone like you would stoop so low as forgery and aiding ACTUAL murderers," Jacqueline snarled.

He folded his hands in his lap. "Ms. Ueda, if someone you knew to be having psychotic hallucinations told you their psychiatrist was an evil monster, would you believe them?"

Hanging over the abyss on a spiderweb, Jacqueline felt another thread snap loose.

"Look at me," she said earnestly, hopelessly, "Look me in the eyes. Tell me I'm lying."

He frowned. "Really, Jacqueline. It is a childish notion that one look can determine a person's relative innocence. I find the romantic idea that eyes are the window to the soul rather beneath you."

"There's an APB out for him, a warrant out for his arrest, call your wife!" she said in disbelief.

"Please lower your voice," he said curtly, "I'd rather not involve the neighbors in this. You should be the last person interested in making a scene."

The numb feeling was spreading, branching out from her brain. She couldn't believe this was happening and neither, it seemed, did her body.

"Why won't you call Clara?" said Jacqueline, her voice trembling with rage.

"I would prefer not to embroil her in our problems

just now. Better to let things run their course."

Our problems. Vagaries and stalling. Clear he wanted something but he wouldn't come clean about the why and how.

"Right," said Jacqueline sourly, bitterly, "Because there's no way you could be wrong."

"No, Jacqueline. I'm not that hard-headed. It's more accurate to say that there's no way you could be right."

He picked up his martini glass as well as Jacqueline's teacup and saucer.

"This a joke to you?" said Jacqueline, "That's all my life is. One big fucking joke."

She hung her head. Doubt was eating away at her insides. Obviously she was crazy. Obviously. Logical. How many dead because of her? One that he knew about. God help her if the others came into question. Someone who looked just like her killing people in her dreams. *Do you hear yourself?*

"Your life is your life. It's easy to abdicate responsibility through self-deprecation, but I'd like to think you're better than that. You're better than half-baked conspiracy theories, better than paranoid delusions. And with a little help, we'll help you get better," he said from the kitchen.

"What does—" Jacqueline replied.

She looked out the window and something that had been nagging at the back of her mind came to the forefront.

"Where's Clara's garden?" she asked uneasily.

Pinkerton called back from the kitchen over the light clatter of the sink. "Oh? It's in—"

"—the back, yes I'm sure," said Jacqueline as several thoughts were racing to catch up.

"Only, I saw your backyard. There's no garden. Just a fenced-in patio. It's not out front either. Nice lawn, though," she said distractedly. He was hurrying back in. Drying off his hands. She looked down at the coffee table. Her memory put the cup back. It was empty. She had finished drinking it, after all. Static crackled around its edges. Something wrong with the background process. It was empty. *It was empty.* No tea leaves. *It was empty.* There had never been any leaves.

Not quite empty. She looked closer, Pinkerton frozen mid-stride in the corner of her eye. Not quite empty, a small powder-blue smear at the bottom of the cup. She looked up, past Pinkerton's shoulder. There was a little orange bottle on the kitchen counter. It was empty. Funny, how one little lie could reveal a much bigger one. Since she got here, she'd been beset by the sensation of falling. Now, it felt like she was floating. She heard the ocean in her ears. The room was turning sideways. The coffee table was rising to meet her. A pair of hands caught her by the shoulders. One last dull stab of pain from her wound there before she stopped feeling much of anything.

"There there," said Pinkerton.

"y fckn sn f btch," mumbled Jacqueline.

"Now now," said Pinkerton as he laid her back. Turned her head to the side. Her eyes darted around the room.

"Okay...okay," muttered Pinkerton as he gingerly sat back down across from her.

"It's likely you're wondering why I waited until now to sedate you when I had ample time before you woke up."

She was taking short, sharp breaths. Auto-pilot.

"I meant what I said earlier. I want to help you. Part of that is making sure you understand your situation completely. It's only fair you get the whole story. By the same token, talking to you has been enlightening."

The edges of her vision were turning black. She felt like she had the world in her throat and couldn't swallow.

"While it's obvious the part you played in all this, I don't think you actually knew what you were doing."

Her arms felt like they were disappearing.

"I didn't think it fair that you run afoul of your demons without any help along the way. Clara would have been heartbroken to learn you were a common murderer, as well. It's better this way. You'll spend some thought-provoking time in hospital, and then we'll all work together on getting your life sorted out."

Fingertips gone. Then the elbows. As her neck turned to dust she had the wondrous sensation of being a severed head. And then she could feel the inside of her skull on her brain. And then nothing.

Fireman carry. Cool night air. Passenger seatbelt.

"Sleep well."

Blessed unconsciousness.

Beatifically.

Yaqui awoke with grass underneath her. It had been a cold morning. The sun was only just starting to come out in earnest, so she wasn't overcooked.

"Hey sleepyhead," said Jimmy.

She sat up, blades of wet grass sticking to her heavy leather jacket and the back of her neck.

"—time is it," she asked groggily.

"Three," said Jimmy, "We were thinking of getting breakfast. Well, I was thinking about it. Nat already ran off to get Mexican."

Soft as it was, the sunlight beating down on her eyelids had now cast everything in blue. Jimmy's hair was verging up through black into lilac, and would soon be red again. The grass on the hill in the park by the street in the restaurant district was dark blue. Yaqui stared into Jimmy's eyes, which were currently as green as the ocean and...

and...

"Who?" said Jacqueline.

The patina of sweat that appeared on Jimmy's pale brow tasted like fear. Smelled like deja vu and regret. *Wait...*

How could...

"Sorry," said Yaqui, putting a hand out. A tinge of relief on his face as he helped her up.

"Still waking up," she grunted as she came to a stand.

"Good. That's good."

He hemmed and hawed. "I thought for a second—"

"Don't," Yaqui said, interrupting him, "We agreed... not to talk about Temple Street."

He gazed balefully at her. Like a kicked puppy. She filled the silence. "Don't look at me like that. I'm clean, okay? I'm clean as shit. I'm fine."

More silence. Sullen for her and helpless for him. She crossed her arms.

"What's eating your ass?" Nat said as she came back up the hill. Awkward silence. The question unanswered, she unslung her backpack and brought out a fat square of colorful cloth.

"Sorry I took so long with the food. I stopped at the car for my pack. I thought we could have a picnic." She unfolded the blanket and fanned it out before sitting cross-legged with her big white paper bag in front of her. She sighed contentedly.

"Seriously though. What the fuck is up? Somebody die?"

Jimmy shrugged, unwilling to break his promise. Yaqui bit her lip.

"Siddown. You're making me nervous," Nat said as she removed the foil-wrapped burritos from her bag. Yaqui and Jimmy sat across from each other like they were beginning a war council. After a moment, guilt overwhelmed Jimmy's trembling lip but it was Yaqui who spoke first.

"I had a bad dream."

Nat looked like she wanted to say something sarcastic at first, but swallowed it. "That's rough. What happened in it?"

Yaqui looked away, over the rolling hills in the park. "I was drowning."

Words wanted to spill over, to tell them everything. But a levee of fear held them back. She didn't want to lose her last few friends to...couldn't even think it. Invisible rules constrained her, an electric fence of panic. Jimmy put his hand out, rested it in the middle of the blanket. Yaqui reached hers out to meet his, but hesitated at the last second. Something held her back, an imminent feeling like static shock. Her body didn't want touch. A strange feeling, but familiar. Feeding the panic.

"Thank you," she said as she pulled her hand back and held it in the other.

Jimmy concealed the hurt expertly, but Yaqui knew him well. Though she was beginning to wonder how well she knew herself anymore.

"Well, you're awake now," said Nat, "And I got your favorite."

Yaqui gratefully took the burrito.

"It's the kind with French fries inside," said Nat.

Yaqui allowed herself a small smile.

"Breakfast of champions," said Jimmy, biting into his.

"Mm," said Yaqui, unwrapping hers, "This doesn't have egg in it, right?"

Nat shook her head, mouth full.

"Right?" Laughed Yaqui,

"Who decided everything with breakfast in the name had to have egg..."

She trailed off. Couldn't stop staring at the exposed flesh of her meal. The tortilla had gotten a little soft. The white skin had a little give as she felt the meat underneath. Nat was talking about her upcoming gallery show and how inspiring it was to have her scribbles alongside guys like Mucha. Jimmy admonished her and said hers were just as good, if not better. Nat looked over at Yaqui.

"You like chorizo, right?" Nat asked. But her voice was muffled. And not because her mouth was full. Yaqui's stomach turned as her mind filled unbidden with all the imagery it took to make something on legs into sausage.

"Yo Yak, you okay?" Said Nat. Jimmy sat up straighter.

Throat full of bile. Tasted like blood. Drowning. Their mouths were moving out of sync. As they sat forward, they left behind after-images, still happily chewing. Their hands were on her. Ow. She'd crushed the burrito, four phantom limbs spasming out of control. One friend on either shoulder. Her hands were all red. Her ears full of ocean, wearing away at her mind. Crucial details vanishing into the tide.

Who am...

who...

"Why can't I have this?" whispered Jacqueline.

"What? What did she say?" said Nat.

Jacqueline greedily drank in the sunlight and the soft smell of the grass and the warmth of their rough hands and almost sobbed.

"Why can't I have this? Why do you keep taunting me with this?"

"Yaqui!" said Jimmy frantically, trying to maintain eye contact,

"This is your life! You're okay. Your friends are here. It was all a dream! Whatever it was, it was all just a dream."

Jacqueline stared into Jimmy's eyes. Couldn't see her reflection in them. She felt hollow. An eggshell. *What was that smell?* Nat's skin. Her perfume. *Pomegranate.*

"You're not real," said Jacqueline with a strangled cry. She kicked and scrabbled to get away from them. Their faces were etched in sorrow. Helplessness.

"You're not real and you're trying to fucking kill me," she cursed. She stumbled backward. Could feel everything moving inside of her. The skin against the muscles against the nerves against the bones. She was trapped inside. She had to get out. She gripped the skin on the back of her right hand with her left. It tore easily. Like paper.

"Makes sense. Not really real," she murmured.

"Jesus fuck!" Jimmy cried.

"Stop it stop it stop it," Nat babbled, nauseated.

She could see the bone underneath the flesh. Almost there. She was knocked off her feet. Jimmy on top of her.

"Please stop," he begged. He was leaning on her throat. Blood choke. Sleep paralysis. Not real.

"Let's go back to sleep. Everything'll be okay," he insisted.

The sky turned back into night. Stars dancing. Their voices echoing.

"Jesus, this is awful," Nat sobbed, "I can't do this anymore."

The landscape rolled by like waves, the car stationary. Her mind caught up, and Jacqueline jolted against her seatbelt.

"Awake? Maybe I got the mixture wrong. Or are you more familiar with these substances than I realized?" Pinkerton chuckled.

"Nnnn," said Jacqueline and slumped forward. Still couldn't move. Still no shoes. Black lockbox. The gun safe was underneath her feet. How thoughtful. Maybe if she was lucky he'd bury her with it.

A fingertip on her forehead and Pinkerton pushed her upright. Reached across her and clicked a button. Adjusted her seat back.

"I know you took issue with my levity earlier, but I think that's exactly what your situation calls for."

Try to think. Jacqueline's eyes darted around the car. Looking down, she discovered she could move her hands. Complete numbness limited their movement to listless spasms and glacial finger curls. Zero chance she could grab or open the lockbox. *What else?* Faux wood dashboard. Soft fuzzy seat covers. A little keychain of a big-eyed cherub hanging from the rear-view mirror. It was one of those gift-shop items with one of a thousand names on it. Its little ribbon said ELAINE. *Clara's car.*

Her eyes roved down. Clara's glove compartment. *Clara's gun.* Her left hand inched forward, dragging itself by one finger. Her eyes shot back up. Met themselves in the mirror. Frantic. Bloodshot. *Don't let him see.* Couldn't feel. The right can't know what the left is doing.

"Look at it this way. You're finally going to be on firm footing with people who understand what you're going through. This is a good thing!"

She looked out her window. Slow, careful turns at ten and two by Pinkerton rotated the world outside like a giant planetarium. It made her nauseous. *Were those street lamps or stars?*

"Trust me. You're going to be fine. A damn sight better than prison, anyhow," he mused.

Definitely street lamps. Still near the city. Still time to escape on foot if she could regain the use of her limbs. All she needed was one street sign and she could chart a course to the nearest muni rail station. *And then what?*

"And then what?" said Pinkerton.

She zeroed back in on him. He looked tired.

"What happens after you shoot me with my wife's gun and run off into the night?"

Her hand hung from the clasp on the glove compartment. She let it fall.

"I want you to think carefully about the impulses you're acting on."

He slowed down as they approached the yellow light at an intersection. Red shifting. There was another car waiting in the left arm of the cross.

"Clara's strong. The strongest person I know. She could survive losing me. But both of us? Could you do that to her?"

Jacqueline met her own gaze again. Could she believe him? Did she honestly believe anything she'd seen in her dreams could be trusted? The question itself was telling.

"This isn't some scheme on my part," he said. The left-turn light changed. The other car waiting in the perpendicular lane could have gone, but didn't. They didn't have their lights on.

"I have no designs for you after you're committed. Do you know why? Because I know you'll do the right thing."

Jacqueline looked back at the other car. Black. *A convertible?*

"You're going to wake up tomorrow knowing you're safe. Free from any bogeymen or conspiracies out to get you."

She tried to get a better look at the license plate.

4792LLL. Her pulse quickened. Their own light changed. Pinkerton began to roll forward.

"There was a time when I'd hit a dead-end in a case I was working or a perp would get off on a bad jury call, and the chief, a great man by all accounts, you know what he'd say to me?"

The windows were rolled up. A silent horror movie was playing out on their left. Smoke billowed up behind Jacqueline's stolen car as it revved up. A hand appeared above the windshield and waved aloha. Hello and goodbye. The car jetted forward. Jacqueline was unable to move, unable to scream.

"Today is the first day of the rest of your life."

Clara's car had seat warmers, air conditioning and a tape deck. What it did not have were side airbags. Pinkerton's half of the car imploded on top of him in a shriek of metal and glass that pierced the silence apocalyptically. Weightless. Way too loud. Overstimulation frying her like an egg. Eating away at her outsides. Acid.

The drug in her system was only just starting to wear off. She'd been totally limp at time of impact. The shock passed through her body almost harmlessly.The seatbelt jerked and clicked like a prize fishing reel. Took her breath away and left a bruise in its place. Pinkerton had tried to put up his arms to defend himself. As if he could lift a car. They spun, and g-force pinned her into her seat. The noise died away.

The smell of blood filled the car, filtered through smoke and the cold wind from outside.

"Here's the crossroads..." said a phantom voice.

The front-facing airbags had not deployed.

"And here's the devil."

An apparition appeared in the flickering headlights. Shaded its eyes, and then waved.

"Hey," said Yakuza. Her voice was as clear as a bell. She was wearing a loose white t-shirt over a black tank-top. As she got closer Jacqueline could see she also had on jean shorts and black high-tops. There was a halo of iridescent light around Jacqueline's vision. No, around Yakuza. The dust and smoke didn't touch her. She seemed to draw light in, and repel everything else. Impossible not to pay her attention. Jacqueline realized she couldn't blink. There was a terrible gravity to Yakuza's face. As life returned to Jacqueline's muscles, she forced her head to turn away. Her skin was on fire. Pins and needles in her bones. She stared at Pinkerton's mangled corpse. Splattered with his own blood, limbs contorted. It looked like the spin of one of the other car's tires had actually rubbed part of his face off.

A gasp escaped his lips and he became alive again. One eye in a ruined socket swiveled about. He couldn't move. No real audible sound but as Yakuza hovered into view again, the ambient bass of the air thickened. The world held its breath waiting for her to speak. At this moment, she merely tutted as Pinkerton struggled to breathe. In one smooth motion, she tore his door off its hinges like the jaws of life.

"What hit...me?" Pinkerton wheezed.

Yakuza laughed like clear water. Like she was watching a kitten play.

Jacqueline looked back at the glove compartment. Clara's gun. If she could just reach *nnnghh...*

An ice cream headache. The back of her eye itched. Dancing spots.

"Good idea," said Yakuza. She leaned into the car and reached across Jacqueline.

"Pardon me," she offered in a movie theater whisper. Her eyes were so big. Almost all pupil.

She withdrew the Saturday night special and stood three feet away.

"Doctor, it only hurts when I move."

She thumbed back the hammer.

"So stop moving."

The sound it made was more firecracker than thunderclap. An auditory thrown punch. It knocked his head to the side as if he'd been slapped. He lay still.

Jacqueline found her voice. "You're real," she croaked.

Yakuza smiled, and her teeth were very sharp. "You sound surprised. Boy, he really did a number on you, huh? Are you in shock? Are you going into shock? I know I would be, well..."

She appeared to mull this over, and then shrug. "Mm."

Her eyebrows perked up. "You don't mind me borrowing your fingerprints, do you? Sorry, should have asked first."

She held up her hand. Splayed her fingers and dangled the gun from a pinky by the trigger-guard. The fine detail of her skin there was scrolling by. Several different textures clipping into each other. It hurt so much to look at, but Yakuza's gaze was infinitely magnetic. A black hole. She put her hand down.

"Don't be upset. I'm only doing this for the benefit of your investment."

Jacqueline started breathing faster, her pulse warming up. "You killed him," she choked out.

Yakuza's eyes welled up, likely only for dramatic effect. "Your concern is overwhelming," she whined. Smiled again.

"Again. It's because YOU care if they think you're a killer that I'm here pulling triggers with your prints. *I* don't give a shit. Means to an end."

Jacqueline didn't have anything more to say. She was tugging at her seatbelt. Visualizing a flying tackle.

"Hey," Yakuza barked, and fired another shot.

It thudded into the dash and sent up a small plume of chemical powder. Jacqueline's airbag deployed, pinning her sideways. She cried out as the rapid expansion of the bag's taut surface dislocated her right shoulder. Yakuza looked at the gun introspectively.

"Crude. But effective. I'm going to keep this. If you want it, you have to catch me." She cocked her head and smiled.

"See you at home."

And with that, she was gone. Not running away, not swallowed by darkness or fog. Gone. Jacqueline had more pressing concerns. The smoke pouring out of the engine block had changed. The smell of pancakes mingling with the stench of blood in the car meant the coolant tank had been ruptured. She struggled backward, forcing open her door with one good arm. The blue tinge to the smoke meant the oil had caught. She forced a few fingers around the handle of the lockbox. Tugged. Managed to lift it over the lip of the door. She fell to the ground outside. The jolt sent daggers through her dislocated shoulder. She rose to one knee, and then to her feet. Worse than the pain was the itch. Knowing her stitches had torn open. There'd be more, yet. She gritted her teeth as she raised her right arm with the help of her

left...

and...

Click.

Thunderous exhalation and a shudder she felt all the way to her knees. Bones moving around not an experience she wanted to repeat.

1934.

The fire safe popped open and she retrieved any evidence she'd been here. No time to repair her gun. It would have to suffice. One bullet wouldn't do Jacqueline much good but could potentially do Yakuza a world of harm. She staggered around the car to Pinkerton's side. Stifled a sudden grunt of pain as she stepped on a shard of glass in her sock feet. Balancing carefully, she slowly withdrew it. She looked up at Pinkerton's corpse, cradling the bloody shard. She wasn't going to get far without shoes. She tossed the shard aside and set to work.

Her face was blank as she tightened her new laces. The cut hadn't been too deep, thankfully, easily bandaged with a torn sleeve tourniquet. She stood, tread carefully in dead men's shoes. Now for the grisly work. Retrieving the slug. She approached him again, hand outstretched. Hesitant.

"...Sorry," she said.

Something caught her eye. A single, minuscule orange campfire fly. A spark. Escaping from the A/C vent. She dove for cover. Rolled. Grabbed up the fallen door as a shield. Heard a *plink plink plink* of metal.

Felt the wave of heat cascade across her back. The roar of the flames was deafening. She climbed to her feet and watched the blaze. Watched it take hold of Pinkerton and lick him clean. Purifying light transformed him into a skeleton devoid of imperfection. She licked her lips, swallowed. She realized since no one else was there, it fell to her to say a few words.

"...You were a damn fool."

The fire crackled.

"But I don't think...you deserved to be murdered. And Clara didn't deserve to have anyone else taken from her."

She looked down at his shoes.

"I'm not sure I can...avenge you, kill her I mean. It's what she wants, I think."

Looked at the inferno again. Still going strong. Red.

"I'll catch her. Fix this whole mess. Make things right for that girl you met on Temple Street. And for Clara. I'll take care of her. I promise."

Jacqueline looked around. No moon. No stars. The fire popped and hissed merrily. Jacqueline couldn't tell where she was. But she knew exactly where *she* was. Yakuza's gravity, or rather the immediate absence of it pulled at her.

"...Goodbye," she said awkwardly.

She stepped into the darkness.

Jacqueline had been walking for years. Lost track of time almost immediately. She'd started counting minutes four hours ago. The sun should have risen by now. She was in wonderland. A hellscape of her own making. Perhaps that was why all she could see was darkness. *No imagination.*

She shook her head. Listened to the sound of her own breathing. She held up her right hand, turned it over and over. *It's still me. I'm still me.* Put it down and stared into the abyss. Yakuza's gravitational pull, the sense that she was near, was everywhere. She was at once surrounded, and terribly alone. Something occurred to her as a chill entered her bones. She looked at her hand again. Her perfectly normal hand. No lights in the sky. No more streetlamps to guide her. Even the ground under her feet was invisible, featureless. But she could see her own hand in front of her face. Sweat beaded on her forehead. A drop fell away. Its glint disappeared into the distance beneath her. She straightened up.

This was a mistake. She was literally in over her head in figurative and possibly hallucinated waters. She was all alone, and it was very dark. Silent tension twanged around her like a pair of hungry jaws, ready to snap shut. Her heart was pounding in her ears. She continued to stare at her hands. A planet without atmosphere in the void. She took a deep breath all the same. Clenched them into fists. Her pulse slowed.

"Fuck you. I'm still alive," she said.

She looked up. If she was dreaming, and knew it, she should be able to dream about whatever she wanted.

"Let's have a moon, then. A big yellow one," she said defiantly.

Black clouds parted, and there was the moon. Biggest one she'd ever seen. She hadn't asked for it to be full, but this one looked ready to burst. A harvest moon. Its light illuminated a multitude of black trees. Mist crawled through their roots. Oddly, Jacqueline felt her fear fading. Likely the wilderness backdrop was Yakuza's doing, if she bought into her own hype as some sort of alpha-predator. Jacqueline could already imagine the game of hide and seek playing out beneath the canopy

"Quaint. But no thanks," said Jacqueline and then thought *CITY* as hard as she could.

The trees fell flat like a pop up book. Ancient

brownstones and gleaming skyscrapers melted out of the air in their place.

The implications of all this were exceedingly dangerous. Such a mutable world would be too easy to sink into on a thoughtless whim. Like quicksand. She needed a lifeline. A totem. No, a tattoo. Something that couldn't be taken away so easily.

"I'm dreaming," she said aloud.

The words appeared on her right forearm. *Permanent*, she thought. Hard as she could. She grit her teeth as I'M DREAMING flared red and then black. Burned into her skin. Satisfied, she pointed her nose into the wind and sighted a likely corner.

"Street sign."

Her words cut open the air as easily as a knife into one of Clara's homemade pies, and the sight was just as comforting. Amigara Street, where Jacqueline lived. She didn't let herself relax though. She felt Yakuza's influence here too. This was another piece in whatever game she was playing. She could follow this path through wonderland, or she could cut to the chase.

"You," she said, framing Yakuza in her mind.

The air shimmered, seemed to resist her will, and then split. There Yakuza stood, exactly as she'd last seen her. The exact moment, actually. A halo of night obscuring the bright brickwork as Yakuza stood in front of the two wrecked cars.

"See you at home," Yakuza said again, and vanished back into static.

Jacqueline frowned. The gap in the world was still there, but she couldn't concentrate her memory on Yakuza for more than a few seconds. The air tasted sullen, bitter. Jacqueline could skip to the end of the book, but her adversary wouldn't let her not read it entirely.

She put her hands on either side of the gap and pulled. The veil parted and the static resolved into a hallway with no ceiling or visible terminus.

"Fine," she said evenly, and stepped through.

The hallway was lined with three-dimensional dioramas. Every scene starred Jacqueline (or perhaps Yakuza since Jacqueline could not recall anything here from her own memory) frozen in the act of this or that esoteric task: Hotwiring a car. Running through a swamp with a monolithic white fortress behind her. Sitting cross-legged in front of a child in a bare room, surrounded by sheaves of paper.

She'd tried to summon Yakuza directly to herself, and she'd gotten this instead. Why was Yakuza showing her this? And what was it she'd said? *See you at home.*

She'd reached the end of memory lane. Not even enough room for an echo. A dead end. She tried to think. *Where did Yakuza think of as her home?* Of all the murder scenes Jacqueline had been audience to, none had an air of familiarity for the killer. Perhaps that was because she treated the whole world as if it was hers.

Jacqueline put a hand on the wall. Glass. With only a ghostly reflection of her fingertips to let her know it was real.

...*Real?* Nothing here was real. Time to stop thinking in terms of what would make for a logical motive and time to start using free association. What about Yakuza stuck out in her memory? Well, out of all her kills, she'd only left two bodies where they could be found. Both killed with purpose, left with purpose—a message, or a stratagem.

There was the butchery, Fong's final resting place. Perhaps Nunogawa's too. But their place was a ruin, now. And Yakuza had never had any attachment to it beyond laying a trap for Jacqueline there. She felt a tug at her subconscious.

Means to an end, said the memory of Yakuza.

Yaqui's boyfriend Jimmy. The second and most personal of the kills for which evidence presumably remained somewhere. Closer, but again, no attachment to it except as a set piece for her lurid puppet show. *Think!* What was it Yakuza actually wanted? The one thing her ravenous id had yet to deliver to her on a silver platter?

There was a noise, a real one that reached Jacqueline's ears. Creaking metal. Cracking ice floes. Wind rushing through a subterranean cave. She looked down. Reality changed again. The floor was turning silver. Hoist by her own metaphor. More ordinary noises now, but no less disturbing. Bodies shuffling. A hand slapped into view from within one of the dioramas.

Oversized. The imaginary snapshot of Jacqueline or whomever hotwiring the car had been a close-up shot from the waist up. The legless torso was joined by several other doppelgängers as it crawled toward her. They advanced slowly, not entirely in control of all their limbs at once. Their eyes and mouths were open, hollow. Jacqueline could see their interiors well-lit. Empty shells of skin.

It's you, baby.

A voice inside her head. Not hers but recognizable at last. Jacqueline couldn't focus on a solution to her situation. Looking at these things was mind-numbing, paralyzing. Viscerally terrifying. Like magnets they repelled her, but drew her gaze in. She couldn't imagine them away. Her control over the dreamscape was slipping. Behind the dolls, black roots and gnarled branches were breaking through the air, choking her escape. Jacqueline turned around, faced her dead end. An empty void. The only part of the dream that was still really hers. She didn't want to be here. She'd rather be out there in space. She felt cold fingertips on the back of her neck.

The wall vanished and she pitched forward into the abyss. No air. No sensation. Just an intense velocity. She did a slow, graceful barrel roll. The hallway had diminished into a tiny white square. And then nothing. No more up and down. She offered a silent thank you that this world didn't have any nausea or vertigo. It was almost pleasant here. Now that she'd gotten used to it. She could stay here forever, she realized.

...She realized she could stay here forever. The full context hit her all at once. This was Yakuza's final test. She'd put her hand on the head of the queen, left it where it was and passed the turn. A winning move if Jacqueline decided not to play. She could stay here in eternal stalemate, or she could go...

"Home," Jacqueline said to the void.

A red star flamed to life in the distance. She knew it was her building before she could even see it clearly. The lattice of story convention stretched out before her. Its veins and pathways gently pulsing with its lifeblood: time. She followed them home. The apartment complex loomed large in her vision. Moving at light speed. No way to gauge her velocity until now. Going to crash into it. Break every bone in her body.

"Good. Do it. I dare you," she said.

Rationality made Jacqueline avoid deadly situations, but she had no innate fear of death. Not anymore. She wasn't anywhere rational. Aesthetically, the image of her body meteor-striking the apartment asteroid and shattering it was weirdly appealing.

Almost as if Yakuza could sense Jacqueline's morbid fantasy, she felt hundreds of little hands grip her arms and tug. Her descent slowed dramatically as if she had an orbital drag chute. She didn't want to look behind her and see what it might be made of. She touched down on the front stoop. Nothing beyond it. Sidewalk crumbling away into nullity. Despite her circumstances, Jacqueline couldn't help but feel comforted by the sight of her home. Perhaps because she associated it with safety in her mind. She felt almost...

Happy.

"I knew you wouldn't kill me."

She looked up at the tower. Her fortress. "There's an enemy at the gates," she said, and opened the door.

The sight that greeted her was dizzying. Literally, a möbius conveyor belt nightmare of intersecting stairs and impossible angles. *I might not kill you, but you might kill you.* She could hear the smile. She watched the stairs go by and crush each other somewhere in the middle distance. She chewed her lip. There was no way Jacqueline could fit through there...but something that wasn't Jacqueline could.

"I'm dreaming. I have to remember I'm dreaming."

She looked down at her totem. The tattoo she'd made was reassuring, despite how odd its implication was for her. She walked forward. There was no space to fit through the maelstrom of stairways as a person. But if she forgot she was a person for a little while and just focused on fitting through every available opening, she'd be fine. She didn't so much duck or dodge as simply occupy every space the rolling crushing stairs weren't. She began to feel light-headed. *Head.* No room above her shoulders for that with...

Shoulders.

She blinked. Tried to will herself away. Dizziness made her look down. *Last mistake.* She read her arm, and its comfort was short lived. A pair of parallel blocks were becoming contiguous again. Caught her just below the elbow there. More crushing, smashing surfaces on the way. Impossible to focus on not being there with the pain coming from her arm. Tighter. Bones popping. *Let go.*

"No," she grunted.

That's fine. Let go or die. Be human and die, or don't. With a cry of pain, Jacqueline ripped free of her pulverized arm and went blind.

If she didn't exist, no eyes to see. A few seconds passed. No noise. Just pain. Pain reminded her she was alive. She commanded her eyes to open. She was in a hallway. Whirring grinding stone far behind her. *No right arm.* Pool of blood and *no right arm.* No right arm, *no right arm.* She clutched at the stump with her left hand. Hand. Something she had to remember. Throbbing pain made it too hard to think. *Blood loss.* Another deeply concerning phrase. Almost as bad as no right arm. She stared into the palm of her left hand. Reflection in the tiny ravine of blood there. Couldn't remember what color her eyes were. Everything was black in the red mirror. Needed to fix this. She remembered she could fix this.

"Oh god," she heaved. *Going into shock.*

"Just make my hand like my other hand."

She looked from her left hand to her left hand to to her left hand. Skin nice and smooth. Did she always have two of those? She got up. She had to keep going. She knew there was something she was forgetting, but the one thing she remembered was that she had to keep moving. Stumbling around the corner, she came across a gap. She could see the other side, but not the bottom. No way she could jump it. But with longer limbs, or perhaps wings?

Her upper back itched.

Yaqui didn't know how long she'd been running. Years, perhaps. This forest was endless. Occasionally she'd come across snatches of familiarity made all the more terrifying by their context. A corner of a car jutting one tire above the black earth, headlight still flickering. An oil painting of a white dress hanging from a tree branch. A pyramid of mason jars, filled with god knew what. She hadn't eaten, hadn't slept in forever. But she couldn't stop. It might catch her.

She'd only caught rare glimpses of the beast. No two were identical, but she was certain the same monster had been tailing her on and off since she got here. When had she got here? The last thing she remembered was sitting alone in her cell and then...nothing. She couldn't even remember when she'd started running. No way to gauge distance. Terrain was variable. Every tree was different. She didn't see the root jutting out of the ground even after she hit it going full tilt. She smashed into the dirt face-first, her ankle screaming. Couldn't black out. *Not now.* She heard rustling in the branches as she scrambled to stand. A preliminary test of her ankle's ability to hold weight was a dismal failure.

It had sensed weakness. Or perhaps it had been playing with her this entire time.

"No, no. No no no," said Yaqui as she frantically tried

to drag her useless leg along. The earth shook as it landed behind her. She didn't dare look. Fucking ecstatic to keep playing its game if that meant she got to live a little longer.

"I found you," they said. Their voice was deep and sonorous. They padded closer. *Four legs. Four legs but it talks.* "Please turn around. I'd like to see your face. It's been so long."

Yaqui was too frightened to speak. Kept limping. A gust of air. They had wings. Stretching them.

"I don't want to hurt you."

Lying. More games. Please don't let it end like this. I don't wanna be eaten alive. She covered her head with her hands. Rolled into a ball. *Maybe it'll bat me around first.*

"Please—" Their claws threshed the underbrush. "—I need you...to remember," they said. They spoke slowly, choosing each word with care.

Yaqui finally regained her ability to talk. "Remember what?" She stammered between her teeth, "I'll remember whatever the fuck you want. I'll reminisce, I'll wax nostalgic. Just please don't fucking eat me," she shouted through cold sweat and hot tears. She felt something heavy on her right shoulder, and she was flipped over onto her back. A massive paw held her there.

"No. I need you. So that I can remember," said the sphinx. Their eyes were blue pinpricks of light in a pair of shadowy eye sockets. Their countenance was skeletal, their features drawn. The two eyes, like distant stars, held Yaqui in their gravitational pull. Frozen. Their skin was a dark and charnel grey. Perfect camouflage for this place. They didn't actually have fur. Not a traditional sphinx then. Didn't have a pharaoh's headdress either. What she'd thought were horns swiveled and twitched slightly. *Antennae?* They flexed their black feathered wings, sheltered the two of them. Stretched their neck forward to examine her. *Were those gills?*

"You're hurt," they said softly.

Stepped back. Yaqui barely moved. Their teeth were sharp as needles. "I can fix you."

Yaqui slowly propped herself up on her elbows. "How?" she said cautiously.

"I've fixed myself many times," said the sphinx, "Eventually, I had the kind of body that didn't require fixing."

Something clicked. "Hey, no. Get the FUCK away from me," she yelped. Tried to scrabble backwards with one good leg. "I don't wanna look like you!"

A single claw popped out of one of their digits and pinned Yaqui by the ankle. The pain was excruciating. She immediately stopped moving.

"Not to worry. I don't think we'll have time for that," they said and depressed their claw gently. There was a soft click, and the pain disappeared. Yaqui's breathing slowed as the sphinx withdrew their claw and regarded her critically. Neither moved for a moment.

"...What's wrong with the way I look?" The sphinx asked almost reproachfully.

"I—what?" Yaqui quavered, "You're fucking horrifying are you kidding me?" she said before she could stop herself.

If the sphinx was even capable of displaying emotion, their death's head visage betrayed nothing.

"Sorry. I sometimes forget there are contexts other than this one."

They sighed.

"It's no good. I thought finally laying eyes on you might bring me back to myself, but there's nothing there for me anymore."

Yaqui thought about the sphinx's comment about obtaining the body they had over time.

"Did...did someone do this to you?" she said.

The sphinx ruffled their feathers and sat back on their haunches.

"In a manner of speaking."

They looked up at the Stygian canopy.

"Yes, I looked a lot more like you than me once. Human. And while no evil witch cursed me...the one who created this place is responsible, in a way."

The sphinx hunched their shoulders.

"I thought I was playing a game with her where the goal was to survive. So I traded away more and more of myself for traits that would ensure my survival in this world, never stopping to think exactly what that meant."

"So, who are you now then?" asked Yaqui.

"Think of me...as your imaginary friend. Or perhaps a spirit animal, if that strikes your fancy. I've been here for a very, very, very long time."

Yaqui swallowed. "Does that mean...you don't know a way out of here?"

The sphinx curled their tail, a prehensile spinal column in ashen black.

"It means that I do, but only you can go through it."

"For real?" said Yaqui as she climbed to her feet. This changed everything. "You probably know everything there is to know about this place. How long have you been here?"

Their eyes flickered. "Centuries," they said gravely.

Yaqui's eyes widened. She had no idea how long she'd been here. Her memories were so confused in this place. Months? Years?

"I sense your disquiet. You're concerned you've been here too long. That if you stay too much longer you'll go mad. End up like me, even."

No sense lying. Yaqui nodded, thin-lipped.

"You needn't worry. Time is relative here. Distorted to such a degree that it moves independently of each of its viewers. While I've been searching for you for centuries, you've probably only been running for about ten years."

"Ten—" Yaqui stumbled. She put a hand to her forehead and sat down heavily. The sphinx didn't seem to notice her turmoil.

"Whereas outside, no time may have passed at all," they mused. Their tail was rippling happily as if a current were running through it.

"That's what gives me hope. Keeps me going. Despite all the mistakes I made, there's still time to set it all right." They looked down at her. "For you," they added.

"How?" said Yaqui, looking up forlornly. "How would that even work?"

The sphinx approximated a shrug. "It helps...if you picture time not as a stream we're wading in, but a ball we're looking at. Imagine we're on the moon, looking at the earth. And there's a large crosshair you can move around it. The line going up and down is Time, and the line going side to side is Place, " They said almost kindly, "Wherever those two lines intersect is where you end up. Our time is separate from the real world because we're on our own little ball."

"Wow," said Yaqui, "Is that really how it works?"

Somehow, the sphinx managed to look guilty. "...It helps, if you think of it that way," they said, "It helps you especially," the sphinx added hopefully, "Because you're the one who's going to be doing the moonjump."

"Me?" Yaqui fretted, "You're the one with wings!"

The sphinx shook their head. "I can't make the leap in logic anymore. This body is too improbable. I've tried to...influence the past once or twice, with...mixed results."

Yaqui suddenly thought back to the first terrible night all this had started. She thought back to the blue stars in the sky then, and how much they looked like the eyes of the sphinx. She kept her mouth shut.

The sphinx raised a claw, and tore a hole in the air. "I can appear in dreams in the past, but the physicality of my presence is, how did you put it? Fucking horrifying?"

Yaqui cleared her throat and looked away.

"Don't be sorry. I inspire fear. It's the nature of the beast."

It was difficult to tell when they were smiling.

"Here. You can make it up to me if you really feel the need to."

They pulled the tear in space down to Yaqui's eye level as easily as one might part some blinds.

"Hop in."

Yaqui eyed the flurry of static beyond as best she

could. It was an eye-watering endeavor.

"Don't be afraid. It's the easiest thing in the world. Once you're immersed, it'll be almost instinctive. Just concentrate on the proper imagery, let it guide you. We're looking for a young woman named Jacqueline. She looks a lot like you."

The wind picked up, clearing away the mist. The sphinx bristled, raising their hackles. Warning spots of bioluminescence flared briefly along their ribcage. Yaqui rubbed her arm, shuffled her feet. Unease radiated from the portal.

"I don't know if I—"

A heavy paw on her upper back.

"I don't mean to rush you," said the sphinx as gently as possible. Yaqui dug her heels in, protested. The sphinx was having none of it. "But we're out of time."

They leaned in, their face half again as large as hers and far too close. "We're going to die. We're going to die here if you don't do exactly as I say. Do you understand?"

Yaqui shook her head, jingling. The stress was getting to her. "I don't understand anything. This is all insane. I just met you and now I'm supposed to jump through some random hole?"

"Not random. Purposeful. Nothing happens here without a reason. Do you hear the wind? It's not blowing for nothing. She's closing in on us."

"Who's she?" asked Yaqui.

"Who brought you here?" asked the sphinx rhetorically, "What living terror took your love away from you?"

"I...I don't know. Everyone thinks it's me, I..."

"It was her!" the sphinx intoned with enough bass to rattle Yaqui back a step.

"She's here because of you. The same reason I'm here. You gave her life and now she can't do anything but take it from others. Do you remember?"

"No-"

Yaqui cried out and then stood stock still at a sudden movement from the sphinx. They had caught her nose chain with a single deadly claw.

"Where did you get this? Can you recall?" They asked pointedly. Yaqui didn't even get to answer, as if the sphinx could sense her fond memory of the evening she'd spent with Jimmy at the piercing parlor. Pink sunset and blue neon evaporated at the sphinx's voice.

"Not what I meant. You didn't come here with this. Can you even remember putting it on?"

Yaqui stared at nothing as the sphinx gently detached the chain from either end of her face.

"This is a dream. Dreams are made of memories. You can guide yourself through them with a totem. Familiarity. A lifeline. Something to ground you."

They whirled the chain overhead and it lengthened, thickened. A mighty chain fit for an anchor now. The sphinx tied it around Yaqui's waist. Daintily, as if dressing a doll. They gripped the other end tightly in their talons. It floated weightless between the two of them. "Here. I can't do too much to local reality without bringing her down on top of us, but this should keep you safe. Tug on the chain if you're in trouble, and I'll pull you free."

Yaqui felt the chain between all of her fingers. "What am I supposed to do?" Yaqui asked numbly.

The sphinx rested a free paw on her shoulder. "Find the person I told you about. Bring her here. Focus on thinking about her, and it'll be easy. Stray...and before too long we'll be discovered."

"By who?" She asked, "I don't get it. If I'm dreaming, there's no real danger, right? I can just imagine it away."

"Yes, you're dreaming," said the sphinx, "But I never said it was your dream."

The sphinx bowled her off her feet and into the breach.

Instinctively, Yaqui thought *home*. She regretted it just as quickly, but her guilt was tempered with defiance. She wanted to see home, why not try to escape this way?

The world loaded in before Yaqui did, in fact she couldn't see herself at all. What she could see distressed her, but she couldn't look away. There was a little girl, strapped to a chair, with a silvery helmet covering her eyes. In front of her, was another little girl. The girl standing free looked nervous. The one in the chair looked drugged, jaw slack. There were other figures, but for some reason, Yaqui couldn't make out their features. *Is this...a memory? Maybe I never saw their faces.*

A voice said "begin," and Yaqui felt an icy spear of pain between the lobes of her brain. The children looked like they felt it too. The one in the chair seized and shook. The one standing alone collapsed as if there'd been earthquake. Clutched her head and screamed. The tall figures ringing the room didn't appear to take notice. One of them held a device like a remote with a screen on it into the circle of light in the center of the room.

"EMF zero," he said.

The figures walked forward and began to unstrap the girl from the chair.

"This should shut Guzman up. Weirdly sentimental for a backer."

"If a pet for charity appearances keeps the blank checks coming, he can have her."

They didn't take any notice of the one who fell. In fact, they walked through her. She stood shakily, looked around in fear, and fled. The room collapsed as she phased through a wall. There was only noise and void again.

Yaqui was floating up, beneath the waves. Spread-eagled. She wasn't breathing, but she didn't need to. She couldn't feel much of anything, except anger. Bitter on her tongue. These visions were confusing, and made her feel sick without knowing why. Like there was a thorn stuck in her brain, blocking the flow of blood to a clot of information.

She was the one dreaming. Why couldn't she dream about what she wanted? Why couldn't she dream about waking up? Jimmy's face flashed before her eyes, and she felt an intense buoyancy. The landscape above her changed. It had land for a start. She could see raindrops hitting the street from below, as if it were glass with turn lanes painted on. A tableau materialized. A body prone. Reminded her of the painting of God and David that Nat had dragged them all to see. More people rendering in. Mid-stride. As the skybox fast approached, Yaqui realized too late when and where she'd ended up. Temple Street. The night it had all started to go downhill. She was back in her body, malfunctioning. Smells and sounds hit her all at once, confusing each other. The taste of harsh yellow light and the buzz of stomach acid. An old man crouched by her side. He held a small flashlight aloft. Shone it in her eyes. First one, then the other. His mouth was moving, but she couldn't hear any words. Here came Jimmy, just what she'd wished for. Another mute specter. Cold comfort. Monkey's paw. She had to salvage this.

"Jacqueline," she said.

"What?" Mouthed both of the phantoms. She said the name again. Over and over. Tried to change the narrative. But it was too late. This wasn't a dream anymore. It was a memory. What had the sphinx said? Tug on the chain, and she'd be pulled to safety. She looked down at her stomach. She was wearing her favorite heavy leather jacket. Burnt to scraps in the real world. Evidence. Soaked through with rain here in the past. Felt each drop hit her out of sync with what she was seeing. And no chain. Her ears popped, and she was holding Jimmy again. Home. Her room. His last moments already stolen from her. Her heartbeat echoed in her ears, but her chest was hollow. Empty. Faster. Faster. No chain.

A tiny wind chime sounded. She narrowed her eyes. Jimmy's sightless gaze vying for her attention but in between then and there, was the chain. Hanging, as she remembered it, from her face. She needed to grab it, but to do that she'd have to let go of Jimmy. Her arms wouldn't move, and she realized this was because part of her didn't want to. She'd been buried alive in her own body. She was part of the memory now, and the urge to stay was crawling up her arms. Inch by inch. Completely numb, she grit her teeth, lifted her hand. Deadlifting a planet. Let him slip, fall to the floor.

"I'm sorry," she said, and grabbed the chain.

Its jingle was so loud, it shattered her eardrums. Everything slid away, turned to dust. Tore at her. Sandstorm blasted her bones clean. Reduced her to nothing. Nothing here was her. She had to leave it all behind. Even the thoughts she was—

Yaqui gasped for air on the forest floor. Her stomach heaved, and she coughed twice before a gallon of saltwater passed her lips. Three ragged bloody breaths as the last of it left her lungs.

She looked up at the sphinx. No change in their expression. Implacable and passive as ever.

"What did you see?" They asked.

"I'm fine, thanks for asking," said Yaqui as she tried to get rid of her sea legs.

"I know you're fine. If you'd died, you wouldn't be here. I can sense that you're shaken, but unharmed. If it happens in my forest, I know the exact nature of it. If I ask a question, you can assume it is because I don't know the answer. This will be a rare occurrence."

They drew closer, and helped pull Yaqui the rest of the way to her feet using the chain.

"I almost drowned," Yaqui snapped,

"Is that why you've got gills?"

The sphinx did not appear to take offense. Then again, their features never appeared to move.

"Partly. That, and the implausibility of this form allows me to move freely through any memory. There's nowhere I fit. I just have to be careful not to visit anywhere after the point in time where I've figured it all out. Recursion and desperation are dangerous bedfellows for time travelers."

They leaned in, eye to eye. Yaqui found she was less afraid of the sphinx now that she'd faced an existential death in the flesh. The sphinx's tone grew hungry. "Did you find her? Did you find the woman?"

Yaqui blanched. She tried to stutter out an "I." Before she could speak, the truth leapt between them in a flash of guilt. The sphinx had no trouble reading her.

The sphinx failed to suppress a growl from deep within their chest. It had the same disruptive effect as someone sticking their finger in your mouth. Yaqui's flight reflex leapt her back a step in spite of herself. The sphinx reared up, but instead of attacking, they put their face in their paws. They began to weep. Anguish poked through their voice like dune-buried ruins.

"I'm sorry. I've failed you. I've run out of opportunities. My timeline is an ouroboros. We're doomed. I'm sorry, I'm sorry, I'm sorry, I'm..." They sobbed gently.

Yaqui hesitantly put her hand out. Bit her lip, and rested it on the sphinx's elbow. "No. I'm sorry. I didn't know what I was doing. I acted selfish, tried to escape on my own."

The sphinx sat back down. Breathed deeply. "I won't lie. I am disappointed, but I have to be forgiving. There's no time for anything else."

Yaqui turned. Movement in the corner of her eye. A tidal wave of red light, thick and syrupy. Washing through the woods toward them.

"What is that?" She cried.

"The sun is rising," said the sphinx blankly.

"Is that bad?" Yaqui asked uncertainly.

"Do I look like I belong in sunlight?" The sphinx asked fatalistically. "She's found us."

"Then, we gotta get out of here, right?" She said, "Is there anywhere we can go?"

The sphinx looked at her, unreadable. "There's one place left, but it will be risky."

They turned and padded over to a tree in the middle distance.

"This way, Yaqui."

Yaqui followed, but jumped back a little bit when the

sphinx pushed the tree sideways with one mighty paw. Uprooted. She watched in silence as the sphinx dug at the earth beneath the roots with the speed of a terrier and the strength of a tractor. As they unearthed another eerie white light like the one Yaqui had just escaped from, she found her voice.

"How do you know my name?"

The sphinx looked up and then back down quickly. "I know about everything that happens in my forest," they said.

Yaqui looked over her shoulder at more movement. The sun was indeed rising. A hateful red eye. In the distance, she could see the black forest being terraformed into gleaming white towers and fortresses. Beautiful, but terrifying. She turned back.

"You said you've been here a long time...do you still remember your name?"

The digging slowed, and Yaqui noticed the sphinx doing something they hadn't before. Breathing.

"...no," lied Jacqueline. She pulled the chain taut. "It's ready for you."

Yaqui stepped into the hole—

—and fell flat on her face in the hallway below. There was an audible gasp to Yaqui's right, so she began the task of painfully climbing to her feet. She met the gaze of the other woman crouched against the bare wall on her way up. She was wearing some kinda old suit, minus the jacket.

"...It's you," they both said in the same breathless moment.

"I can't believe that worked," Yaqui said to herself.

"I've got so much to tell you," Jacqueline said. She tried to sit up, but fell back with a groan of pain.

"You're hurt," Yaqui said with concern as she moved closer.

"I fell," said Jacqueline, pointing upwards. Several meters above them was a square of light in the dark.

Yaqui looked around, and her eyes were naturally drawn to the left, following her ears. A great roiling tesseract of stairs and doorways was eating itself into noise. *No going back that way,* Yaqui thought. "Where did you...come from?" she asked.

"Another hallway, like this one. Maybe the same one," Jacqueline replied. She pointed forward, and Yaqui realized her new friend had two left hands. *Still not the weirdest thing I've seen.* Ahead, a chasm loomed, the same size as the one above them. "I have to keep trying, until I get it right," Jacqueline said.

Yaqui shook her head, "No you don't. Hey, look at me." She tugged Jacqueline's chin back toward her. "If you're trying to escape, I'm here to help." She held up an arm's length of chain. "I've got a lifeline, see? And a friend on the other end who really wants to meet you."

Jacqueline shook her head. "I'm not going anywhere, not like this. My knee's been dislocated."

Yaqui's hands hovered over Jacqueline's leg uncertainly. The other woman was sweating.

"I don't know how to fix that. Um, sorry."

Jacqueline swallowed. "I do. I just wasn't looking forward to it. Grateful for the extra pair of hands, though."

She gestured for Yaqui to move into position by her ankle. She placed both hands underneath her own thigh and pulled it towards her chest. Grit her teeth. Braced her back against the wall. She took a deep breath.

"Do you have anything I can bite down on?"

Yaqui hesitated for a moment, before offering her arm.

Jacqueline cocked an eyebrow. "That's...very sentimental of you. And more than a little silly. We don't need two injuries to deal with. Just, grasp the patella and gently move it back to the center."

Yaqui flushed slightly, but sat back. She gently placed her hand on Jacqueline's knee and—

Jacqueline winced, hissed through her teeth and Yaqui immediately pulled away. Tried to apologize.

"It's okay. You can try more than once, so long as

you go slowly. Don't force it," Jaqueline said.

Yaqui steeled herself and nodded. Jacqueline closed her eyes, and there was a soft click. The pain was sharp, jagged, but swallowed almost immediately by relief endorphins. Like a reef under a wave. She felt Yaqui's hand in hers and opened her eyes as she was pulled to her feet.

"Thank you. Now let's get out of here."

Yaqui smiled and held up the chain that trailed from the knot on her hip to a small warp in space.

"Glad to. And my friend'll be glad too. You can call me—"

"—Yaqui. I know," Jacqueline interrupted. "This might sound weird. But I'm really happy to see you. My name's Jacqueline."

Her last word rattled and reverberated the chain. Jacqueline, now used to the sensation of change in the dream, tried to react in time.

"Watch—!" She managed to say before the chain came alive. Black scales over an endless undulating neck. A serpent's head. A serpent, in fact. It whipped itself from around Yaqui's waist. Spun her about so fast she fell to her knees. Struck Jacqueline in the side. Knocked her to the ground. Yaqui looked up in time to see Jacqueline rising off the ground in the coils of the black snake. She reached for Yaqui in vain as she disappeared into the darkness above.

"NO! NO!"

"NO!" Jacqueline screamed as she was hauled out of the black earth like a corpse. The serpent withdrew into the fog, and she rolled as she hit the ground. Came up right away, rushed forward. Mouth dry with screams. The strange beast that loomed out of the mist did not frighten her. Their chimera tail and alien features did not faze her after all she'd seen. She pounded upon their chest as hard as she could.

"Why! I was so FUCKING CLOSE!"

It was like punching rock. Her knuckles came away bloody.

"Who are you! Who the fuck do you think you are!"

Her breaths were bloody now too.

"I think...you know," said the sphinx.

Jacqueline looked up at their eyes. Into them. Into her own. It was another her. She didn't know how she knew, but suddenly she did. Bit by bit, past details fit together and unlocked the puzzle. Those blue stars, haunting her visions. They'd been staring down at her out of black skies in her dreams. She hadn't pieced it together until now because the only person she never saw in her dreams was her.

"Oh my god," she said brokenly.

The knowledge directly imparted. Like looking in a mirror. She could see the evolutionary path that had twisted this future version of her, like a sordid diagram.

"How did this happen?" she asked, drained of emotion.

The forest was melting around them. The sphinx didn't seem to notice or mind.

"It's good to see you. Though I wish it could be under better circumstances. Do you like what I've done with the place?" they said.

Jacqueline spat expertly, striking the sphinx right between the eyes. They flinched slightly.

"Fuck you," quavered Jacqueline, wide-eyed with rage,

"I was closing in on the first and last lead in this fucked up case, and you ruined everything. Bring her back, now!"

"You've misplaced your priorities. I maintain that's what started us down the path to misplacing my face."

The earth was crumbling away in a ring around them. An island, an asteroid meadow.

Jacqueline balked.

"Don't even try and be funny. Don't say ANYTHING cryptic or engage me with bullshit riddles, just fix the fucking mess you made!"

The sphinx leaned in. "I am. You are. As I said, you've misplaced your priorities. But it's the one thing I never forgot. Survival is the only important thing. Its why, for instance, one of the many adaptations I evolved was a sense of humor. It can help you stay sane when you're running for your life for hundreds of years."

"Hundreds—?" Jacqueline whispered in horror.

"Seven hundreds. But who's counting?"

The sphinx's laugh—HER laugh, was as rough as ever.

Jacqueline shook her head as the atmosphere of mist around their tree-clutched rock began to disperse in earnest.

"You've changed too much, then. You sacrificed an innocent life for nothing. Yaqui was the whole reason I came here!"

"I agree that she's responsible for what happened, but she's no innocent."

"What's that supposed to mean?"

"She created this whole mess. Created the demon who's been hunting us. Dreamed you up and then forgot about you. But she's not important anymore. Only you are."

Insistent. Almost smiling.

They were falling. Drifting down towards the cyclopean cityscape below. The sphinx gestured at the exploded diorama all around them.

"I've failed, but you get another chance. To escape, possibly with your life. I made this forest, and now that you're here I am being unmade. I'm out of moves, but you're not subject to the same biases I am. Yakuza won't be expecting you."

Jacqueline did not bother to conceal her disgust. "Do you honestly think that'll work?"

"Knowing what you know now? You have a much better chance than me. I played to win, but I was playing by Yakuza's rules. Ultimately, she was the House. Banker. Dungeon Master."

The city was settling in around them. Rotting away the trees. Washing the earth down its storm drains. The sphinx was beginning to fade, too. Twinkling yellow street lights visible through it like a blanket of stars.

"You didn't answer my question. How. How am I supposed to beat someone who controls the whole world?" said Jacqueline.

"I don't know. But that's my shortcoming. It doesn't have to be yours. You've got time to escape, think up a new plan. Maybe you'll do it in time this go-round. Who knows?" They Cheshire-grinned.

"Third time's the charm."

Gone.

Alone.

Ahead, a festival of warm yellow phosphorescence called to her. The electric light of civilization. Deception. Exposure. Heat death. A dark alley beckoned behind her. That seemed more her style. But then it would, wouldn't it? Cool and inviting, more importantly it represented an opportunity to run from her demons a bit longer. Continue the cycle.

What did the lights represent, then? Exposure meant death. The end. She could think of no worse fate. She couldn't even picture what might happen if everyone knew everything about her. Death would be preferable.

Death. And what happened when you died in your dreams? A grim smile appeared on her face. She wiped it off, and walked forward. The lights grew brighter as the street tapered to a smaller and smaller point. An optical illusion meant to make it seem as if Yakuza could create more of a city than she actually could. Not a road stretching to the horizon but the corner of a diamond. Funny. What good was controlling a whole world if it wasn't even that big? She pressed against the walls of the diamond. White hot. The lights trying to fry her. Her fingers sunk into the walls of the dream. She couldn't feel them anymore. One last test. The further into the membrane she pushed, the more she realized the less she had of herself. One last bullshit test.

Arms gone. Almost all the way through. What

happened when her brain passed into nothingness? Trick question. Not her real brain. Not her real body. Nothing here was real. Not even her. To be herself again, she had to leave it all behind. She passed through the membrane—

—and into cold rushing wind. The smell of gasoline, the rustling of trees. Planted by the city twenty odd years ago in a misguided attempt to beautify Amigara street. They'd been left to wrack and ruin. Overgrown roots buckling the sidewalk. You'd always trip over at least one if you weren't careful. All of these things, mildly unpleasant on the senses as they were, were real. Inimitable. She followed the cracked and creviced street with her eyes all the way down to a tower almost as wide as it was tall. Her apartment building.

"See you at home."

Still dark. The night-shift commuters were coming home. Outside of the dream world, existentialisms were less distinct. Fear had no taste. She couldn't really feel foreboding in her bones. As she stared at the barred door set deep in the concrete, she didn't sense any inexorable path leading there. The only thing remaining in her mind that felt out of place was the fatal certainty that Yakuza was waiting for her in there. Irrational to think of life like a story, but that's how one would end. She closed her eyes.

No. That was a dream. She'd woken up. She opened her eyes. Same street.

She could turn around and leave, if she wanted. If Pinkerton was to be believed, she'd been missing for several days. He faded to monochrome in her memory. Dead, she reminded herself. They might be looking for him now too. Might be better to arrive with his killer in tow. If that insane circus of a murder scene could even be believed.

Her head throbbed. If she felt anything, it was tired. Her bed was also in that building. Another reason to get closer. To open the door. To go in. Her ears rang from the silence in the dingy lobby. She took the stairs. She didn't trust liminal spaces right now. Especially one as claustrophobic as an elevator. Hot dusty air billowing up through the stairwell. Descending into hell. No proper ventilation. Headache throbbing, getting worse. In the roof of her mouth, and behind her eye. An ice cream headache. *What do you expect to find down there?*

She paused in front of the doorknob. *My bed. My clothes. The trash I haven't taken out yet.*

She opened the door. Exactly as she'd described. The dozens of drawings of faces had barely stirred. The bathroom door was open. Yaqui sat next to Yakuza on her bed. The lights had been left on. Damn, her bill would be a little heavier this month.

"Glad you could make it," said Yakuza, "Though it was certainly entertaining watching you stumble about playing games against yourself. I'm easily bored but not impatient."

Yaqui struggled against the bonds around her wrists and ankles. She'd been gagged. They were both still wearing the same outfits Jacqueline had last seen them in. Now that they were all together, Jacqueline wasn't sure how anyone could confuse the three of them. Same face, sure, but they all wore it differently. Yaqui's occluded hazel eyes were wide with fear, Jacqueline's were tired and bloodshot, and Yakuza's were completely black now. Taking in everything. She was stroking Yaqui's unwashed black hair. Her own flowed like it was underwater.

Jacqueline looked at the two of them for a moment and then went in the bathroom to wash her face. *Not real.*

Yakuza stepped out from behind the shower curtain. "Hey what the fuck," she said.

Jacqueline ignored her. The water was really nice and cool on her face. She felt a gun barrel against her temple. A hand turned the water off.

"I hate that you're making me do this." She guided Jacqueline's head back up with the gun. Gestured at it.

Clara's .38 special.

"I mean, look at this stupid fucking thing."

Yakuza put it to her own head and pulled the trigger three times. In the tiny interior of the bathroom, the shots were magnified tenfold. Ringing in Jacqueline's ears. Shortness of breath. Headache exploding. A flash of cold. Fong and Nunogawa in their icy tomb there for one moment. Plaster cracked around three impacts. Blood dripped between Yakuza's teeth.

"So disappointing." She waved the pistol around as if she hadn't just shot herself three times.

"I mean, in so many ways you're way more advanced than me. You can reflect light! I only started doing that recently."

She stuck the gun in Jacqueline's ribs. Forced her back out of the room. "And yet a toy like this still holds power over you. Even though I just demonstrated what little effect it has on us."

Yaqui screamed against her gag when she saw Yakuza's ruined skull. Blood was dripping out of her nose and eyes now too. Didn't seem to bother her, or impair her speech.

"You've surrounded yourself with the trappings of a human. Weak and feeble. But I know the truth. You're just like me. We belong together."

Jacqueline shook her head. *Nothing like you. I'm not some shark toothed monster.*

An icy tear of pain forced its way out of her left eye. Yakuza spoke as if answering.

"You never smile. How do you know what your teeth look like?"

She gently forced the gun into Jacqueline's hands. Folded her fingers over it like a gift.

"Now, if you're done hamstringing yourself, why don't we get to why I brought you here in the first place?"

"What are you talking about?" said Jacqueline, reeling. Trying to flex the muscle in her brain that would allow her to realize this was all a dream. Yaqui couldn't take her eyes off the gun.

"You've built me up as this grand antagonist, but the truth is I'm your greatest friend. You spent so long trapped in your head, instinctively running from me, even trapping yourself, hurting yourself to keep me from you...without really knowing why. I'm here to show you."

Jacqueline swallowed. "This is—this doesn't make any sense. This is a nightmare, it—"

Yakuza slapped her. Hand like brickwork. "Focus! Use that big brain of yours. Think back. You can see the past clearly. Your perfect memory is the result of existing in all times and places at once. A quality humans lack."

Jacqueline gripped the gun, pointed it at Yakuza like it was going to do something.

"You're just trying to confuse me."

"No, I'm trying to enlighten you. Think. Back. All those times you were trapped in your own mind, who got you out? What kept you going!"

Yakuza nodded as real memories of imagined events filled Jacqueline's head. The face in the window. The stars in the void.

"Yes...subconsciously, you'd rather be a solipsist. But I want you out here. Tasting what life has to offer. That's why I chase you. Drive you on. Play the villain in your absurd story. You need this."

Jacqueline's memory wasn't entirely complicit, though. It offered a counterpoint. "You kill people," said Jacqueline, horrified that she felt the need to say it like she was arguing a point,

"You expect me to believe all of that was out of some kind of infatuation with me? Like that's what I'd want? No. YOU want to kill people. Is that what you'd call 'tasting what life has to offer?'" she said, disgusted.

"No," purred Yakuza, "I already know what lives taste like. I wanted YOU to taste them."

Jacqueline's eyes widened. Realizations flying between her and Yakuza without words. The murders. The bodies. The butchery. Bone marrow. Locally sourced protein. She didn't have to wonder how deep this conspiracy went anymore. It had all been laid out for her. Like a banquet. She felt violently sick.

"You—" She staggered back, tried to wave Yakuza off with the gun.

"Shh shh shh…" Caught her wrist like a vise. Forced the barrel towards Yaqui, who squirmed to get away.

"I worked really hard for this," said Yakuza, "For us. You didn't make it easy. Really hard to sneak that stuff into your diet. Particular that you are. But I had to try. So that you could understand how important this is. So you could take the next step. So you could be like me, be free. Once you learn how to taste memory in blood like I do, make dreams real like I do, there'll be no stopping us."

She thumbed back the hammer for her. "You wanted answers. You wanted truth. The nature of life is transactional. If you stick your hand in the fire, you get to be burned. Isn't life wonderful?"

Jacqueline dug her heels in, tried to force the gun away. "What…are you? Why are you doing this!"

Yakuza could not be moved. "You need to be ready. Ready for the taste of life and what it can give you. This will be the most important meal of the day. The first one for the rest of your life. As for your other question…"

She swiveled Jacqueline like a weathervane. Held her in a tango embrace. "We were imaginary friends, you and I. A stupid little girl with a funny brain and a power she didn't understand dreamed us up. No clay required. Divinely conceived from drawing board to storefront."

She nodded the gun at Yaqui as Jacqueline continued to struggle.

"Golems with no words. But now it's time to kill our god. Be truly free."

Yaqui's eyes were darting between the two of them.

"Do it!" Said Yakuza gleefully. "Kill your mother!"

Jacqueline grit her teeth. "No!" She shouted.

Her shout echoed to the very core of her being. Empty. A line of code searching for contradictions. Finding none. Yakuza heard it too. She pulled away, startled. Simply stared into Jacqueline's eyes.

"...you really won't, will you?" She said almost incredulously. Tinge of sadness. Doused in naked sincerity. Jacqueline didn't care.

"Of COURSE I won't! Fuck you! There is no universe where I'd ever consider something so cluelessly insane!"

"I honestly thought I could change your mind," said Yakuza, eyes stunned. "Thought I could steer us away from the end of the story I knew was coming." Her jaw set.

"But that's fine. I know this story too. It's an old one. The oldest one. It's the first one I learned. How to deal with a threat."

She raised her hands, clutched the air. Her corona of light intensified. Inside, colors brighter than real life ever could be. More real than reality. Outside, everything washed out. Weak as wet tissue paper. Mutable.

The foundations cracked. The walls split. Jacqueline hurriedly stepped to the right as the ground between her feet suddenly became two widening cliffs. Her drawings kicked up in a maelstrom and then fell away as the walls crumbled.

Into the sea. They were on three spires over the abyss. Yaqui was still on the bed. From the way her eyes were glued downward at the sheer drop, Jacqueline could guess what she was seeing was at least somewhat real.

"You like that? You were so concerned with what reality could offer you, you never stopped to think what you could offer it," Yakuza gestured at the sea,

"I may not understand your fascination with sleep and oxygen, but I bet you never thought you could bring your dreams to life. Make your own reality, make reality your own!"

"I don't want to," Jacqueline called back over the howl of the wind. It tore at the rock of her spire, turning it bit by bit into dust.

"Well too bad. Here I am! You're the kind of person who cries and says 'I never asked to be born.' Well I did!

I've wanted this, to exist, since my first moment of I AM. But you, you've squandered your gifts!" Yakuza said as if the wind weren't there.

"And once I'm through with you, we'll see how reality handles what I can do to it without holding back."

The gale was not content with eroding Jacqueline's perch. It wanted to knock her off her feet, sweep her away. She looked into the sky. Swirling pinks and yellows. Sunset. She could fly, if she wanted to. Let the wind carry her. From there, she could take the fight to...

No. Look at the sky again. The sea mirroring it. No, not a mirror. One solid mass. All one abyss. If she flew, fought here, it would be a game where Yakuza dealt all the hands. If there was one thing she'd learned from the sphinx, it was that the only winning move was not to play.

She closed her eyes. Surrounded herself with four walls. Clicked the floor and ceiling into place. The wind's howl turned into a compressed shriek, and then vanished. Jacqueline opened her eyes, and tackled Yakuza to the floor of her apartment. Just as she'd left it. They rolled around, kicking up her drawings. A silent gladiatorial audience. Yakuza was incredibly strong, but only where it counted. Her punches were deadly, cracking the floor with each miss. However, her disregard for everything human—the way they fought, the science, the dance of it was Jacqueline's advantage. Yakuza had never used her hands to defend herself, only to kill. A fact made clear when the well-trained Jacqueline caught her in an arm bar.

She locked both fists around it and leaned back, until she felt bone creak.

"You have the right...to remain...Silent!" she crowed.

No more nonsense. Simple. Clean. Disregard everything before this one moment. Nothing else mattered. She'd won. The murderer in manacles, behind bars, before a judge, strapped to a chair. Dead. Gone!

Yakuza was laughing. Jacqueline looked down, swimming in endorphins. Drowning.

"What's so funny, punk?" She grunted through

gritted teeth.

"You!" guffawed Yakuza. She turned her head, and Jacqueline realized she was still talking to a corpse. Fighting a corpse. No matter. No fear. They'd just dissect her in a lab somewhere. A fitting end.

"We've already established that I don't respond to physical stimuli," said Yakuza. Her elbow cracked. Bent the wrong way.

Jacqueline let go and scrabbled back in spite of herself.

"Even in your most daring fantasy, you can't hurt me. But that's not the funny part." She stood and gestured bonelessly at the apartment. "It's that this was the best you could do. This hovel. These stains. Those piles of garbage. You could have been anyone, anything. And you chose this. And, and! You were so quick to reestablish control, you forgot a rather crucial detail."

She pointed, and there was no one on the bed.

"Where did she go?" Yakuza laughed,

"Why was there no room for her in your fantasy?"

Jacqueline blanched, and bolted for the door. *Not a fantasy. Real. This is real,* she told herself.

"Oh don't make that face. Of course it's a fantasy. You couldn't even touch me otherwise. Let alone arrest me."

She dissolved the last word into laughter. Tears in her eyes. Red.

The door swung open. The void. Nothing out there.

"Can't believe I was worried about how you felt toward her. Clearly you want her out of the picture. Acting like the big goddamn hero when really you couldn't be happier stealing her life. See why it's so funny now? This was the best you could do!"

Not quite willing to believe she'd actually fucked up this badly, Jacqueline still had to commit to the delusion so she could mold it. Change it. A pinprick of light became a body. Washed closer on the tide of darkness. Jacqueline pulled Yaqui through the door. Sodden. Not breathing. This was still her fantasy. It had to be, so that she could know the specifics of CPR. A well-trained supercop here, not some desk jockey with abandonment issues.

She pinched Yaqui's nose shut and began the cycle of chest compression and breathing into her mouth.

Focusing on reviving Yaqui broke her concentration on the room. The faces in her drawings became indistinct, grotesque, alien. Yakuza looked around at the pixelating scenery. As Jacqueline's confidence wavered, the walls began to melt.

"And it's that easy," Yakuza remarked as Yaqui coughed and spluttered her way back to life. Jacqueline looked up as the atmosphere changed. Yakuza had vanished, but her presence remained, coagulating the air. Pressure bearing down on her. Bottom of the ocean. Outside her rapidly shrinking island of sanity, something moved. Something massive. Great waves of dread washed over her as its wake drew closer. A great leviathan, a benthic mermaid. With a tail that could swat a ship to pieces, two long arms that could pop her head off like a doll. Lantern eyes, needle teeth jaws too wide closer and closer and closer and—

Jacqueline closed her eyes and clutched her hands to her head. *Not here not here not here anywhere but here.*

Yakuza's voice pierced through the darkness. Through her mind.

This was never your moment of transformation. I'm the hero of this picture.

Jacqueline dug deep, sought out the most nonthreatening, the most comforting image she could. It wasn't a story about a nightmare anymore it was a—

There were two identical little girls facing each other, waist deep in a field of flowers. One of them looked down at her hands. Her black pigtails. Her traditional dress. It was a beautiful day. She looked up. The other girl was already running away, pigtails streaming behind her in the wind. Running towards the forest. There was a river there, and a small bridge. The little girl who'd been left alone picked up a sharp rock.

"Oh no you don't," said Yakuza.

She gave chase. Jacqueline knew if she could reach the bridge, she'd be safe. She felt a hand grab one of her braids and tug her backward. She shielded herself with her hands. Caught the rock as Yakuza tried to plunge it into her heart. They wrestled each other to the ground. Playing by Jacqueline's rules, Yakuza had been robbed of her monstrous strength. They were evenly matched. Further, Jacqueline didn't have to kill Yakuza, only hold her off long enough to get away. She kicked awkwardly, caught Yakuza under the chin. It bought her a second, but she'd have to turn her back to escape. Her suspicions were correct, and she caught a swipe from the rock to the left eye. In return, she swung a backhand and caught Yakuza with an unripe crabapple fist. Started running. Little lungs already burning. Little legs too short to cover the ground she needed. Yakuza lunged and grabbed Jacqueline by the ankle. She tripped flat on her face.

"Alright, I take it back. I'm impressed," Yakuza said in a high-pitched voice.

Jacqueline scrabbled under her, tried to push her away.

"Setting it up so that the first thing I'd wanna do is chase you? Inspired. I play by your rules, I can't use any glam. Smart." She raised up the rock. "But I don't need super strength to kill you."

Jacqueline tucked both her legs up and booted Yakuza in the stomach, hard. She took off like the wind she'd just knocked out of her adversary.

Yakuza glared balefully after her, trying to hate her to death.

If Jacqueline reached the bridge, she'd won. That simple. No telling what winning might mean in this context, but Yakuza would be a fool not to recognize the importance of symbolism to their kind. She licked her lips. Symbolism...there was a weakness to this story. If you were running to the safety of a bridge, it was likely because you were running FROM something. Every game had its exploits.

Jacqueline was almost to the tree line when a colossal hand slammed down in front of her.

"NOT SO FAST," the benthic titan said. Its other hand snatched up Jacqueline like a doll.

"I REALIZED MOST STORIES ABOUT RUNNING HOME HAVE A MONSTER BEHIND THEM."

Yakuza cast her lantern gaze around the meadow. From up here, she could see the edges of the dream. Trees that gradually shrank to nothing against a featureless gradient to give the impression of distance. Sloppy.

"AND WHERE IS OUR LITTLE FRIEND HIDING? DON'T TELL ME YOU FORGOT HER AGAIN."

Jacqueline struggled in her grip. "She's safe. Somewhere you can't see.

This was bad. How did children defeat monsters? Jacqueline looked at her reflection in a giant milky eye. Swallowed.

They had to grow up.

She reached out with her mind's eye. The exploit Yakuza had used still hung in the air. Unused code.

"WHAT ARE YOU DOING?" Yakuza menaced through her prison of teeth. But Jacqueline wasn't in her hand anymore.

"Just like I encouraged you to chase me and play by my rules. I encouraged you to cheat and break them. Now I can too," said Jacqueline's disembodied voice. It wasn't a child's anymore. It grew deeper, wiser. Took shape as she reappeared midair in front of the monstrous mermaid.

Now Jacqueline was the witch, the agent of change, the storyteller. Yakuza swiped at the specter to no avail; Jacqueline was IN the sky and she raised her hands as the scenery blackened into constellations. Forming the outline of a cottage around them. She was the mother who would banish this shadow. Yakuza screamed and leapt for her foe, piercing the veil.

"You forget," Yakuza hissed, "This was my canvas first." She clutched herself against Jacqueline. Tail wrapped around her legs. Forehead to forehead. "I think in still-life. My body is art, my blood is paint. You? An amateur."

True as her word, she was a master at warping narrative. In seconds, she'd hijacked it all. She was the witch, queen of all she surveyed, the eye and the hand of god. Jacqueline shrank back as the cottage finished taking shape around them. A child again.

"This is rich," said Yakuza, as their roles in the story solidified,

"Any last words?"

Jacqueline smiled. "No," she said, and pushed Yakuza into the oven.

Her screams weren't enough. A wave of the hand, and it was the furnace from Yaqui's basement. Flames licked higher and formed into the bodies of every man and woman this story had killed. Yakuza's memories inside of Yaqui's memory inside of Jacqueline's story. A three layer vault from which there was no escape. Jimmy and Fong held Yakuza down as the idea of her was consumed in flames. Remorseless and single-minded to the end, she screamed defiance from the bottom of Hell. "DIE! DIE DIE DIE!" Over and over. Spoken with the same force of will they'd both used to mold each other's reality.

Jacqueline felt her pulse stutter. She put out an arm, and a vein pierced her skin from within. Became a branch. Flowered multiple hearts like fruit. The rot took each one. They dropped off and became ash. Life outpaced death, and Yakuza's words melted in the air. She ceased to exist at the heart of a new star.

"Should've said 'live.'"

Jacqueline whorled her fingers, threading space into time. With no one to contest her, she could use her newfound power over dreams to return to reality. Pages flipped over the scene and turned the star from the past into the little gray water heater from her building. Closed the chapter. She turned, and shut the door after her. The hallway was dim and flickery. Dim because there were no windows. There were no windows because it was below ground. This hallway was real. The sewer below it was real. The street above it was real. Her door was real. She opened it.

The dozens of drawings of faces had barely stirred. The bathroom door was open. Yaqui sat alone on the bed. Her bindings lay in pieces around her.

"Hey," said Jacqueline kindly,

"I was worried that—"

"Oh, no. No worries," said Yaqui, rising from the bed. Red-eyed. Voice tired, rough. Cold as a tomb. Jacqueline's adrenaline was spiking and she realized her gun was in her hand before she saw the one in Yaqui's. Clara's 38.

"I should've guessed, really. It was obvious, stupid of me. A lion with a thorn in its paw is still a fucking lion," Yaqui said.

"Put the gun down. You're safe now," Jacqueline pleaded.

Yaqui shook her head and laughed bitterly. "Not while you're around. In my head. Fucking it up."

"I'm not her!" Jacqueline shouted.

"I know who the fuck you are you fucking THING." Yaqui was breathing heavily.

"I had seven hundred years trapped in your dream to figure it out. Nothing to do there but think. Couldn't die. Couldn't sleep. Couldn't even go insane. But I could go back. I can't change things like you can, but I saw."

She cocked the hammer. "I saw everything."

"What are you talking about?" said Jacqueline, "Everything's fine now! I saved you!"

"You put me in THE FUCKING DANGER YOU SAVED ME FROM YOU FREAK," Yaqui screamed.

She took a deep breath.

"No. You're just like her. Worse. Driving me crazy. Trying to bleed into my life. Steal it because you can't have your own. We can't coexist. Even now, I can *feel you* inside of me, like a parasite. Killing me."

She was wild-eyed. Jacqueline couldn't look away. She forced herself to respond.

"That's not true! It—it wasn't on purpose...she was just saying those things to get in our heads. I— I'm real! I'm real!"

Yaqui didn't blink. "I dreamed you up, and you came to life. You were my imaginary friend. You were my friend and she was... when I got mad. I know it sounds crazy and... and I wouldn't believe it myself if I hadn't seen the evidence. Even without her help. It was when I went to the station. That was the first time. I was sitting in your chair."

"Stop," said Jacqueline.

"She was right. She's a monster too but she was right. I saw it all. It's just like she said. Surrounding yourself with human things without context. No mirrors because you're the only thing you can't stand to look at. No real understanding. Born fully formed, pretending to be human by copying what you see. Stealing habits and cues through mimicry." Her voice was climbing.

"I said stop it!" Jacqueline had clicked off the safety without realizing it. But Yaqui's words were a deathblow without fear.

"You had a picture frame on your desk. But there was nothing in it."

The last layer peeled away. Nothing left. Neither tide nor tether. An empty frame. A stolen car. Attachment with no memory. Knowledge without experience. Documents carefully forged with an eye for duplication. Before she'd started working, dreaming: an empty gulf. The void, ever present. No childhood. No parents. Until this very second.

"This..." Jacqueline struggled for words. "Isn't fair," she choked out. "I'm human."

"Are you?" Yaqui asked, "On the way here you broke your leg and suffered a stab wound. But I don't see you limping now."

Jacqueline's breath was deafening in her ears.

"Go ahead, check."

Slowly, Jacqueline opened the top two buttons of

her shirt and gripped the bandage there. Tore part of it free.

Smooth unbroken flesh. No stitches. Not even a scratch. Yaqui's hand was moving.

All at once, Jacqueline could see the chain of events in motion, all out of the corner of her eye. Believing she was human, her last faint flickering belief, was going to kill her. A monster like Yakuza could outrun a gunshot, but not Jacqueline. She didn't want to.

"Good bye," Yaqui said, and fired.

Jacqueline could take no action. She wouldn't, couldn't fire. Not at Yaqui. Not willingly. The bullet spun slowly, and for the second time she saw her reflection in it. It impacted her heart. Her reflex, her human reflex, the one she still believed she had, squeezed the trigger.

It loosed its final shot before jamming in her hand, broken. She'd been aiming low, but the impact sent it wild. It struck Yaqui between the eyes.

They fell, and lay there.

For several hours, their blood pooled together between them. Yaqui was dead.

Jacqueline wasn't breathing.

Jacqueline sat up.

There was a great pain in her chest. She dug two, then four fingers into the bullet hole. She pulled the slug out of her heart. It started to beat again.

She got up, left the room, and went to the service elevator down the hall. Took it to the roof. The sun was rising. She looked behind her. Trail of bloody footprints. She looked down. *Lost a lot. Should be empty.* She closed her hand around the bullet.

Opened it.

Gone.

ABOUT THE AUTHOR

TRISTAN SELLERS began writing because there were too many ideas that needed to be real. He picked the genre of psychedelic thriller for his first novel because it was the broadest brush for the picture he wanted to paint.

His muses vary but include other authors like Terry Pratchett as well as the music of Run The Jewels, Neil Cicierega and Death Grips.

Tristan Sellers was born in Northern California and has since moved. He currently lives with his four cats and three dogs.

Intrusive Thoughts is his first published novel.